THE CHERKLEY COURT CONUNDRUM

BENEDICT BROWN

Storm
PUBLISHING

Ebook ISBN: 978-1-83700-270-2
Paperback ISBN: 978-1-83700-271-9

Cover design: Rose Cooper
Cover images: Shutterstock

Published by Storm Publishing.
For further information, visit:
www.stormpublishing.co

ALSO BY BENEDICT BROWN

The Marius Quin Mysteries

Murder at Everham Hall

The Hurtwood Village Murders

The Castleton Affair

A Body at the Grand Hotel

Arsenic and Old Lies

The Holly Village Murders

The Yacht Party

Lord Edgington Investigates…

Murder at the Spring Ball

A Body at a Boarding School

Death on a Summer's Day

The Mystery of Mistletoe Hall

The Tangled Treasure Trail

The Curious Case of the Templeton-Swifts

The Crimes of Clearwell Castle

The Snows of Weston Moor

What the Vicar Saw

Blood on the Banisters

A Killer in the Wings

The Christmas Bell Mystery

The Puzzle of Parham House

Death at Silent Pool

To my wife Marion and our incredible children,
Amelie and Osian.
You make the hard work worthwhile.

ONE

I don't believe I'd set foot inside a theatre since my uniquely unlucky play had closed before it had opened and nearly left me bankrupt. *A Killer in the Wings* had the finest cast I could ever have hoped to assemble, but then two of the actors were murdered, which rather put paid to my theatrical ambitions.

As I stood in the cold outside the Theatre Royal, I thought back over the months to what may have been the darkest period in my life. The war was no picnic, of course, and I certainly wouldn't recommend getting blown up, no matter how pretty the nurses who attended me turned out to be. But the time when I could barely write a word, and I was sure I would have to sell my home to cover the debts I'd accumulated... Well, that was a low of canyon-like proportions.

And yet, a little over a year later, my world felt as though it made sense again. Certain pieces that I had considered shattered beyond recognition and repair had begun to fit together. Which is why, as I froze off my coattails in the street, and the great and good of old London town streamed past me into the theatre, I barely noticed how cold it was.

"My! Don't you look dashing, Mr Quin," the woman I awaited informed me as we caught sight of one another through the throng.

I like to think I have a smooth tongue and can badinage with the best of them, but I was almost speechless just then.

"Good evening, Bella," I mumbled as I took in her full-length black velvet evening gloves and matching choker – whilst fighting with all my might not to admire the shapeliness of the emerald-green dress she wore under a thick nutria shawl.

She continued staring at me for a few moments before apparently remembering what we were doing there. "Perhaps we should go inside? I haven't nearly enough clothes on, and I can no longer feel my elbows."

"Allow me," I said and quickly held out my arm, in case she thought I was offering to feel her elbows.

I'm quite convinced that, as we swept through the pillared loggia and into the glittering bright theatre, every man we passed stared either at me in envy, or my dear Bella in admiration. The train of her dress followed us at a respectful distance – much as my dog wouldn't have if he'd been in attendance – and I had the very real sensation that I was accompanying a princess to a ball.

Had I entered that building alone, I would probably have apologised to the check-taker on duty – simply for expecting him to do his job – before shuffling along the row to my seat, muttering to my fellow theatregoers as I went. But with Bella beside me, it was as if every last person there had been waiting for us to arrive. The staff rushed forward to inspect our tickets, grateful for the appreciative smile with which my companion rewarded them. The fact that Bella had booked the royal box didn't hurt either, and we were soon escorted upstairs.

Although it is only a short walk from my house, I'd never been to the Theatre Royal before. It is just as sumptuous as its name suggests. The thick red carpet on the stairs felt as if it had been upholstered with puffy cushions underneath and, after the door to our box was thrown open, I confess that I drew a breath. I goggled at the gilded proscenium and the curving amphitheatre, which was filled with impressed, expectant faces, just like mine.

I moved aside for Bella to take her seat, and she gave my arm a grateful squeeze. I watched her own look of excitement as she peered around the theatre, and my emotions doubled. I don't need to describe the feeling that swelled within me; I've loved her since we were children.

The happy buzz and mumble of the other spectators added to the atmosphere as the orchestra tuned their instruments. It sounded as if they were performing a discordant but beguiling piece of music in a genre that has yet to be defined.

"I've heard it's a wonderful production," Bella eventually muttered, "but every time I read a mystery novel or come to see a play like this one, I find myself being disappointed that our own endeavours as detectives haven't improved my skills when it comes to spotting the guilty party."

"Perhaps this will be your lucky night." I waited for the count of three. "Especially as I read in the newspaper that the culprits are revealed in the first act."

She turned back to look at the stage. "In which case, my chances are good."

I should probably have been envious of the playwright. As if A.A. Milne hadn't made enough money with his tales of a talking bear, his play that we were about to watch, *The Fourth Wall*, had been running for months to enthusiastic reviews. It was a mystery about a pair of plucky amateur detectives who try to get to the bottom of a vicious murder in a grand stately home. You know: just the kind of story that I write, and no one will ever see in the theatre.

And yet, as the house lights dimmed, and the audience fell silent, I couldn't have been happier for Milne. It struck me that, if he could do it, then I could too. I might never write anything as appealing as *Winnie-the-Pooh*, but the fact that so many people crammed into a theatre six nights a week to watch a murder mystery showed me that I was on the right track. And besides, if he hadn't written his play, I wouldn't have been sitting there with the woman I loved.

"It's starting," Bella whispered with the excitement of a child as the curtain rose.

I can't tell you a great deal about the plot, characters, staging or musical accompaniment. I spent the whole time watching my mesmerising companion out of the side of one eye and wondering how I could be so lucky as to spend any length of time in her presence. I'm sure there were all sorts of unexpected revelations as the story went on, and I certainly did my best to pretend that I was riveted to each of them.

"So? What did you think?" Bella asked when the play had reached its conclusion and the whole place had risen to applaud. "Was it up to your high standards?"

"I greatly enjoyed every moment of our time here," I replied, choosing my words carefully as the encore concluded and the noisy rabble quietened. "I haven't had such a fine evening in a long time." None of this was a lie.

"Yes, it was a lot of fun, wasn't it?" She put her hand out towards me as if to take my arm but only rested it on the back of her chair. "I especially liked Susan. It's good to see a spirited young woman solving a mystery for a change. Far too often, it's left to the man to tie up the case as his beautiful assistant looks on through heart-shaped eyes."

"Would you say that's what happens on our cases? Do you stand around waiting to heap praise upon me?" I stepped back so that she could exit the box and join the long, snaking queue to descend the stairs.

She still didn't take my arm, but she did hit me playfully around the shoulder. "The only response to such a ridiculous suggestion is that I'm sure you wish such a thing were true."

I dropped my voice to a whisper, not just because we were no longer alone, but because I wanted to show that I was sincere. "I was only teasing, Bella. Any success I have had in our amateurish enterprise is thanks to you."

Showing no such discretion, she burst out laughing. "You sop, Marius. You mustn't take me so seriously."

Two rather hairy gentlemen in opera cloaks looked at us disapprovingly over their shoulders, and their attention served to make us both shy. In fact, we didn't say another word until we were out in the frozen air of a London night.

We stood with the pedestrian traffic passing us in both directions. I didn't know how to say goodbye, and Bella didn't seem to feel like saying anything at all, but I finally managed to utter a few clumsy words.

"I suppose your ghoulish chauffeur is loitering nearby." I knew this was the wrong thing to say, but it was somehow less painful than the silence that it had replaced.

"Actually, I told him to park in front of your house. I thought we might enjoy a short walk after all that sitting."

A stiltedness had entered our conversation, and I didn't know how to fix it. "Wonderful."

I looked up at the sky to check for rain, though we were still standing under the grand porch of the theatre.

The gesture evidently amused her, as she snickered and seized my arm. "Marius Quin, you are the most curious man I've ever met." She somehow managed to make this sound like a compliment. "Many of my favourite people are odd, but you constantly find new ways to outdo them."

I would have asked what had caused her to say such a thing, but I was afraid of the answer. "*You*, the daughter of a man who has his own frog pond and a woman who, on their first meeting, made Queen Mary feel rather common, are accusing *me* of eccentricity."

She was not dissuaded from her position. "Precisely. Deep down inside you, there's a madman straining to come out. The fact that you hide it makes it all the more apparent."

I was the one laughing now. The bitter wind blew harder, but she pulled me close, and I barely felt the cold.

"Don't think of it as an insult, Marius. I wouldn't find you interesting if you were just like everyone else. Of course, that doesn't mean I don't worry about you from time to time."

"So I'm eccentric to a worrying degree. Is that it?"

When she didn't answer, I was momentarily tempted to discuss the life that we could have shared. A life in which I'd asked her to marry me when I'd had the chance and not sabotaged my happiness. Just like all those years ago, I spurned the opportunity.

The cold had penetrated my suit, and I was glad that I lived so close to the theatre. We turned into my road, and I caught sight of her Sunbeam car on the far side of the leafless garden square.

"Do you ever think about the role we play in this world?" Bella asked this question quite out of the blue, and there was real purpose in her tone. It was as if she knew exactly what she needed to say and was determined to get it out no matter what obstacles I put in her way. She looked at me with great earnestness, and I realised that my chance may not have passed after all.

"I think about it all the time." Why do I find some things so hard to discuss? Why is it that the words I would happily utter in front of a mirror desert me as soon as I'm with her?

"It sometimes feels as though everything is laid out for us at birth, and there's nothing we can do to break free." She turned away from me for a moment. "I'm not complaining about my lot in life. I just wish that..."

It is hard to describe the change that had come over her. She'd seemed so carefree as we left the theatre, but now her strained, serious tone made me want to soothe away her troubles.

"I often think of another life we could have led." With each word I spoke, my heart beat a little faster. "I imagine a world in which the friendship I prize so highly had changed over time."

We were only a few houses away from my own, and I stopped to study her flawless face. She looked frightened, but she held my gaze.

An unexpected streak of confidence ran through me, and now I knew what I needed to say. "I think about how different everything would have been if I'd found the courage to ask—"

"Marius!" a voice shouted across to us. If this newcomer had spent her life waiting for the perfect moment to rankle me, she couldn't have chosen a better one.

I didn't take my eyes off Bella, even as the call repeated. Or rather, I couldn't take my eyes off her. Her glossy black hair seemed to have captured the darkness of the sky overhead, and her soulful green eyes shimmered under the glow of the electric street lights.

"Marius, it's me!"

When I heard my name for the third time, I could no longer ignore it. I turned to see a primly dressed young woman running towards us just two seconds before she opened her arms to wrap them around me.

"Oh, Marius," she murmured as she placed her head against my chest. "Thank goodness I found you."

TWO

"Nerea?" I pulled back to look at her properly.

"Didn't you recognise me?"

The truth was that, though eight years had passed since I'd last seen the woman I'd once loved , she hadn't changed a bit. The shock of finding her there was so great that, for a moment, I forgot what had almost just happened.

"Marius," Bella said to break the spell, her voice noticeably fragile, "would you care to introduce us?"

I looked back and forth between the two women who (after my mother) had most shaped my life, and I didn't know where to begin.

The best I could do was, "Bella, this is Nerea."

Either fortunately or regrettably, Nerea did the rest. "So you're the Isabella who tore us apart all those years ago?" Her Spanish accent was less noticeable than I'd remembered.

Bella took a step back then. I couldn't really blame her for being surprised. There was a whole period of my life of which I'd never spoken.

"So you and Marius were..." I imagined that she was too polite to finish this sentence. A more optimistic part of me hoped that she couldn't bear to consider the possibility I'd ever spent time with another woman.

It was Nerea's turn to sound apprehensive. "We met in Madrid after the war. I followed him to Paris, and we spent the best two years of my life there." She was certainly no less bold than I remembered. "I'm so happy to have found you again."

Bella had barely looked away from the beautiful interloper, but she now cast her eyes over to my house where her chauffeur, Caxton, stood glaring in my direction. He couldn't have overheard the conversation from thirty yards away. He simply always looked that grumpy.

"Very well. It's late and I should be leaving." Bella stepped further away from me, and it was as if someone were tearing me in two.

The force was so great that I was worried my limbs would rip off, and I would end up as a bloody heap on the floor. I'm glad to inform you that nothing so dramatic (or gratuitous) occurred.

"No, Lady Isabella, please don't go," Nerea surprised us both by saying. "It is not just Marius I came to see. I..." All of a sudden, the Spaniard lacked the verve and bluntness that had once come so easily to her. "I need to tell you that..." Her second attempt was no better, and her eyes turned glassy.

Whatever feelings the woman's unexpected arrival had provoked in her, Bella couldn't ignore a soul in need, and she put one hand on Nerea's shoulder. "What's the matter? I'm sure there's no need to cry."

My former... well, I don't really know what to call her, actually. Some would opt for the word *girlfriend,* and while I'd very much wished to use that term myself once, she had rarely agreed to any so traditional a description. My former love pulled back her shoulders and wiped away her tears.

"It is kind of you to try to comfort me, but the events of last night make any happiness difficult to believe." The rhythm of her, if not broken, then ever so slightly cracked English sent me shooting back through time and space to the tiny flat in Montmartre where our lives had slowly but surely become entwined.

"Are you all right?" I managed to say, but there was little real emotion in the words. Whatever I'd felt for Nerea had long since faded, and I could only recall our time together with regret.

She must have noticed, as she began to back away, and the look in her eyes was one of fear and disappointment. "I should never have come here. I read in the newspaper about what the pair of you did in Highgate, and I thought that you would be able to help me, but I see now that I had no right to intrude."

Nerea turned to Bella again, and I realised how desperate she was. I suppose she'd tried to hide it when she first approached us – she was good at that sort of thing – but it was obvious that she was in a bad way.

"What's the matter?" I asked again, trying to show more concern. "If there's something wrong, then we will do all we can to help you."

She turned away from me, and I thought she would break into a run. Instead, she stopped and looked back over her shoulder. "I didn't mean to interfere."

Her soft footsteps on the pavement grew quicker, and I wanted to stop her, but I didn't know how. Bella showed no such hesitation and stepped into the fleeing woman's path.

"We can't possibly let you leave without hearing what's happened. You'll come into Marius's house, and he'll put the kettle on while we talk."

I know how hard it is to say no to Bella. I've been trying to resist her charms for a quarter of a century. There's something about the way she makes everything sound so simple that means it is impossible to argue with her. I could see that Nerea was having that very same problem.

The pair wandered off along the pavement together, and I couldn't hear what they said, but it was clear from the way Nerea turned her head to look at Bella whenever she was speaking that she would not run away again. I followed them at a fair distance before remembering that I was the only one with keys to my flat and increasing my pace.

Caxton noticed and stepped from the spot where he'd been skulking to make his presence felt.

"Easy, boy," I said, not because I would ever wish to denigrate a servant, but because I knew how likely the objectionable chauffeur was to snap at me otherwise. "No one has any intention of attacking your mistress. We're merely escorting the young lady inside to offer her something to drink."

What I had hoped would be a fairly innocent explanation clearly appalled the man even more. His nose scrunched up, and he made sure that I saw the two immense fists dangling at his sides.

"I don't care what you hope to get up to, matey. I've got my eye on you, and I won't let anything happen to Lady Isabella."

We seemed to have reached something of a stalemate, but it was too cold to stand glaring at one another, and so I stepped past him and went to open my front door.

I let the ladies in ahead of me and was about to follow them when I realised that Caxton was still outside. I almost felt sorry for him.

"Would you prefer to come in out of the cold?" I suggested, calling on a well of compassion which had never been tapped for a man like him before.

"That's just what you'd like, isn't it!" he claimed, and I really couldn't fathom how to reply. "There's nothing you want more than to convince me that you're an all right sort of fella, but I'm wise to your games, Quin. I will stand out here even if my blood freezes and my body turns to ice."

He folded his arms and turned to face the street.

"Jolly good," I finally managed. "I'll send out some tea once it's boiled."

THREE

My basset hound, Percy, was very much enjoying the attention my visitors lavished upon him. I wasn't worried about Nerea meeting him so much as my mother, who would now appear from the kitchen.

"Marius, would you like me to—" She stopped herself as she stepped into the sitting room and realised that we weren't alone. "Oh, hello, ladies. I didn't realise that you were here."

Nerea looked up from Percy to take in my other flatmate. There was a moment of stillness, which I spent wondering whether this might be the end of their interaction, but I knew them both too well to hope for any such thing.

"You must be Mrs Quin," Nerea said brightly.

Bella was enjoying my embarrassment. She sat on the sofa with a wide smile on her face as she continued to pat Percy.

"That's right. You are very welcome here..." Mother held the final note to make it clear that she wished to know our guest's name.

"This is Nerea, Mother," I finally explained.

"Oh, Nerea. It's so nice to meet you." She came into the room to shake hands before realising whom she was about to greet. "Oh, *Nerea*."

"We knew one another when I lived on the Continent," I said to make it a fraction less awkward.

"Yes, of course. I remember." Mother did her best not to reveal that I had talked of Nerea when I had first returned to England and that not everything I'd said had been positive.

I've always thought of my mother as a wise sort of person. She has no great level of education and certainly hasn't had the opportunities in life to show off her natural intelligence, but she possesses something which no academic qualification can guarantee. One example of this was the speed at which she realised that the best course of action available to her was to retreat from the room post-haste.

"Perhaps I should boil the kettle. I imagine you have something serious to discuss."

"It's lovely to see you, Mary," Bella murmured, and I believe there was a hint of possessiveness in her tone. She would never boast to Nerea just how important she was to me, but she didn't mind showing the woman who had (quite literally) grabbed me in the street that she and my mother were old friends.

Mother winked as she turned and made her exit, and the uncomfortable atmosphere I had first noted on the pavement returned.

"Perhaps you can tell us why you came here," I said with far less compassion than Bella would have injected into such a statement.

For a moment, Nerea reminded me of a cat whose tail had just been pulled. She flinched, and a certain look passed over her features as though she had to remind herself to keep up her guard.

"If it's not too painful to discuss," Bella added, to sand off the edges of my blunt suggestion.

Nerea was still on her feet and would no longer look at me. Instead, she walked over to the window that gave on to the narrow strip of concrete that led to the garden at the back of the property. It was too late at night to see anything through it, but that didn't stop her looking. Her lively eyes seemed to prod and penetrate the darkness.

"I really don't know why I thought it was a good idea to come here." Her normally deep, resonant voice had become faint. It sounded for a moment as if she were speaking to us from the room next door. "The simple reason is that I read about you in the newspaper. There was an article about what the two of you achieved in Highgate over Christmas, and I told my friends very proudly that I knew you. I had no idea back then that I would find myself in need of your assistance."

A brief note of optimism in her tone instantly faded, and she looked as disconsolate as she had at any moment since she'd found us.

I looked across at Bella, who, for the time being at least, was willing to overlook whatever objections she had to my behaviour. Before she could say anything, Nerea spoke again.

"I've only been living in Britain for two years. I was tired of Paris, and Spain is no place to make a life right now. I have a cousin nearby and remembered how fondly you had always spoken of your home, Marius, so I looked for a job here."

She turned back to me then, and that mix of hope and desolation that I'd already seen running through her was apparent once more. "I've been working in a house in Surrey for the last year, and I don't mind telling you that – perhaps for the first time in my life – I felt as if I'd finally found the right place for me."

"What sort of house?" I asked, when what I really meant was, *Where in my home county have you ended up?*

"It's a large family home in the Surrey Hills – a real beauty, in fact. Perhaps you've heard of Cherkley Court?"

Bella answered her before I could. "That's Lord Sheridan's house. Do you work for him?"

She looked shy for a second and admitted, "I suppose he's the one who pays my salary, but we've rarely spoken. I work as the language mistress. I teach his youngest son French and Spanish.

Little Lionel is a dear, sweet boy, and I couldn't have a better position. I really couldn't."

Every sentence she spoke brought back memories of Paris. I knew just what she was doing – I'd spent so much time with her that I could practically read her thoughts. She'd always pretended that everything was fine when it wasn't. Even as she stood there, building up the courage to ask me for help, she felt the need to communicate just how well she was doing.

"But it wasn't just my job that suited me. It felt for a time that my whole life had fallen into place. I get on very well with my colleagues at the house. They have become like a family to me. I could have been aloof and kept my distance, like the governess does, but by mixing with the other workers in the house, I have found my place."

Her English had improved immeasurably since we'd first met. It amazed me to hear her uttering phrases that wouldn't have sounded out of place coming from her wealthy pupil.

"That doesn't explain why you would accost us in the street late in the evening," I felt I had to point out. And no, I was not at my most welcoming, but if you had seen us screaming at one another the last time we were together, you would understand why.

Her chin dipped again, and she gazed down at the floor. "You're right. I'm very sorry to come here like this. I really wouldn't have dreamed of... What's the word?"

"Intruding?" I was trying to be helpful, but it probably didn't sound like that.

"No, that's not what I... I had no intention of disturbing you, but I didn't know who else to ask. You see..."

She took a deep breath, and fifty different possibilities for why she had come flashed in and out of my mind. Thanks to my occasionally cynical nature, several of these explanations involved her asking me for money.

When she was ready to speak, she spun on the balls of her feet like a dancer and looked straight at me. "Marius, Lady Isabella, a terrible thing has happened, and I don't know how to describe it."

"Don't distress yourself." Bella stood up from the sofa to cross the room, leaving Percy looking quite heartbroken. I knew exactly how he felt. "Whatever it is, we will listen without prejudice and do our very best to assist you."

Normally, I would have been disappointed in myself for not coming up with something so calm and reassuring. Bella was an expert at putting people at ease, but these were not normal circumstances, and I wasn't too concerned about Nerea's feelings.

"You are so kind, Lady Isabella." Her big brown eyes were terribly expressive just then, and I could see what effect she was having on my friend. "Marius often talked about how special a person you are, and I noticed it instantly when we came face-to-face."

Bella looked across at me as Nerea continued, and I saw a faint blush on her cheeks.

"Cherkley Court has been shaken by a horrific incident. It all started at a party last night. I had nothing to do with the gathering that Lady Sheridan had organised, and I can't tell you exactly what happened. All I know is that, by the end of the night, one of the maids had been beaten half to death, a valuable box had been stolen from the mistress's boudoir and..."

She had revealed all this in a torrent to prevent herself from hesitating any more than she already had, but there came a point at which her words faded out.

"I told you, Nerea," Bella tried once more. "You can trust us."

Her words didn't work this time. Perhaps Nerea noticed something hollow in them. Either way, she didn't respond. She just stared at me, and I realised that I would have to be the one to encourage her.

"It's true, Nere," I said, finding the old, affectionate term on my tongue, though I hadn't so much as thought of it in years. I should have left it at that, but I've never known when to keep things short.

"Does someone suspect you of being involved in the crime? Is that the problem?"

She looked just the tiniest bit horrified and pulled away from me even as she answered. "Not me. Why would you think that, Marius?"

I could feel myself being drawn into an argument, just as I had been a thousand times when we lived in the same city. I believe I even opened my mouth to answer, but I remembered my previous mistake and stopped myself.

"As it happens, I was visiting my cousin in Guildford on the night of the crime. But I have a friend," she continued somewhat blushingly, and I already knew what kind of friend she meant. "His name is Dennis Apps, and he's the head gardener at Cherkley. Well, he was until…" She raised her hand to her mouth, and the horror returned. "Until he disappeared soon after the theft."

"And I take it he's fallen under suspicion?" I said, but I managed to soften my tone enough not to alarm her further. "Do the police have any evidence that he is to blame for what happened?"

Without checking what was behind her, Nerea crumpled back onto the sofa. It looked like a strong wind had knocked her over. "I can't say for certain. A young inspector from Scotland Yard came to talk to everyone this afternoon. He clearly didn't believe me when I defended my Dennis, but I'm sure that the dear sweet man I've come to know this year would never do anything to hurt poor Penny."

"Is that the maid who was injured?" Bella asked in a whisper.

"Yes, Penny Baker. She's a kind-hearted creature, and it's hard to imagine who could have savaged her like that. It seems unlikely that she will recover."

"When exactly did all of this happen?" I had already screwed my detective's head firmly into place on my shoulders. "You mentioned a party. Were the guests in the house at the time?"

Nerea needed a few moments to compose herself. I could see that she was still trying to make sense of what had happened. "Yes, it was late in the night. Around midnight, in fact. I believe that Lady Sheridan's friends were engaged in some sort of game – a trick or prank or something of the like."

"Then they were all together when Penny was attacked and the box was stolen?"

"No, not then." She interlocked her fingers as though she were praying and began to mutter a string of fast Spanish words, of which I may have caught half but understood far fewer. "They were scattered about the house when the attack itself took place. Apparently they were cackling with excitement as they ran through the corridors."

"And what of the other staff?"

She looked back up at me. "All I know is that the nursemaid, Hilary, had trouble putting little Lionel to sleep. She remembers hearing a thud from the mistress's boudoir shortly before the clock on the landing struck for midnight. She didn't think anything of it at the time, but as soon as she discovered what had happened, she put the pieces together."

Bella had been listening intently and now broke her silence. "So she was the one who discovered the injured woman?"

"No, that was our mistress, Lady Sheridan. Hilary had taken Lionel back to bed, and fell asleep beside him, but they both woke up to a shriek."

I realised that there was one person who had barely been mentioned. "And what of Lord Sheridan? Where was he when all this was going on?"

She looked at the door then. I wondered what the gesture meant – whether the mention of her employer frightened her in some way. At the very least, a sense of discretion washed over her. "He'd been with his wife at the beginning of the evening, but he isn't the type who enjoys playing host to young visitors. From what I've heard, he'd retired to his library."

Her revelations came in dribs and drabs, and it was clear she would need prompting to say anything more.

"So then the house was roused," Bella prompted. "Is that right?"

Nerea nodded.

"And what happened next?" I asked to be more direct.

"All I can tell you is what I heard from Hilary. You do understand that, don't you?" She waited until we'd both provided confirmation. "Lionel stayed in bed, and she hurried downstairs to see who had made such a dreadful noise. She found the mistress in her negligee."

"Her negligee?" I was quick to parrot. "I thought you said she'd been entertaining guests."

"I can't explain it; I only tell you the facts. Lady Sheridan was standing in her boudoir with a hand clamped over her mouth and poor Penny on the floor at her feet. They all thought she was dead." Anticipating the inevitable question, she added, "Francis and Frederick the footmen had just arrived, and one of the guests was there too."

"Do you know the name?"

"No, I have nothing to do with any of the young crowd that Lady Sheridan so adores. They seem..." She evidently had no wish to finish that sentence, but she pushed herself to do just that. "Well, they seem flighty and frivolous: not my type of people at all. If you want to know anything more about them, you'll have to ask the mistress."

"Yes, we will," Bella replied resolutely, and it took Nerea a moment to realise what she had just heard.

"Are you saying that you'll come to Cherkley Court?" Her incredulity was apparent, and I wondered what this said about her perception of me.

"Of course we will." Bella sounded perfectly accepting of the idea. "We haven't got anything else to do this week."

"Wait," I interrupted before either of them could get excited. "There's something you haven't told us. When did your boyfriend go missing?"

"He's not my boyfriend," she said in much the same tone as if

I'd accused her of battering her colleague and stealing whatever valuables had gone missing. Regardless of this, her demeanour changed once more when she spoke of the gardener. "I'm very fond of Dennis, but there's no formal arrangement between us. He's not asked me to marry him, and I've no reason to think that he will." She uttered these words in the manner of someone who fully expected this to come to pass before long.

"Fine." I adopted a blunter tone. "When did the man of whom you are very fond but in no way connected to disappear?"

She rolled her eyes in a way I distinctly remembered. "No one has seen him since Penny was attacked."

"And yet you're sure that he isn't to blame?"

This matter-of-fact persona had served me well enough for the last few questions, but I could see from the emotion that now coloured her cheeks that I'd taken things too far.

"If you knew Dennis Apps, you would realise that he is the most honest, well-meaning and reliable man you could ever hope to meet." She stood up to deliver her defence. "I can tell you this for nothing: Dennis Apps makes Marius Quin look like a lowly, squirming worm, and I do not believe for one moment that he attacked our friend or stole from Lady Sheridan."

The room fell silent as she glared at me with pent-up, breathless energy. Even Percy didn't make a sound, and his near-perpetually waggy tail fell still. I felt terrible that I had hurt her so. Whatever had passed between us in years gone by couldn't excuse such cynicism on my part. An agonising pang stung me, and I was just about to speak when my mother bustled breezily into the room with a tray.

"Now, who'd like a nice cup of tea?"

FOUR

Bella escorted our foreign visitor from my home that night with a scowl on her face the like of which I hadn't seen since we were children. I hadn't meant to be so curt. I hadn't meant to show how much Nerea's reappearance had affected me, but some things are hard to conceal.

I lay in bed, unable to sleep, replaying the incidents and emotions of a complicated evening. I can't say it was the first time I had experienced such tumult. The year since I'd reunited with Bella had been filled with highs and lows, losses and joy. Her fiancé's murder in my own home months earlier still weighed on us both. My lack of knowledge on my father's whereabouts, despite feeling that I was closer to finding him than I had been in a decade, certainly didn't help, and yet... Well, I was going to say that, with the turn of the new year, I had seen hints that Bella might be able to see a life for us beyond those tragedies.

I know she will never truly recover from Gilbert's unfathomable demise, but I still allow myself to dream that there is a future in which we can love one another as we did before the war. I'm fully aware that life is far more complex and confusing than it was in our infancy. I know that we can't travel back in time, but I cling to the belief that the woman I've loved for so long could feel the same way.

The appearance of my former love only reinforced my feelings.

I must have fallen asleep eventually, though the night passed restlessly. I remember picking over the details of my father's case for the thousandth time, and then suddenly it was morning. I woke to the sound of the telephone ringing in the hall. When it didn't stop, and no one answered it, I knew that I would have to rouse myself.

"Yes?" I responded a little sharply upon putting the receiver to my ear.

"Well, that's a fine greeting," a voice answered. I'm happy to say it was not another ex-love but a relatively new friend. "This is Lovebrook. I could really use your help with something."

"Hello, Valentine," I eagerly responded. "Let me think; there's been a terrible crime." I paused as if considering what could have happened. "But not a murder. At least, not yet. I'm going to say that someone has been attacked. The fact that you're ringing me at this ungodly hour..."

"It's ten o'clock in the morning, Marius."

I ignored him and kept talking. "...suggests to me that whatever has occurred is connected to someone important." I made a humming sound as I (supposedly) put the pieces together. "I'm going to make a wild guess and say that a woman was attacked in the home of a wealthy and influential man. Am I close?"

"That's remarkable!" He was so impressed that his voice grew louder, and these two words crackled down the line. "How did you do it?"

"I couldn't possibly give away my secrets."

I must have taken the joke too far, as he didn't say anything for a moment and, when he did, he was wise to my subterfuge. "Come along. Who told you?"

"You've got me. I knew Lord Sheridan's language mistress when I was living in Paris. She came here last night."

"I see," he replied a little blankly, and the slightest inflection told me that he was wondering exactly how well Nerea and I had known one another. "Señorita Barriuso and her colleagues have been very helpful, but the whole thing remains a mystery."

"Where would we be without a little mystery?"

"Well, quite. Your books would be short and very dry if all they included were descriptions of fancy houses in which any crimes that occurred were instantly solvable. My point was rather that this particular incident is as perplexing as they come, and there are several elements that don't make sense. On the surface, it looks like a simple case of a burglary gone wrong. The maid presumably interrupted the thief and received a bash to the back of the head."

"As you say, that sounds straightforward enough. How is she faring?"

"Penny Baker is lucky to be alive. The doctors can't say what sort of existence she will have if she does regain her faculties – and there's no guarantee of that."

"The poor woman. It's somehow worse that she was going about her job when the incident happened. Had she arrived a few minutes later, she would probably have avoided her fate."

"Quite."

I realised that we'd strayed from our original discussion. "I beg your pardon; you were about to explain what made the crime unusual."

Before he could answer, there was a knock at the door, and I had to interrupt. "Actually, Lovebrook, we'd better talk in person. Someone's here. I'll come to Cherkley Court as soon as I can."

"Jolly good." He didn't sound his usual optimistic self and, to be honest, it was worrying. I'm normally the taciturn one, not the cheery inspector. "Lord Sheridan has already given his permission for you and Bella to assist me."

We said a swift goodbye, and I ran along the corridor to the front door.

"You're awake, so that's a good start," Bella told me as she took in my rather fetching pyjamas. "I believe there's somewhere we ought to be?"

I got ready in a time that was acceptable to my punctual companion. And when I reached her car, she even seemed to approve of my choice of suit, though she maintained the same air of dissatisfaction that she'd had the night before.

"What are you doing here?" I asked my dog through the window. He was sitting in the front seat, tongue hanging out, raring to leave.

I'm sure it will surprise no one to learn that he did not reply, but Bella explained the situation. "We couldn't just leave him behind. He brings us luck," she claimed without evidence.

I find it surprisingly difficult to argue with baseless superstition, and so I waited for her to get into the car and then did the same. I can't say that the atmosphere was in any way improved by the fact we would be travelling with Caxton at the wheel. He had not opened the door to grant me access to the vehicle, and he certainly didn't utter a cheery greeting when he saw me. He grimaced in my direction and grunted a little as we pulled away from the square.

The freeze of the previous night had given way to a dull, overcast day. It was the kind of weather that gives London a bad name as a grey and dreary city. In weeks like this, it is hard to remember that the sun ever shines here, despite the fact that, when it does, it is surely the liveliest and most inspiring place to be.

One of the undoubted charms of the capital is just how quickly the cold stone buildings begin to space out, and the natural world floods in around the human footprint. In no time at all, we were south of the river and whistling along past Wimbledon Common and the great green enclosure of Richmond Park.

I will never tire of London, but it's even easier to appreciate when I get the chance to travel beyond the city. I'd been trapped at home writing and editing my last book – set for release any day now, if anyone should be interested – and hadn't travelled much further than Fulham for months. While it was sad that we were off to investigate a vicious assault, I looked forward to having some fresh air in my lungs.

And if it's fresh air you're after, there are worse places to get it than the county of Surrey. Cherkley Court is only twelve miles from the village where I grew up, and yet the beauty of the scenery still bowled me over. If I had to pick one part of England in which to spend the rest of my days, the area around the Mole Valley would be an excellent choice. There's a smoothness to the lines of nature there. It's as if all the faults and imperfections have been corrected, leaving perfectly rounded hills and curving lanes. On this visit, the trees were fighting back after a long, cold winter, and the first signs of emerald greenery had appeared on branches along our route.

Caxton pulled off the road near Leatherhead and drove up to the Cherkley Court gate, which was attended by two overly suspicious guards. It took our driver some time and a telephone call to the main house to convince the men on duty that our presence would be tolerated within, but they finally let us through.

It turned out that there was plenty more of the countryside I so admired behind the high walls of the estate. Vast swathes of field, forest and parkland stretched before us. We drove for several minutes before getting our first glimpse of the house where the crime had taken place. Cherkley Court was well named, as I imagined its wealthy industrialist owner living like a king, removed from the humdrum world outside.

"Did you drive Nerea back here last night?" it occurred to me to ask Bella as we rolled down the hill towards the northern façade of the property.

"No, I spent the night in my brother's flat in London. She stayed in a hotel and had a train booked for first thing this morning."

We'd already passed various smaller buildings, and they only served to make the opulent house ahead look more impressive. It was eclectic in style – not some ancient pile from Elizabethan times, but a modern mansion with features borrowed from French châteaux and Tuscan villas.

We looped around the property to reach the main entrance

with its balustraded porch and a large crest of the Dixon family carved into the wall above. Bands of rustication contrasted with the ashlar around the large sash windows that dominated the façade of the building. It was very appealing, if you happen to like nice things.

Even as Caxton pulled the car to a stop, I noticed Detective Inspector Lovebrook bounding out to meet us with his usual reserve of energy. What was missing, however, was any of the levity which normally marked his demeanour.

"I'm relieved you're here. I don't know what it is about this case, but it's given me the fantods." He didn't even say hello. He started jabbering as soon as I'd opened my door, and he wouldn't stop until Bella joined us and decorum dictated that he was obliged to welcome her more formally. "I'm so glad you could come, Lady Bella." He spoke in a grateful tone and even bowed his head.

"I hope we can alleviate some of your..." Bella needed a moment to recall the term he'd used. "...fantods."

My dog took this as a sign that he was needed in the house, but I soon explained the lie of the land. "I'm sure you would love to nose around inside, Percy, but we are barely guests here and cannot expect the owners to allow every curious dog onto their property."

He looked at Bella in the hope she might side with him. She was of no use, nor was the inspector, and so, as I had moved to block his way, he turned with all his usual disgruntled grace and went to inspect the gardens.

Lovebrook was in a hurry. "I'll take you to see where it happened. Lord Sheridan will want to meet you, but let's start at the beginning, shall we?"

This wasn't really a question. I followed him into the house as Bella muttered some parting words to the side of meat we left guarding her car. I imagine that Caxton snarled in my direction, but my mind was already on other things.

"You said on the telephone that there are elements of the case that don't fit together," I reminded him. "Perhaps it's time to elucidate."

We saw an elderly butler standing as motionless as a stuffed bear in the small entrance hall that gave on to a larger hallway. Lovebrook apparently didn't want to answer whilst there was anyone to overhear, and Bella caught up with us before he could say anything.

"So, Inspector. What do you have to tell us?" She made her request for information a little more cheerfully than I had.

We passed through a marble-columned archway, and Love-brook stopped at the bottom of an impressive three-flight staircase that took up one half of an open gallery in the centre of the building. The doors I'd seen so far had all been closed, so this was my first true impression of the interior. It couldn't have been more different from most other stately homes I'd visited. In place of paintings of long-dead forebears, there were black-framed photographs of famous visitors, from politicians to sportsmen and other people who don't spend their lives playing games. A highly patterned woollen rug occupied the space there, and the only other noteworthy artefact was an alabaster statue of what looked to me to be a woman in the throes of death.

"What I have to tell you," Lovebrook finally said before trotting on up the stairs, "is that I've never felt so out of my depth before. I had recently allowed myself to entertain the foolish notion that I was a competent detective, but I believe that this is the case to disabuse me of such false confidence."

"Don't be so hard on yourself, man," I tried to reassure him, as he had done the same for me in the past. "It can't be that bad. Why don't you start from the beginning, as you previously offered?"

He paused at the second turn of the stairs to consider this. "I'll do what I can." This was followed by a truly weary sigh, and I could tell that he hadn't slept a great deal the night before. "The victim is fifty-year-old Penny Baker. She has been working at Cherkley Court for the best part of a decade. We will look more closely at her personal life, of course, but I have learnt nothing to suggest that anyone held a particular grudge against her or even thought badly of her work. In short, I can find no motive for the attack beyond that to which the scene attests."

I already had a few thoughts, but I decided not to interrupt him as we walked around the arched balcony on the first floor to the wing of the house where Lady Sheridan's boudoir was surely located.

Lovebrook still sounded mournful. "Perhaps I've spent too long around the pair of you. It's hard for me to think that the simplest solution could turn out to be the correct one."

"That's wonderful!" I said, even though he clearly wasn't happy about it. I was talking as a mystery novelist, rather than his friend, and Bella soon got us back to the core of the case.

"How exactly did the attack occur?"

Even this required him to think for a few moments before nodding. "Let me show you." He accelerated towards a closed door on the other side of the gallery. He didn't knock or call out to tell anyone we would be entering, and I took this to mean that Lady Sheridan had relocated to another part of the house. Once we were inside, I did not blame her one bit.

The room was furnished in a far more traditional style than I'd seen until now. Floor-length damask curtains with a baroque gold design upon them covered the windows – perhaps out of respect for what had happened there two nights prior. There was a suite of furniture around a wide fireplace, where I could picture the lady of the house entertaining her friends. The walls were hung with tapestries, and the carpet underfoot was thick and springy and covered in blood.

FIVE

I admit that I knelt down to examine the stain, even though I was no expert when it came to studying the colour or shape of the dirty red mark before me.

"Am I right in my impression that someone may have been hiding out of sight as Penny came into the room?" Bella asked as she examined the position of the stain, its proximity to the entrance, and the alcove beside the door that was just big enough for a man to conceal himself. "As soon as she entered the room, her attacker jumped out with a weapon of some sort."

"Precisely. The maid seems to have been hit from behind and fallen forward. We found a blood-stained metal bar discarded by the sofa over there." Lovebrook pushed his fringe from his eyes and pointed to the far wall.

Though the world outside was bright, the dim room, lit only by two electric bulbs in glass tulip shades, gave me the feeling that it was late at night. It was easy to imagine the maid stepping into the room to meet her fate.

"Were there any fingerprints on it?" I asked, looking up at the inspector.

I could tell that Lovebrook was conflicted again and, rather than answering my question, he moved around me to draw our attention to a locked cabinet between the two tall windows. "This is where the thief stole the silver box. It was a real antique – worth thousands – and there was nothing else here that was quite so valuable."

"Even then," Bella began, "wouldn't it have made more sense to look for jewellery? Surely a woman like Lady Sheridan has a small fortune in rings, bracelets and necklaces. Items which are more easily transported and sold."

"Well, quite." Lovebrook leaned back against the glass-fronted piece of furniture. "That's one of the things that struck me as strange. Why come in here in the first place? From what I understand, the stolen box wouldn't have been obvious when the criminal stuck his head into the room. And he had to break a pane of glass to access it, thus risking the possibility that he would be heard."

"Perhaps he was, and that's why Miss Baker came inside?" I managed to turn this statement into a question, and Lovebrook pointed at me encouragingly.

"I considered the very same thing. For the sake of argument, let's say the criminal is an opportunist – either he's Dennis Apps, the gardener who's disappeared, or a vagabond who somehow made his way onto the estate and up to the house."

I thought this last possibility unlikely, seeing how well secured the place was and what a walk it would be just to get from the high walls we'd seen to the house itself.

Lovebrook had a third option to put forward. "He could even be a professional criminal, but I think that's unlikely judging by what happened. Whoever he was, he came in here looking for something to steal. He broke the pane of glass, presumably using the metal bar that we found behind the sofa and some fabric to dampen the noise. At that point, Penny Baker, who happened to be up here for another reason – let's imagine she'd forgotten something in one of the bedrooms when she'd been going about her duties – Penny heard a noise and decided to see what it was. The sound of her approach alerted the burglar, and he ran to the door to hide before she entered."

He broke up this list of hypotheses by acting out the scene he was describing. "As soon as she had made it a few steps into the room, the attacker swung his makeshift weapon through the air."

We waited for something more and, when it didn't come, I allowed Bella to point out the obvious.

"That doesn't seem like a complicated case to me." She spoke hesitantly. It wasn't like her. "I mean to say, there are few real inconsistencies in what you've told us."

Lovebrook reacted as if he'd just had an electric shock. He suddenly stood up straighter and shifted away. "I haven't got to that yet, though I imagine Marius has already worked it out."

They both looked down at me, and I tried to fathom what I could have missed. It was surely something to do with the blood, as I was the one who'd stared at it for some time. Or perhaps Lovebrook had such a high opinion of me he assumed that I'd be able to guess what he was thinking.

"We know she was hit on the back of the head," I muttered in the hope that something more would come to me.

"That's right." Lovebrook mimed the action again, and the gesture was so macabre that I was glad his hand was empty. "Her assailant brought the bar down with some force, fracturing the top of her skull with what we believe, from its position, was the first blow."

I've read enough books about famous murders to know that there are scientists and even some police officers who can read a whole story in the blood that is left after a killing. As a superintendent in the Metropolitan Police, Lord Edgington was well known for it, but I couldn't imagine where to begin.

"Look at the sprays that lead off at diagonals from the main halo of blood," Lovebrook said to help me. "What do you make of them?"

In an instant, a detail revealed itself. "She was hit again on the floor?" I asked to be sure.

"My goodness." Bella sounded more surprised than shocked, but I can't deny that it was a gruesome topic to consider. "That poor dear woman."

"That's just it," Lovebrook reflected. "The assailant did enough with one blow to knock her out. So why would he have continued hitting her?"

A noticeable hush gripped the elegant room, and it seemed to call attention to the lack of frivolous voices which might ordinarily have rung out in Lady Sheridan's boudoir. To be perfectly honest, I'd never known what a boudoir was before. I'd imagined it being full of dresses and powder-puff make-up for some reason. I suppose what I'd actually been picturing was a dressing room in a theatre, but it turned out that a boudoir was like any ordinary sitting room, though perhaps decorated in a more feminine manner.

"A burglar's motive is to gain as much as he can without putting himself in unnecessary danger," Lovebrook explained when we failed to answer his question. "The doctor who inspected Penny believes that it was the attacker's intention to kill. He considers it a miracle that she's survived as long as she has. So why would the burglar have carried out such a violent attack when it is far more likely to send the police after him and lead to a heftier and maybe even deadly sentence if he's apprehended?"

"Perhaps she caught sight of him," Bella put forward. "Perhaps he wanted to make certain that she couldn't identify him to the police."

Lovebrook backed up a few steps to return to his concealed position beside the door. "I don't think that's possible. First, we have already concluded that the attacker was standing behind her at the time, and she was looking forward. Second, if he'd been anywhere else in the room, she would have turned around to flee."

"Hide yourself in the alcove," I told him. "I'd like to test something we haven't explored." I went back to the gallery, closed then reopened the door and entered the room just as Penny Baker would have. On stepping inside, I had a look around, as one might when entering a new room. "It's possible that she forgot why she'd come in here and had a glance about the place."

"And?" Bella asked as she looked up at me from a crouched position beside the bloodstain. "What does that prove?"

The air (and excitement) went out of me. "It proves she was unlikely to have seen her attacker." I turned my head ninety degrees, and the hidey hole in which Lovebrook was standing still didn't give up its secrets.

He finally stuck his head out to continue the conversation. "That's the very thing. I don't believe the victim saw the person who brained her. And so I ask once more, why would the attacker have delivered further blows on the floor when there was little chance of Penny raising her head to see him?"

"What if the attacker was known to her?" I knew I hadn't answered his question, but I thought it might be of consequence. "Perhaps the mere sound of his breathing, or his shuffling footsteps, or something like that could have given him away."

Lovebrook moved across the carpet at this moment to show how little noise he could make. "Even if that were the case, he would most likely have held his breath and moved more quietly. I find it very hard to believe that the violence perpetrated against Penny Baker was necessary."

Bella walked to the windows and drew back the curtains to have a better look at the room. "Have you ruled out the possibility that the burglary was a distraction from the real motive? Could someone have called Penny up here in order to attack her?"

Lovebrook pulled his lips into his mouth for a moment. He looked just as deflated as when we'd arrived. "That possibility can rarely be eliminated until the culprit has been identified. However, I have spoken to her colleagues and, as I've no doubt Señorita Barriuso will have told you, Penny was loved – truly loved – by everyone who works here. And sadly, none of the other staff saw her in the half hour before she was attacked."

We did indeed already know this, but I've discovered in my short career as a detective that ruling out the same thing a number of times is often a good idea. Before I could draw their attention to something in the inspector's behaviour that didn't make sense, Bella did it for me.

"What haven't you told us?" Her voice was oddly flat, as though she were afraid that she wasn't supposed to have worked out what she'd worked out. "It clearly isn't just the wounds on the back of the maid's head that have upset you. It's foolish to assume that every killer is motivated by the chance to perpetrate senseless violence, but that doesn't make it impossible. So tell us what else you know."

"Fine." He glanced at his hands as if trying to work out this conundrum. "There is something. The weapon we found is a cast-iron garden stake." He paused again, and I still didn't understand why he would be so reluctant to share this with us. "We took Dennis Apps's fingerprints from a cup in his bedroom, and they're all over the weapon too."

SIX

He continued to set forth his feelings on this apparently vital revelation as we travelled back downstairs. "The most significant thing as far as I'm concerned is that there are no fingerprints on the cabinet. Finding evidence that the gardener had been in the room would have been damning, of course, but the presence of prints on the weapon and nowhere else alarms me."

Bella reacted as though she wished to answer him, but no response came. I could imagine why she had held herself back. All we'd been doing since we'd got there was responding to Lovebrook's concerns with vague explanations for what might have happened, and it hadn't got us very far. I even thought I knew what she would have said if she'd continued the practice. It would have been something along the lines of, *Apps may have taken the silver box then removed his gloves for some reason. Perhaps he wanted a better grip on the metal bar.*

"Yes," I found myself replying to my thoughts aloud, "but if he'd removed his gloves, he wouldn't have left the weapon behind." They both looked at me as if I'd lost a good part of my mind. "I agree with Lovebrook. Something isn't right here."

"I'm glad you feel that way, Marius," the inspector replied, and he picked up his pace as we reached the open hallway at the centre of the house. "I was beginning to think that I'd read one too many of your tricky books."

"You've only read two of them!"

"I just meant that I keep looking for complicated solutions when the simplest will often do the job."

Perhaps wisely, Bella ignored my over-sensitive remark and changed the topic. "It's time to pay deference to our host; isn't that our next task?"

"Well, yes," Lovebrook looked a little uncertain again. "I feel we should stay in Lord Sheridan's good books as much as possible."

"What can you tell us about him?" I asked, aware that we only had seconds before we arrived at our destination. "I know that he's a baron and some kind of businessman but nothing more."

Lovebrook nodded to accept his task. "His name is Virgil Dixon, and he's a high cockalorum in the City. He's not what you would call *to the manor born*. From what I understand, he was awarded the barony for his services to British trade. He exports and imports metal goods back and forth to the Continent and has made an absolute fortune..." He looked about at the splendour of the house. "...as you can already see."

"Are there any rumours of corruption wafting about him?" I tried, on the off-chance the case would be that easy. "Any hint of double-dealing or impropriety?"

Lovebrook had raised his hand to knock on a door that was set back in a shady hallway towards the rear of the building. "Sadly not."

"Come in," a flat voice called when we made our presence known, and the inspector soon pushed the door open so that the sunlight flooded out to us from a large, well-appointed library.

At first, all I could see was the silhouette of a man against the wide French windows which covered one wall. My eyes needed several seconds to adjust to the light, and even then, I had to squint to pick out any details of the scene.

"Ah, Detective Inspector Lovebrook. It's good of you to come back." Lord Sheridan rose and stepped out from behind his immense desk that looked as if it were a good few centuries older than the house in which it stood. "I see you've brought your friends."

"I prefer to think of Lady Bella and Mr Quin as colleagues, if you don't mind, sir." I'd rarely heard Lovebrook sound so deferential. He was not the type to fear the rich and powerful figures we encountered on our cases, and it surprised me that he should treat our host in such a way. "It may not be standard practice for police inspectors to involve members of the public in our investigations, but the three of us work extremely well together."

"I will trust your opinion on the matter. What I want more than anything is to find the savage who was responsible for this heinous act." Lord Sheridan remembered us at this moment and came over to greet Bella. "You are very welcome here, Lady Isabella. Your father and I are members of the same club. I haven't seen him for some years, but he always spoke highly of you."

The pale, precise man took her hand and kissed it rather flamboyantly. Bella had been trained how to react to such formalities from a young age and knew just how to respond. "That is kind of you to say, but Daddy isn't the most impartial judge when it comes to his children. I hope we can be of help, nevertheless."

I enjoyed watching this exchange without having to contribute anything. It gave me a chance to study the man before us. No matter where the mystery of the (nearly) murdered maid might take us (and yes, I might consider using that as the title of a future book), Lord Sheridan would undoubtedly be pivotal to our time there – if for no other reason than that he had the power to eject us from the estate whenever the feeling took him.

He was less tall than I'd pictured him: a good foot shorter than me, in fact. He had grey hair that was oddly wan and wispy. It was as though someone had taken the time to remove the colour from it. And yet, despite the initially wishy-washy impression he gave, when his eyes landed upon me, he communicated a great internal strength. They were a deep blue colour and had an intensity to them that sent an unsettling fizz through me. His smile did nothing to hide the fact that he was sizing me up.

"And you must be the mystery novelist," he said, holding his hand out for me to take. "I believe that my Imelda has read your books. She enjoys lighter forms of literature, whereas I tend to be buried under a pile of papers." He'd managed to insult my work without sounding as if he had any wish to offend.

"It is an honour to meet you, sir," I told him, aware of just how much I sounded like Lovebrook already. Sheridan was a man around whom everyone remained on their best behaviour.

He pointed to the three chairs before his desk, and I was quite sure that a servant had arranged them there in preparation for our visit. I took a moment to take in my surroundings but, except for books, and a portrait of a rather commanding figure with a great bushy beard, there wasn't much to see.

"You must explain how I can help you and what you need," Sheridan told us when we'd all sat down.

"I think the first thing we must do is repeat the interviews I conducted yesterday," Lovebrook replied on our behalf. "It may sound unlikely, but the very same information could lead to an important discovery when examined in another light."

A distant look bothered Sheridan's features for a moment and, rather than responding, he took us in a different direction. "Now that I think of it, I believe I read about the pair of you in the newspaper." He scratched his head as he tried to recall the details. "It was in Hurtwood Village, wasn't it? I recall you solved an unsolvable crime there around this time last year."

"As Detective Inspector Lovebrook explained," Bella answered for the three of us, "we all play our part, as we have on several cases since then."

The baron seemed amused by this. His hand covered his mouth but, from the curve of his sallow cheeks, I could see that he was smiling. "Go ahead then. Ask me your questions. I have nothing to hide."

Lovebrook sat back in his chair, and I could tell that he wanted one of us to lead the interview, so I did just that. "Perhaps you could begin by describing the events of Friday night as you remember them."

Sheridan took a deep breath. "I wasn't directly involved in any of it, I'm afraid. By the time I was told what had happened, the servants had realised that Penny was still breathing and moved her somewhere more comfortable whilst the doctor made his way here from the village."

We didn't need his vague proclamations. We required facts and details. "I believe your wife was entertaining guests, is that correct?"

"She often does." He shuffled in his seat, and I could tell that he wished this were not the case. "She is devoted to the arts, you see. She'd invited three young hopefuls up here to compete for her..." He paused to allow us to imagine how he might finish this sentence. "...patronage. I believe she has a project in mind for one of them."

This immediately had me thinking that two of the guests would go home empty-handed and might have fancied helping themselves to a consolation prize from Lady Sheridan's boudoir. I wasn't about to share my ideas with a potential suspect, though.

"Can you tell us how the evening unfolded?" Bella asked, as I'd spent a little too long picking over our host's words.

Sheridan crossed his arms across his chest. "We ate dinner together. I tolerated the conversation for as long as I could, but all that talk of expressing oneself and realising a creative vision was too much for me. As soon as we'd finished eating, and it was clear that neither of the young gentlemen was interested in retiring to share a cigar and a glass of cognac with me, I made my excuses and left."

"What time would that have been?" I moved my head to look at him from another angle. A cloud had blown away from the sun, and a strong beam of light shone directly into my eye.

"Around eleven o'clock, I would imagine. I came in here to look over some files. My wife can confirm that. She called in to speak to me during the game they were playing, that was perhaps twenty minutes after I'd finished dinner. I continued my work, and it was gone midnight when my head footman, Francis, knocked on the door to tell me the sad news about Penny. I went straight upstairs to the boudoir to see what had happened. I don't know who called the police, but I'm sure my butler, Ponsonby, can tell you."

I wanted to excavate some nugget of intrigue, but I could see he was not the sort of man to indulge such tawdry desires in those around him.

Bella must have realised the same thing, as she changed tack. "What can you tell us of the victim?"

This question evidently annoyed him, and he answered more sharply than before. "What would you like me to tell you? She was employed as a maid. I rarely consulted her opinion on the price of British steel or movements in the French Bourse."

Bella managed to hide just how much she disapproved of this attitude. Had she been required to give her opinion on a member of her staff at her home in Hurtwood, she would have been well positioned to comment on anyone from the pot boy to the head of household. "Very well, then. Can you tell us whether there were any problems between the workers here? Did anyone take issue with Penny Baker for any reason?"

He tapped his long, skinny fingers on the top of his desk a few times as he considered the question – or whether he wished to reply. "She gave me no cause for concern, but the staff here are the same as anywhere else. Despite the stereotype of loyal British maids and footmen, they all have their failings."

I could already see that he was not a warm-hearted sort. I wondered whether there was any point in continuing the interview as, despite what he'd said about wishing to help us, I felt that he considered it a waste of his time.

"To concentrate on facts alone," I began in the hope that a new approach would meet his approval, "where was everyone at the time that Penny was attacked?"

He glanced over at the inspector at this moment, and I'm sure he would have liked to dismiss my question. Instead, he frowned and muttered, "As I've already told you, I was busy in here. My butler is much better positioned to tell you what you need to know."

Bella sat forward in her chair. "Do you often stay in here working late at night?" Even she looked surprised by the question, and Sheridan nodded as he reflected on his answer.

"I do indeed. It's quite common for me to work until the early hours of the morning and get to bed some hours after my wife. On Friday, I'd had a fair bit of wine with my dinner, so I believe I may even have nodded off. Red always goes to my head." He seemed pleased with this, though it was hard to imagine whether it was the neat rhyme which tickled him or the general sentiment.

"Is that your father?" I asked out of the blue, pointing up at the stately painting that was surrounded by shelves on the right-hand wall.

"No, that is the Earl of Clonmel, my father-in-law. He was a great man. A visionary, in fact, who saw something in me when I was young and invested in my first commercial idea. If it weren't for him, I'd never have made anything of myself. I'd also never have married my wife. He gave me a job, helped me establish my company, and I ended up winning his daughter's heart."

I had another glance at the stern, bearded gentleman, who was dressed in the gloomy black suit of an undertaker. He and Sheridan had the same steeliness about them, but with his washed-out colour palette, the younger man was like a negative photograph of the earl.

I was about to say something polite in reply, but before I could, the door flew open and a woman with wavy auburn hair stepped confidently inside.

"Virgil, my darling, I'm so sorry to disturb you and your guests, but I wanted to take my friends for a drive before lunch."

Lady Sheridan was a fetching woman of perhaps fifty. She was dressed in modern fashion, and I could just have imagined Bella wearing the airy red dress she sported. As she came closer, I realised that her hair owed more to a jar of henna than – judging by her freckled skin, green eyes and her father's title – her Irish roots.

"I couldn't find the keys to the Daimler, so I was hoping you'd have them," she continued, nodding to us by way of apology.

It was at this moment that two grinning buffoons appeared behind her. They wore smart suits and had neatly parted hair, but they were buffoons nonetheless. You could tell from the way they giggled without making a sound that they were coxcombs of the lowest order. Though they were undeniably of voting age, the younger man looked all of twelve years old, the older perhaps seventeen, and they could barely stand still as they waited for their matron to give them instructions. And if I were being more honest, I would admit that they were both around twenty-five years old, but where would the fun be in that?

When her husband still hadn't said anything, Lady Sheridan spoke again. "I thought they'd like to experience a little of the countryside." She sounded less confident for a moment. "The lanes around the estate are so pretty at this time of year that it would be a shame for them to come all this way without seeing anything of the place."

Her husband still hadn't spoken a word, but he pulled out the drawer in front of him, reached inside it and tossed a tasselled key ring across to her. She snatched it with one hand, then ran to kiss him on the cheek. Lady Sheridan had a youthful energy about her that matched her clothes, and I wondered whether that was what she gained from spending time with such infants.

With her objective achieved, she was even livelier than before. "We'll be ever so careful, won't we, boys?"

"Rather!" one of the idiots yelped with excitement. "As my daddy told me after I crashed my first Bentley, a car is not a toy." The man was a caricature of how a carefree young toff is supposed to look and sound.

"And yet he still bought you a second one," his baby-faced friend replied with a chortle. "More fool him."

The three of them fell about laughing at this moment, even as they strolled back through the doorway in which they'd been loitering. As she passed, I saw the amusement on our hostess's face. She wore the look that a mother gives her children as they tread the fine line between cheeky and naughty. However, not everyone was amused by the two men's frivolity. Their departure revealed a young woman in the doorway with short black hair that cut across her face in a diagonal fringe. She remained where she stood for a moment as though she wished she could stay there with us.

"Louise?" the art patron called when the fourth member of her party was slow to follow. "Are you coming?"

I caught the exceedingly modern young woman's eye for a moment, and I noticed a sorrowful look there. It is a hazard of my trade to believe that every person has a story within him, and I'd just encountered four perfectly good ones. I was aware that I might be jumping to conclusions, but I saw Lady Sheridan as the wealthy widow of a still-breathing businessman who sought her pleasures outside of the home. Then there was the spoilt heir to some untold fortune who was rebelling against his rich family by pretending to be an artist, the put-upon woman in a man's world, and last but not least the marginally older of the two men who, despite his talk of wealth and his exceedingly smart accent, did not fit in with the others. It was if he were trying harder to impress and be noticed than his friends were. I had all I needed to sketch out the characters for a book, without even mentioning our host, who was about to say something truly interesting for the first time since we'd arrived.

"I'm well aware of how all that must look," Lord Sheridan informed us. "You surely think that I have returned home to my Penelope on Ithaca and the suitors are doing their best to win their prize. I can assure you that my wife and I are just as in love as when we first met."

I must admit that, as I had a less than classical education, it took me a few moments to realise that he was comparing his situation to that of Odysseus in Homer's epic tale. My general knowledge was just strong enough to bridge that gap, but it didn't help that his metaphor was a poor one. For one thing, he hadn't recently returned from an epic voyage.

"We wouldn't be inclined to cast any such aspersions," Lovebrook replied most diplomatically (and, in my case, dishonestly).

"That's neither here nor there." Sheridan pushed his chair back to stand up. He seemed surer of himself as he paced in front of the window – turning into a smudge of darkness amidst the bright light as he did so. "I know how it looks and, were I sitting on the other side of that desk, I'd think the same thing. My wife enjoys the company of young people, just as I enjoy the company of anyone who will help me make more money from my existing enterprises."

He paused then, as though weighing up whether to say more. "But you can think what you like. Imelda and I are a perfect pair. Without her, I would never have made anything of myself."

We'd all been so polite for so long that it was becoming unbearable, and I couldn't resist a probing comment. "So you wish it to be known that you aren't jealous of the two spirited young men with whom your wife just drove off into the countryside."

Something fired in him then, and I could see that he liked the challenge. "I didn't say that I wasn't jealous. I'd be a fool not to be. All I wish you to know is that I trust Imelda implicitly. Whatever went on two nights ago had nothing to do with us."

It was Bella's turn to overstep the bounds of civil conversation and venture into darker territory. "But it might have something to do with the three strangers who were running about the place when your maid was beaten?"

Sheridan stepped in front of the long blue curtains, and I could see his face once more. Though my eyes were still a mess of burns where the sun had marked my retinas, I could make out a smile. It seemed to suggest that he appreciated Bella's deft conclusion, but he wasn't going to fall any deeper into her trap.

"I may be a poor host, Lady Isabella, but I'm not about to accuse my guests of criminality. They seem like solid sorts – all three of them – and I have no reason to suspect any particular person of being involved in the theft."

"What about your gardener?" I was quick to ask. "Do you have any reason to suspect Dennis Apps?"

Far from pushing to reveal a lingering secret, this did little to upset him. He simply pulled back his shoulders and looked a little bored. "I don't know the first thing about Mr Apps, or his muddy colleagues for that matter. I've had deeper and more revealing conversations with the man from the dairy than with that gloomy, shuffling gardener. I pay him to keep the view from my window looking beautiful and, until two days ago, he did a fine job of it. I'll leave it to you to find out anything more."

It was clear from his tone that he considered the interview to have concluded. The three of us rose without uttering another word, and ever-courteous Lovebrook was preparing to say something when Lord Sheridan spoke again.

"If you want to know about the gardener, you should talk to the Spanish woman. Miss Barruso, is it?" He'd got her surname wrong, but he wasn't the type of man you corrected. "The pair were practically glued together outside of their working hours."

SEVEN

"I have to ask, Lovebrook," I said as we walked through a sizeable salon at the rear of the property to access the gardens, "has anyone verified exactly where Nerea was at the time of the assault?"

"Really, Marius!" Bella was angry again. "Are you genuinely asking whether your former girlfriend is a violent criminal?"

"Yes, I am." I looked back at her, uncowed.

Lovebrook was evidently tickled by the exchange. "What did this woman do to you? I've been broken-hearted from time to time in my life, but I don't think I'd accuse any of the charming young ladies who spurned me of being violent maniacs."

I struggled for an answer then. "I'm not suggesting that I ever saw her commit a crime, and she was certainly never violent in my presence, but..." For more reasons than one, it was difficult to finish that sentence and so I decided not to. "I'm really only asking to be sure of our facts."

Bella and the inspector exchanged a glance, but I remained quite cowless.

"So, has anyone confirmed where Nerea was on Friday night?"

Lovebrook made a fuss of reaching into his inside pocket and extracting a small ribbon-bound notebook as though it were a great inconvenience. Perhaps it was heavier than it looked.

With his eyes on me, he flicked through the pages before drily responding, "Yes."

"Dash it all, Valentine. I'm not being difficult. I just want to know that we can rule her out."

It was Bella's turn to think badly of me. "Would you like her to be the culprit, Marius? Is that what's got into you?"

We stepped through the tall French windows that led outside, and I sighed. "No, of course not. Do you really think I want to accept that a woman I adored for a significant period of my life is a lunatic?"

We'd come out on a stone terrace that spanned the width of the formal gardens at the back of the property. A lawn sloped down from where we stood, and there was a great expanse of woodland in the broad valley, with the closest sections surely planted to the owners' tastes. I noticed Atlas cedars and Japanese maples mixed in with the native yews. I could also see a four-stone basset hound lumbering over to us to pad along at Bella's side.

Percy's adopted mistress now looked even angrier with me, and I decided not to mention Nerea again for some time. Unfortunately, as we circumnavigated the house, we came across the woman in question with her young ward.

"Is there any news of Dennis?" she asked without ado. She was unquestionably disturbed by the gardener's disappearance, and I felt guilty to have judged her so harshly.

"My men are doing all we can to find him," Lovebrook reassured her. "They're investigating reports of a sighting at Euston Station, but that is quite common whenever the police go looking for someone. The reality is that there are many young men of average height and build. And, since the war, a good few of them have faint scars on their cheeks."

"You must do all you can to find him," she said, and I remembered that her Spanish accent used to grow stronger whenever she begged a favour. "He could be in danger."

"I promise that we are trying our very best, señorita." Lovebrook used his usual affable manner to put her at ease. It seemed to work.

"It's nice to see you again, Nerea," Bella stepped closer to tell her. "And this must be young Lionel."

I hadn't looked at the boy until now. He was rather a blank sort. Dressed in an unremarkable brown suit – his trousers a half inch too short above his stout leather one-bar shoes – he looked like any boy of ten years old. When Nerea had described him the night before, I'd imagined a tiny infant, but there was nothing little about "Little Lionel". He was as round as Billy Bunter, with the thick-lensed glasses to match.

"Is the maid dead yet?" the boy asked, and I immediately took a disliking to him.

"Miss Baker is still in the hospital," Lovebrook replied without showing his feelings on the brat's question. He had no doubt developed this talent twice over: first from being born into a wealthy family, and second as a police officer.

"Baker?" Lionel let out a snorting laugh. "Was that her name? I always just called her Piggy because she was such a porker."

"She isn't dead," I reminded him. "Nor is it acceptable to speak of other people in such a disrespectful fashion." I was tempted to tell him that he was no chiselled athlete himself, but as rude as I can be, I draw the line at disabusing children of their misconceptions. I also wasn't about to tell him not to believe in Father Christmas.

Nonetheless, he looked at me in dismay. "She's a servant! How do you expect me to speak of her?"

There were several things I could think of to reply to this, but I bit my lip, and Nerea scolded him in the softest manner imaginable. "Come along now, Lionel," she said in French. "Don't be a naughty little cabbage." I should probably explain that the French word for cabbage is a term of endearment. She put her arm around the boy and then, switching back to English, told us, "I won't be far away if you need anything," before leading her pupil off towards a large greenhouse at the end of the gravel-strewn terrace.

I watched her leave and tried not to remember what I had once found so attractive about her. Even in the simple blue dress of a teacher, she cut a striking figure.

"Where are we going?" I asked when we continued on our journey, though I should have probably questioned this some minutes earlier.

"I thought you'd like to meet the other gardeners. They knew Dennis Apps better than most."

I must admit that I felt like a tourist being guided between famous sights.

"When was he last seen?" Bella surveyed the spectacular land-scape as she asked this question. You could see for miles over the tops of all those fabulous trees.

"The butler, Ponsonby, said that Apps retired before the others on Friday. No one saw him for a few hours after dinner, and when one of the other gardeners went to fetch him from the annexe to help look for the attacker, he wasn't in his room."

"What time was that exactly?"

Lovebrook looked back at us as he replied. "Around one o'clock in the morning. And I know that all the evidence says he's our man, but a whole other part of me – perhaps not the most rational part – keeps yelling that it doesn't make sense." We'd reached a gate in a tall hedge, and he stood with his hands on top of it to watch us pass. "If Apps wished to rob his employers, why would he do it when there were so many people around? In addition to the party guests, there were still several servants about the place. If he went upstairs to his mistress's boudoir, he could easily have been caught."

"There they are," I said to distract from the forlorn mood his comments had roused.

I pointed to two men in bottle-green serge dungarees, and we followed the path down a set of steps with high stone balustrades to the spot where they were cutting back an immense hydrangea bush.

"Morning, copper," the older of the two said when he saw us.

Delivered in another tone of voice, the gardener's address might have sounded disrespectful, but I had the feeling that he called each person by their profession, and would have greeted his postman, butcher and dentist in the same manner. Actually, I take back that last one as, judging by his crooked, yellow teeth, I doubted he'd ever visited any such person.

"Good morning, Gareth, Gavin," Lovebrook said to each man in turn.

"And 'ow can I 'elp ya today?" Gareth had a strong country accent. He reminded me of my cheery uncle.

"We'd like to ask you some questions," I said to get to the point. "You may have said all you can remember to the inspector, but we're trying to uncover anything that has been missed."

Gareth didn't seem bothered by this, but his younger colleague couldn't bring himself to look at us. "Do I have to stay, or can I get on in the rose garden?"

Gareth shrugged without turning around, and so the younger man remained where he was.

I jumped straight in. "Do you know whether Dennis Apps had any money troubles?"

Gareth smiled. "I doubt it. 'E never spent no money on nothing as far as I know. 'E lived 'ere in the annexe and rarely went up t' town."

"He was fond of a flutter on the horses," the younger man, Gavin, muttered with his eyes off down the hill somewhere. I must say, the Dixon family could have made life easier by choosing staff with less similar names. We'd had Francis and Frederick the footmen and now Gareth and Gavin the gardeners. Aside from this making it more difficult to remember which was which, I felt like a character in a children's book.

Gareth removed a pipe from his pocket and began to fill it with tobacco. "That is true. I'll give ya that, but only in the summer. There wouldn't 'ave been any risk of 'im losing much money at this time o' year."

"What about his interactions with other members of staff?"

Bella asked, and the previously cagey Gavin blushed, leaving his giggling colleague to answer for him.

"If you're talking about his 'interactions' with that foreign lass over the last month—"

"Spanish," Gavin corrected him.

"Well... I can say they seemed to be interacting quite 'appily."

Gareth was at least sixty, so it was funny to hear a note of embarrassment enter his voice, even as he joked about the affair between Nerea and their colleague.

Bella showed no amusement or shame. "I was thinking more of the staff in general. We know that he and Señorita Barriuso were fond of one another."

This really made Gavin titter, and I decided it might be necessary to calm them down. "Come along, both of you. Penny Baker may yet die from her injuries. You were the people who spent the most time with Dennis, so what can you tell us about him?"

My comment did sober them up somewhat, but I was still surprised when Gavin looked at me and provided a clear answer. "He's a good man, Mr Apps is. He's head gardener and treats me and Gareth well. He fought in the war – I were too young for that – he sends money home to his old mum in Basingstoke, and I've never heard him say a bad word about no one." He delivered this short testament with a rather noble air – regardless of his poor grammar.

"Tha's right!" Gareth agreed. "'E's a good man, our Dennis. I won't 'ear no one say nothing against 'im!"

"So you don't think that he could have been the person who robbed your mistress on Friday night?"

They looked at one another then and appeared less sure of themselves before Gareth provided a response. "Now, I wouldn't say that neither. Most men I know'd pocket a free dinner if they saw one lyin' around. But Dennis'd never've smacked our Penny. That woman is a better person than most priests I know. Everyone round 'ere loves 'er."

"She wuz like a mother to us all," Gavin added. I had to assume that his shyness had either worn off, or his fear that we were there to cause him trouble had subsided. "It's hard to imagine anyone hurting her."

"Did either of you see anything yourselves on the night of the attack?" I thought it bore asking, even if Lovebrook and his men had already interviewed them.

"We wuz here in the shed playing cards till Francis the footman came to tell us the bad news. We didn't see nothing all night."

"Thank you." Bella spoke with little animation. "If you can think of anything that might help, please come to find us at once."

They agreed, and we left them to their work. Lovebrook had remained silent throughout our discussion, presumably to give us a chance to probe the gardeners in our own way. As we walked further on around the property, he came back to life.

"I didn't know about the gambling," he admitted. "They didn't mention that when I spoke to them. I suppose that, so soon after the incident, it is natural they wouldn't have given me a full picture."

"It's still not enough, though, is it?" I put to them. "An interest in horse racing isn't the same thing as being hundreds of pounds in debt because he can't stop himself – especially if he only gambles in the summer."

"I would tend to agree." Bella was cautious in her reply. "Unless the man suddenly lost his mind or received some terrible news that changed his life for the worse, it's hard to imagine him giving up a steady existence here for the sake of whatever money he could make by stealing that silver box."

"Exactly." Lovebrook was a step ahead again and looked back at us over his shoulder. "If he'd got the whole jewellery collection or a pile of money from Lord Sheridan's safe, it might be feasible, but we keep coming back to that same problem. I still feel it's unlikely that Apps is our man."

"How long has he been working here?" I asked, as this seemed like a significant point we were yet to discuss.

"Ever since he returned from the war. He'd worked on another estate near his home in Hampshire before then."

I suppose that, like me, the others allowed their thoughts to take over as we walked through a short avenue of trees in silence before coming to a red-brick building that was set away from the main house. It couldn't have been more than a couple of decades old and, in contrast to everything else we'd seen until now, was unembellished and utilitarian: a brick box in which to store the staff when they weren't needed.

"So this is where he lived," Bella practically whispered as Lovebrook produced a key and unlocked the green front door.

We followed him into the building and up the stairs to a room off the first-floor landing.

"This was where he lived," Lovebrook confirmed somewhat unnecessarily.

It was a bare and basic space. There was a small wardrobe in one corner, a hard bed, which Bella sat down upon as if to test the firmness of the mattress, and a single small window with a view of a messy piece of land behind the annexe. Aside from a large mound of earth which looked as if it had recently been turned over, the ground out there was black, so I assumed it was where the gardeners lit their bonfires.

The room itself was no more welcoming. The walls had once been white, but they had turned beige after years of exposure to cigarette smoke and sunlight. There were no photographs or paintings hanging. It was as impersonal as a place can get, and I wondered what that said about the person who had lived there.

I opened the wardrobe to see what, if anything, our missing man had left behind. There was a set of overalls very similar to the ones we'd seen on his colleagues, a scruffy black woollen jumper, a pair of work boots and three empty coat hangers.

I turned to look at the inspector. "So he took clothes with him?"

Bella glanced up at the open wardrobe. "How can you be so sure?"

"His Sunday shoes are missing," I replied quite confidently, whilst secretly doubting the accuracy of what I was about to say. "The only clothes here are for work. He may be wearing his casual outfit, but at least his church clothes should be here."

"I came to the same conclusion," Lovebrook said from his spot beside the window. "And I confirmed it with Señorita Barriuso. He had a brown suit for best, and there's no sign of it."

"So he definitely hopped the twig then?" My words came out louder than I'd intended and echoed back to me off the cold, hard floorboards.

"If you mean he absquatulated," Lovebrook said with a wink to show that he was fancier than me, "then, yes, Apps has vanished like a snake in the desert."

"Or someone wants it to seem that way," Bella replied, but it was becoming increasingly difficult to hold on to that belief.

"I think we're trying too hard to prove the impossible," I told them. "We can't stomach the idea that a seemingly normal, decent chap could be tempted by the chance to make more money than he'd ever had before. He probably thought that he could get away with it. Had Penny not gone up to his mistress's boudoir when she did, he may well have. The fact he took a silver box and not a case full of jewels is hardly surprising either; it would be a lot easier to carry one valuable thing than many little ones. In a place like Cherkley Court, its disappearance might not even have been noticed."

Lovebrook defended his feelings on the case, and I didn't blame him. "The glass was broken on the cabinet, so I doubt the burglar was trying to be subtle. And he must have known the risk of being caught, as he was carrying the metal bar with him."

Bella said nothing. She just stared out of the window at the encroaching woodland, and I could tell that she was stuck between our two arguments.

I kept talking to see whether I could win her over. "Nerea never had the best taste in men..." I realised how this sounded and soon corrected myself. "Before me, I mean. When we first met, she was with a terrible fellow. From what she told me, he wasn't the first rotter who had stolen her heart."

Lovebrook pursed his lips, waiting for some evidence to spring to mind that could contradict all I'd said. "It still doesn't explain why he would have attacked the maid so brutally. Whatever else you might think, that is hard to explain."

I walked over to him and perched on the windowsill. "Maybe he thought it would shift suspicion from him. Perhaps he thought it would look more like a real burglary if she were unconscious. When he realised what he'd done, he accepted the plan wouldn't work and ran from the premises as fast as he could." I tried one last time to strengthen my argument. "Was there anything else in here when your men inspected this room?"

"Yes, an empty envelope with his name written in block letters. The only fingerprints on it, except for his, were too faint or smudged to identify, and there was nothing inside."

"There you go," Bella said, to push him back in the other direction. "Perhaps he was being blackmailed. Perhaps he received a letter telling him that his family would be in danger unless he followed certain instructions. The letter must have been important, or he wouldn't have taken it with him. It's more than possible that he was told to leave the estate and go to a particular address. I'm sure that, in a day or two, we'll hear from him and everything will make sense."

I felt that Bella was supporting Lovebrook's position out of sympathy, but she wasn't the sort of person to box the compass. "Think about it. He can't have passed through the main gate when he left, or the men on duty would have reported it. And it's an hour's walk to the nearest town. Even if he'd got there without anyone seeing him, it was the middle of the night. There were no trains running or taxis to be had."

She'd put some fire back in him at least. Lovebrook sounded quite animated again. "Yes, we spoke to the station master at Leatherhead, and he's had no reports of a man fitting Apps's appearance."

"Leatherhead is a small town. He couldn't have gone unnoticed," Bella replied, relying on her local knowledge to encourage him. "Someone would have called the police after they heard what had happened here. And if there's one thing I know about small towns in this part of the country, it's that word of a scandal travels fast."

She was up on her feet, eager to indulge in a bit more of the old investigating, when a cry carried across from the estate, and Percy began to howl.

EIGHT

"Please, Lord Sheridan," Nerea begged as we reached the terrace before the house. "You're not listening to me. I had nothing to do with what happened on Friday."

Her employer looked away and would not return her gaze. "That's easy to say, young lady, but the fact is that you can't possibly prove it. Your fellow was involved in all this to some extent, and I find it hard to believe that he could fail to tell you his plans if he intended to disappear."

"But it's true!" Nerea's voice became shrill and distorted as the anguish poured from her. "I didn't know anything about it. Whatever has gone on, I was as oblivious as you were."

His sharp eyes caught sight of us as we hurried along the path to them, but this didn't break his concentration. "A moment ago you told me that you were certain Apps was innocent. Now you're saying that you had no idea what he was up to. Which is it?"

We'd just reached them when Nerea released another tortured cry. Recognising the nice young lady from our flat the night before, Percy tried to sit on her feet to comfort her, but she was moving about too much for that.

"Please, Lord Sheridan," she tried. "I need this job. It's the only way I can afford to stay in the country, and I believe I've been a good teacher to little Lionel. I'll do whatever you demand to prove my innocence."

Her eyes were red, and I had to think that this discussion had gone on for some time before we became aware of it.

Inevitably, Bella came to the young woman's defence. "Lord Sheridan, I beg you to reconsider. Señorita Barriuso is a personal acquaintance of ours. As she has already told you, there is no reason to think that she had any prior knowledge of the attack. I'm sure that there's a solution that would remove the need for you to stand here shouting the place down."

"We wouldn't be out here if she had accepted my decision with good grace." This was the first time I'd caught a glimpse of the anger that was hidden behind the baron's placid façade. He directed the comment at Bella with great venom, and I knew what it was to get on the wrong side of a man like Virgil Dixon.

I truly believe that he would have stuck to his guns and dismissed his language mistress had it not been for a face we both spotted at one of the upstairs windows. Not-so-little Lionel banged on the glass to communicate his disapproval of his father's hasty decision, and a change came over the man.

"Very well, Lady Bella. If you are willing to vouch for this young person's good character, I will give her a second chance." He turned to address his employee, and I was terribly glad that I wasn't the one on the receiving end. "You may stay, Miss Barriuso, but if I hear the slightest report against you, nothing will make me change my mind a second time. Is that understood?" Though he was not much taller than the woman he'd just threatened, Lord Sheridan was a terrifying presence when his hackles were up.

Nerea nodded and pressed a crumpled handkerchief to her eyes. "I appreciate your leniency, my lord." I knew her well enough to detect a faint hint of sarcasm in these words. "I can assure you that you will have no trouble from me in the future."

He observed her for a moment, and I thought perhaps he enjoyed this whole affair more than he would have wanted to admit. Some men take a certain thrill from ordering around help-less women. It made me wonder whether this was enough to connect him to the violence of two nights earlier.

"I'm very glad that's settled then." Bella was exceptionally good at pretending that nothing was wrong when everything was clearly wrong. I really should learn to hide my feelings like that.

"Yes, of course." Lord Sheridan wasn't quite as accomplished as she was in this respect, but then we'd heard that he didn't have the same conditioning that she'd had from birth. As I know only too well myself, certain things are hard to learn later in life. "I suppose you'll require some refreshments," he continued more cordially. "When you finish with your current occupation, lunch will be served in the dining room."

"That's very good of you, sir," I smarmed so that Bella didn't have to.

He regarded Nerea with that same mix of cruel pleasure, pride and perhaps a little lust thrown in for good measure. He clearly luxuriated in the power he held over his subordinates. I could see that, more than the fortune he'd amassed, it was the influence he wielded that motivated the rich industrialist.

Nerea was the first to turn away. I thought she might cry again, but Bella was there to comfort her. Lord Sheridan nodded to me, his face blank as he returned to the house.

"I'm so sorry," Nerea whispered as she tried to recover her composure. It was quite unlike my memory of that bold and implacable woman, and I finally had to accept that we'd both changed since our time in Paris.

"You have no reason to apologise." Bella put an arm around her shoulders, and Nerea willingly buried her face in the thick mauve woollen coat that my friend wore. "The man was quite unreason-able, and if I'm alone with him again at any point, I will tell him just that. You can't be blamed for your boyfriend's actions."

"What actions? He didn't do anything!" Nerea pulled away, and the words came out of her almost as noisily as the shouts we'd heard.

Bella tried to comfort her again, and Lovebrook looked quite sympathetic, but I saw that there was something I could do to help. I held her with both hands and looked her in the eyes to say, "I believe you, Nerea. If you truly think Dennis is innocent, then we will do all that we can to prove it."

Her response caught in her throat for a moment, but when it came, it occasioned a wide smile, even as the stress of the previous confrontation still affected her. "Thank you, Marius. I knew that I could rely on you."

Five minutes earlier, I'd been trying to persuade my friends that the time had come to give up on Dennis Apps's innocence, but the wind had changed direction.

Young Lionel appeared at this moment with his governess at his side, and it was clear from the look of determination on his face that he had forced his way out of their lesson. "What happened, Nere?" I thought perhaps he loved her just as much as I once had.

Her eyes still sore, she attempted to hide her despair for his sake. "There's nothing to worry about," she told him in Spanish, and as I never learnt as much of the language as I probably should have, I can't tell you what she said after that.

The stern governess watched this exchange from the steps that led up to the grand salon, and when Nerea had reassured the boy that she would not be leaving him, the three of them returned inside.

Percy had been rolling around on the floor this whole time, ignored by everyone there. I'm sure he found such a prospect unfathomable, but when we began to disperse, he got to his feet to work out whom he should now reward with his company.

"I hope you enjoy your lunch," Lovebrook said without any suggestion of jealousy. "Riff-raff like me don't get to sit down to eat with lordly types." He leaned closer and dropped his voice lower. "Which is one of the reasons I brought you here in the first place. You can hobnob with the toffs while I lunch with the commoners. The food below stairs is more to my liking anyway."

He seemed quite happy with himself and walked off whistling, which Percy took as a sign that he should follow.

"And then there were two," I said to Bella, who sighed a little and looked as though she would have preferred to go with them. "Is anything wrong, dear friend?"

I motioned to the house to embark on our next piece of detective work: finding the dining room.

"Wrong? Why would anything be wrong?" She asked this sincerely before immediately undermining her question. "Aside from the fact I will never be able to understand the savagery that exists in man." I could only assume she was referring to our species in general, but I did worry for a moment that I was the man in question. "At times, our investigations feel like jolly escapades that someone has planned for our entertainment – with plenty of riddles and puzzles for us to solve. And I know we've seen a lot of dead bodies over the last year, but when I think of the woman who was attacked here lying in hospital, it makes my whole body throb at the injustice of the thing. I keep questioning the cruelty required to carry out any such assault. The very idea of someone bludgeoning her when she was already on the floor is too terrible to contemplate."

"You're quite right." I managed to sound sympathetic, but there was always going to be a caveat. "Of course, the only way to make it better is to concentrate on what we're doing here. Perhaps every murderer we've met was born with a minuscule piece of his heart missing. Or perhaps their consciences were wired incorrectly at birth. Even if we knew, it wouldn't change the fact that the man who attacked Penny Baker is still running free."

She bit her lip and considered my point. "I know you're right, but sometimes..." She didn't finish this thought. Instead, she moved towards the house and up the stairs as though pulled by an invisible thread.

"If the group we met earlier comes to lunch, there's a decent chance that we'll be sitting down to eat with the culprit," I said in the hope that this would help her concentrate on our task. "Let's do everything we can to find the evidence that will help us catch him."

She sighed a little more optimistically this time. "I'll try my best, Marius."

I felt there was more to her bad mood than she was willing to reveal, but I've never been the type to crack open a Pandora's box unnecessarily, so I kept quiet. We walked through that elegant salon, which I now noticed had a well-stocked bar within it that I hoped we would soon get to enjoy. From there, we returned to the corridor, and following the plan in Bella's head – based on her visits to countless such stately homes – we located the dining room. It was long and narrow and had a wall of glass doors at one end that, judging by the verdant display I could see through them, gave on to some sort of tropical garden, housed within a large glass extension.

We were the first of the guests to arrive, and so I took the opportunity to speak to the butler, who was inspecting the table settings.

"Mr Ponsonby, isn't it?"

He nodded at me with all the pride and reverence expected of a man in his profession. "That is correct, sir."

He was so resolute in his tone that it was hard to know what to say next. "Jolly good."

As Bella clearly wasn't sure where to sit, he hurried forward to pull back a chair for her. "Lord Sheridan informed me that you would be eating with him today. I believe he will be along forth-with." The man had alabaster skin and approximately seven hairs on his head which had been swept across his dome to dull the shine a little.

"I don't suppose there's anything useful you can tell us about Dennis Apps or the assault on Penny Baker?" I thought I might as well ask him.

He looked even haughtier for a moment, put his hands together in front of him, and in that ever-so-smarmy voice, which was far posher than his master's, demanded, "What did you have in mind, sir?"

"Well, perhaps you know something of his background. Or maybe you're aware of past problems that the maid suffered with other members of staff."

He looked as though he were sucking on a particularly sharp lemon drop for a moment as he attempted to answer. "I'm afraid not, sir. Penny is a much-loved member of the household. I have worked alongside her for many years and never had the slightest problem. Like me, she prides herself on never missing a day of work to illness or personal matters."

This made him look even smugger, but I noticed that he hadn't fully answered the question. "And Apps?"

His curling smile disappeared. "Hmmm, what can I say? The gardeners do a good enough job, but they spend much of their time smoking their pipes and talking. I don't trust a single one of them."

I doubted this would be the dramatic revelation that would turn the case on its head and lead us to the guilty party. The butler seemed like the type who would find his own mother suspicious if she failed to live up to his high standards.

"Thank you for your time, Ponsonby," Bella said when I didn't reply. "I'm sure that will be very helpful."

He may have blushed a little then. "You are so welcome, my lady. If there is anything more I can do, you need only ask."

Rather than recognising this as the perfect moment to return to his duties, he lingered with the same self-satisfied look on his face, forcing Bella to respond.

"No, thank you. That will be all for the moment."

He gave an unfeasibly low bow, and I got the impression he had a bad back. He seemed to get stuck halfway on his return journey and needed to support himself with one hand on the table before making it to full height. He left us with an awkward smile on his lips, and I was about to comment on the exchange when our host arrived. He had changed his clothes in the short time since we'd last seen him and now appeared to be dressed for a business meeting.

He stopped at the head of the table when he saw us looking at him. "I have to go into London. I was hoping to avoid it, but I've just had a call from my secretary and they need me there. A supplier we've been using has... Well, it's really not very interesting. Little about my job is to people with lives like yours." He pulled his chair back and sat down. "I do not like leaving at a time like this, but I see no other option."

"At least we get to have lunch together, first." Bella said this as though we were there for a social engagement.

I couldn't help but smile at her. I'm certain that she would have told me off – or possibly kicked me under the table – had we not heard voices carrying down the corridor to us.

> "We lunch at Maxim's
> And her mother comes, too.
> How large a snack seems
> When her mother comes, too."

I could hear two male voices singing, and a woman joined in for the final line of each verse.

> "And when they're visiting me,
> We finish afternoon tea,
> She loves to sit on my knee,
> And her mother does, too."

"What a hoot!" I heard the younger of Lady Sheridan's twin nincompoops holler from just outside the room.

I watched for any reaction from her husband, but our host was quite inscrutable, even as the others arrived.

"Oh, hello there!" the slightly older of the two men declared as they stepped into the room with Lady Sheridan on their shoulders.

Except he didn't say it like that. Because he was so posh, what he actually said was, *"Air, hair lair there."*

With our hostess raised high, the men held their arms out as if they were a particularly unconvincing circus act. When they realised who was sitting at the far end of the table, their expressions turned sheepish, and it was only then that Lord Sheridan showed another hint of his corked-up anger.

"Why don't you sit down, gentlemen," the blunt baron muttered through gritted teeth. "You know you are always welcome at my table."

NINE

"We're terribly sorry," the younger fellow said as they set the man's wife on the floor.

Lady Sheridan evidently found the look of displeasure on her husband's face amusing. Before either of them could say anything, Louise, the third of the young artists who had come to win the favour of the lady of the house, trailed in after the others. She didn't sit down but lingered a few feet from the table, perhaps trying to decide whether she was welcome. It reminded me of Bella's attitude a few minutes earlier.

The cockier of the two male guests had no such problem and plumped himself down in the first free seat to which he came. "The name's Thomas-Richard Harrison," he said as he flicked out his red damask napkin and placed it on his lap. "I don't believe we've been introduced?"

He appeared quite happy to ignore his awkward entrance into the room and smiled broadly as he awaited my reply.

"Marius Quin," I told him without revealing anything more. "And this is my good friend Lady Isabella Montague."

"Another lady! How wonderful." He was evidently pleased at this and winked across at our hostess. "Of course, I like hobnobbing with people from all walks of life, but there is an abundance of refined folk around here. Even the policeman who interviewed us gave me the impression that he knows his way around a croquet lawn."

I believe he mainly said this to communicate the fact that he was familiar with such places himself. He had an almost comically posh accent and over-enunciated his Ts as though someone had once accused him of being a Cockney and he never wished for it to happen again.

"Lord Sheridan," the younger chap interrupted, hesitation and perhaps even desperation apparent in his voice, "please let me express just how sorry I am for..." He found this sentence too difficult to complete and gave up on it. "I mean to say that I am very much mindful of your hospitality and have no wish for you to think badly of me... or my friends, of course."

Looking rather bemused by the reaction, Lord Sheridan took a contemplative sip from the glass of red wine a footman had just poured him. "I'm glad to hear it, Quentin," he replied, though he didn't sound particularly sure of himself.

Bella had been watching the various exchanges with interest and surprised me – as she so often does – by divining something useful. "I say, you wouldn't happen to be Quentin Urquhart?" she asked. "If so, I know your sister."

"That's right!" the near-infant beamed. "Which must make you Belly Montague?"

The only other person I'd heard refer to my friend as "Belly" was her fiancé, who was subsequently murdered (though I doubt the two facts were connected). It still surprised me that she would tolerate any such nickname.

"It does indeed, and I must say, it's dreadfully nice to meet you at last!" She didn't sound like herself all of a sudden. She sounded... what's the word? She sounded a little airheaded, and I had to think she was putting on an act. "I have heard so much about you over the years. Your sister and I met a lifetime ago at Madame Augustine's."

Bella has all sorts of friends I don't know, so it came as no shock whatsoever that there should be a branch of them of which I hadn't even heard. Who, what and where was Madame Augustine's, for goodness' sake? Aside from her links to various important families through her parents, there are her riding friends, the ladies from the London Rotary Club, and the Dorking WI. She is involved with the administration of a number of charities, plays tennis with the same pack of opponents twice a week and is a well-known attendee of Baroness Amberson's literary salon. However, I doubted any of them would be connected to the theft of a silver box, the assault on Lord Sheridan's maid or the disappearance of his gardener.

In fact, I was struggling to comprehend why Bella was chattering such nonsense in that glib new tone of hers, and I wasn't the only one.

"I'm sorry, Virgil," Lady Sheridan whispered intentionally loudly so that we could all hear, "but who are these people?"

Lord Sheridan turned his impatient gaze on his wife. "I would have thought you'd approve of my inviting friends over to the house, dear. You always tell me that I should be more sociable."

She clearly enjoyed his retort, and her pleasantly plump cheeks rounded even more. "You are a tease, Virgil, but you haven't answered my question."

"You're quite right, my darling." He stretched out a hand to pat her affectionately across the corner of the long table, and I could tell that their marriage was built on a healthy amount of ribbing. I felt that, were I ever to be so fortunate as to call Bella my wife, we would develop a similar rapport. "But I know you have heard of Mr Quin before." He paused then to increase the impact of his revelation. "You've read one of his mystery novels. Away from his literary endeavours, he and Lady Isabella investigate murders for fun."

It was a nicely delivered line, and Lord Sheridan enjoyed the shockwaves that he sent through the room. Louise, the dark-haired artist with the sharp fringe, pulled back from the table. Quentin Urquhart was apparently horrified by the news, and Thomas-Richard Harrison found the whole thing amusing.

"How jolly!" the giggler intoned as he stroked the long side-burns on either side of his face. "There's nothing so exciting as a murder mystery. Perhaps we can all participate in solving the crime."

"Really, Tom!" Louise replied, making no attempt to hide just how macabre she found his reaction. "It's not a joke. A woman is dead."

"Is that right, Lord Sheridan?" Innocent little Quentin continued to look and sound quite terrified. It was about time that someone reacted to the seriousness of the events that had led to our visit to Cherkley Court. "Is she really dead?"

"Dear me, Quentin!" Thomas-Richard Harrison was still chortling. "Are you afraid that you'll be taken off in irons? I don't know why you're worrying. It was a maid who got bashed. It's got nothing to do with us, and the police know to leave our sort out of the affairs of the little people."

He was increasingly unbearable, and I was about to tell him just that when Lord Sheridan took charge.

"Stop talking this second." His gaze seemed to stab at his guest. It was a sharp reminder of his temper, but I can't say I minded. "I started life as a 'little person'. I grew up with nothing, and people like you, who have had every imaginable advantage, should consider the lot of others once in a while."

It took a few moments longer for the hirsute young gent to realise just how serious his host was. And yet, rather than cast his eyes to the floor in shame, he continued laughing. "It's all a bit of fun."

"A woman was attacked!" Louise rephrased her earlier misstatement and pushed the long fringe from one side of her face to see the reprehensible figure before us more clearly.

"Please tell me she isn't dead though," Quentin's voice came out as high as a whistling kettle. "Tell me it's not true."

His nervousness rather distracted from the lesson that Lord Sheridan had been trying to teach. "Calm down, Quentin. It's not true." I could tell from his tone that he'd rather have continued dressing down young Harrison. "Penny isn't dead, is she, Marius?"

Everyone turned to look at me then, as if, due to my job and morbid pastime, I had knowledge of every dead body in Britain.

"No," I informed them, clearing my throat as I did so. "As far as I have heard, Penny Baker is still alive but in a serious condition in hospital. That doesn't change the fact that the attack is a serious crime."

Quentin released a long, tormented sigh. He must have realised that the others in the room found his reaction strange, as he sat up straighter and, in a wavering voice, explained, "I don't like to think of anyone being hurt. It's simply too sad, no matter whether it's the Queen consort of the United Kingdom or an unlucky maid. I disapprove of violence in all its forms."

This was a less than natural response, but a trio of servants had arrived to serve lunch, and silence fell. It was a shame, really, as I'd been planning to put a bit of fear into the youthful trio. Lord Sheridan was a formidable character. His wife seemed quite unfazed by anything she'd heard, but her guests were just the kind I enjoyed interviewing.

I felt that, were we to get them alone for half an hour, Bella and I could extract any number of secrets from them. I normally try not to rush to judgement, but it was clear that Quentin was a faint-hearted custard, Tom was far less sure of himself than he wished everyone to believe, and Louise was a tightly closed nut that might be worth cracking.

Instead, we had a course of scallops served in their shells in a white cheese sauce. The only good thing about the distraction was that the food was delicious. I'd eaten far more meagrely in presti-gious London restaurants, and I can't deny that the meal offered some comfort, no matter how eager I was to uncover the mystery we were just beginning to investigate.

With conversation reduced to a minimum, I took the opportu-nity to watch our suspects up close. Quentin didn't raise his eyes from his plate once as he ate. Some of Tom's brashness had evidently rubbed off in his clash with Lord Sheridan, and Louise kept peering along the table at her potential benefactor, as though afraid what Lady Sheridan would think of her. I locked eyes with Bella at one point, and she was doing just the same as me. Of course, it was all very well gaining access to the key figures in the house, but it wouldn't do us much good if no one spoke.

"In my experience of murder cases," I forced myself to say, "you can't rule out anyone based on class, wealth or upbringing." I'd got their attention at least. "Take you, for example, Mr Harrison."

Thomas-Richard Harrison tipped his chin back to regard me across the table. "Please do, Mr Quin."

With his rather lionish aspect, he did not appear intimidated in the least, so I leaned forward to show that I wasn't either.

"You suggested that the police will draw a line between the staff and residents when it comes to looking for the culprit of Friday's attack. Yet as it occurred at such a late hour, it would be more likely to find one of you upstairs than a gardener or hall boy."

"Why do you all keep implying that this was anything more than a bungled robbery?" Quentin's whining was becoming irritating.

"Hush, boy," Lord Sheridan snapped. "I want to hear what Marius has to say for himself."

"Just because a gardener has gone missing, that doesn't mean he's to blame," I said to calm Quentin down before continuing with what I had to say. "Looking at the scene of the crime, we saw several small discrepancies which, in my mind at least, make Dennis Apps a less likely culprit."

"Are you typically so forgiving of men who run away immediately after a violent attack?" Harrison had lost his jovial tone and sounded quite combative. "If you ask me, your sort look for problems when there are none to find. You've never done a day's work in your life, and so you seek out fun where you can find it to fill your time. It's quite perverse, and I don't approve."

I was yet to get a feel for this ever-shifting fellow. Having previously detailed the gulf between himself and the staff of Cherkley Court, he was now acting like a man of the people.

"Perhaps you're right," Bella conceded on my behalf. "Perhaps we do treat our investigations as too much of a lark. There's no denying that we enjoy our work, but we wouldn't have to go looking for tricky solutions if killers didn't do all they could to obscure the truth."

Her words left me buoyed and emboldened, and I returned to our discussion. "There is no such thing as a perfect crime. Criminals have spent thousands of years trying to find one, but if it existed, men would get away with murder far more often than they currently do."

"How very interesting." Lady Sheridan turned her head so that half of her face was illuminated by the red glass lamp hanging from the ceiling. "You're saying that people like yourselves, and Inspector Lovebrook of course, must keep searching for new solutions because criminals keep making your job more difficult?"

"Something like that, yes."

"Very well, then." Louise moved the hair from her eye once more. She did this practically every time that she made a comment, and it made me wonder why anyone would choose to have such an impractical style of coiffure. "You've said your piece. Now explain why one of us would have had anything to do with the attack on the maid."

The mood had shifted, and everyone was eager to hear the response. It didn't surprise me one bit that my brave Bella would be the one to deliver it. "You mustn't overlook the immediate facts of the case. A valuable item was stolen, and the police will already be inspecting your finances to discover any discrepancies. Perhaps one of you has amassed mountains of debt."

"They will?" Quentin hadn't changed. He was still unnerved by anything anyone said. He put his hand to his forehead as though he was having a funny turn and his tortoiseshell glasses seemed to tremble on his nose.

Quite the opposite to her shrimp-hearted guest, Lady Sheridan was greatly enjoying herself. "It was not just a valuable item. It was a sixteenth-century jewellery box, forged by a legendary Toledan silversmith for Catherine de' Medici herself. It was left to me by my father and is quite irreplaceable."

She said all this with a smile, so she didn't seem too disturbed by the loss. In fact, I couldn't ignore the impression that this whole affair was an entertainment arranged for her pleasure. Just as she dangled the prize of her patronage over three artists to see who would jump the highest, I wondered for a moment whether Lady Sheridan might have perpetrated the attack on her own maid for the thrill of seeing what would happen next.

"As Bella said, the police will leave no stone unturned," I put in, mainly to support her rather than because of any faith I had in our friends in blue. "Unearthing financial irregularities is an area of investigation in which we are unable to engage to the same extent, but that will not hold us back."

I winked at Bella. She fought a smile and won. "We have other means to bring criminals to justice."

Lord Sheridan looked less interested in these bold claims, but he encouraged us all the same. "Do tell us more."

I made sure to look around the room just then to register the reaction to what I was about to say. "I have no wish to crash my own cymbals, but I have been told by a professional detective whom I greatly respect that I have a unique ability to see through even the most sophisticated of subterfuges." I didn't feel it was necessary to point out that the detective in question was my friend, Valentine Lovebrook.

Bella knew exactly what I was doing and kept up this arrogant harangue. "That's the real reason why no case has beaten us until now. I'd like to claim some special talents of my own, but it's really Marius here who has led us in the right direction each time."

I feel I should point out that we were both lying, and Bella was equally important to our financially unrewarding but generally enjoyable detective enterprise. If we'd told the truth, that wouldn't have created quite the same air of mastery around me, so she kept going.

"I'm sure you'll all come to see just how exceptional he is as we interview you one by one about the events of Friday night."

It was at this moment that Thomas-Richard Harrison gripped his knife more tightly, Quentin dropped his head to the table, Louise held her breath, and our hostess clapped her hands together to say, "Oh, what fun!"

TEN

"I'm sorry to interrupt you, Lord Sheridan." Ponsonby the butler came after our dessert to do just that. "There have been more calls from your office, and Foster has prepared the Daimler for your departure."

Lord Sheridan looked quite fatigued by the idea of going to work, but he fished into his pocket for his gold hunter watch and, with an accepting shrug of the shoulders, rose from his seat. "I'm sorry to leave you all, especially as I found the discourse quite fascinating, but I must attend to business in the City. I will try to come back this evening, but I may have to spend the night at our flat in Maida Vale if there is more work to do tomorrow."

He put his hand on his wife's shoulder. She took it in hers and looked up at him lovingly. "A good businessman has no idea how to delegate, isn't that the saying?"

"I wouldn't know, dear." He kissed the top of her head and held her for a few seconds, as though reluctant to go. I remembered my father doing the same thing whenever he went to work. Even as a boy, I'd found it rather sweet. "But I'm sure you'll have plenty to keep you entertained here. I've never known you to be bored."

There was a wicked look in her eyes before they darted

momentarily around the table. "I do my best, darling." She kept looking as he walked quietly from the room.

I thought that this would lead to another period of uncomfortable silence, but Lady—

"Now, Marius, Bella, you must call me Imelda."

—but Imelda, didn't go in for such things.

"So who do you plan to rake over the coals first?" She folded her hands expectantly on the table in front of her, and her lively eyes widened. "I'm terribly excited for my turn."

Bella and I looked at one another. We certainly weren't used to suspects volunteering to be interviewed, and it rather threw me.

"If Louise and the gentlemen have no objections," Bella replied, as if we were doing them a favour, "you are welcome to go first."

She gave her guests the chance to object but, when none of them did, she shot to her feet. The others looked both nervous and confused but, with a cheery wave, our hostess escorted us from the room. She didn't tell us where we were heading but led us through the house via a corridor we hadn't previously taken.

"This is my sitting room," she said rather proudly, and I tried to remember the name of the space she owned upstairs where Penny Baker had been coshed. How many rooms of one's own does any one person require?

The décor was thoroughly modern once more, and it left me feeling cold. I'm no traditionalist, but I do prefer to be able to recognise furniture just by looking at it. There were some wooden geometrical shapes in the centre of the room that I had to assume were chairs as they were approximately the correct height, but they might just as well have been sculptures of some variety. And please, tell me why so many modern buildings have to be painted white? Are the owners scared of blending in with their surroundings? Is it a tribute to arctic climes? I'm sure I sound grumpy and reactionary, but I'm a man who likes wallpaper, and I'm not ashamed to admit it.

Imelda stood in front of the enormous mirror over the plain

brick fireplace, leaving us to tussle with the potential furniture. I eventually worked out how to sit down, but it was not at all comfortable, and I may have been sitting backwards.

Unlike her husband, whose jagged edges had never been totally smoothed away, Imelda rivalled Bella and even Thomas-Richard Harrison for high breeding. Her diction was as sharp as crystal, and she held herself with such poise that I questioned whether her deportment teacher was hiding in the shadows to check she was standing up straight enough.

Any hope that our masterful manipulation of the conversation over lunch had intimidated her was immediately dashed when she asked, "Which of my many motives would you like to discuss first?"

We were lost for words again. Bella opened her mouth to respond but got no further, and I believe I might have had a brief laugh.

"I'm sure you'll be able to think of something. You are a mystery novelist, are you not, Marius?"

For all her fine breeding, Imelda was relaxed in her manner and clearly lived life on a first-name basis.

"I am, but my work with Bella is quite different," I answered with care. "I could make up any story about you, but that wouldn't help us to identify the violent criminal who was here on Friday night."

"Please do."

"I beg your pardon?"

"Please make up a story about me. As my beloved husband implied at least once during our meal together, I very much enjoy diversions. If he had his way, we'd live like hermits here at Cherkley. And if I had mine, we'd live like Bacchic revellers. The middle ground we have charted suits both and neither of us just perfectly."

I have to say, she was an entertaining character, and it was hard to take our very serious job seriously enough when she was so quick with quips. I did as she'd requested all the same, aware that half an hour earlier, I had imagined standing over her as she quaked at the force of our questions.

"Very well." I began my task. "Let's imagine that you were about to go bankrupt and needed the money from the silver box which you have already told us was extremely valuable and therefore almost certainly insured. I thought it strange that the thief didn't just steal your jewellery collection, but perhaps you couldn't bear to part with it. So instead, you robbed yourself so that you could sell the box and simultaneously benefit from the insurance payment. You hit your own maid over the head in order to—"

She was not convinced. "That's a little prosaic, don't you think?"

Enjoying herself once more, Bella replied before I could. "Definitely." Her emotions over the last twenty-four hours had been bouncing around like an India-rubber ball. As long as she wasn't scowling or tutting at me, though, I had no intention of complaining. "It's not so much an idea for a story as a conclusion to which you've lazily jumped."

"That's right." Imelda turned away from us to admire her silky red hair in the mirror. "After all, I was born as rich as a sultan's daughter and inherited the lot when Daddy died. And even though Virgil may have remained as poor as a beggar's son if my father had never lent him the money to start our business, he's magnified and multiplied our wealth much as if he had his own magic lamp. It is a preposterous idea that I could need the insurance money from one stolen item when my substantial inheritance is just sitting in my bank account."

Her noticeable sense of pleasure as she said this told me that, just like Thomas-Richard Harrison, she enjoyed people knowing how rich she was.

"So what would you suggest?" I asked in as dry a tone as I possess.

She bit her bottom lip and considered the possibilities. "I'm afraid to tell you that I'm a romantic at heart. Perhaps love could come into it somehow?"

I continued to humour her. "Then perhaps you were secretly in love with your gardener and, to save him from the pain of seeing you with your husband, whom you still adore, you gave him your silver box and set him free."

"That makes no sense whatsoever." Bella frowned at me – she'd gone a good five minutes since the last one, which was probably a record. "Why would she have knocked out the maid if she was simply giving the box away?"

It had been some time since I'd planned a new book, and I must admit that I savoured the opportunity to exercise my creative muscles. "I didn't say that Lady Sheridan—"

"Imelda!"

"—attacked the maid. It was obviously her husband who did that. He was incensed at the thought of not just his wife falling in love with another man, but the loss of a valuable artefact from the home, and so he made it look like a robbery for the insurance money."

Imelda walked closer with her nose ruffled. "I see you're back to insurance again. That really doesn't fit with the romantic atmosphere I had in mind for my tale."

Bella replied with a cheerful look. "You mustn't blame him. There is an oddly humdrum streak to his thinking at times. Despite the fact he has fought in a war, spent years living on the Continent, and investigated a series of head-scratching murders, he can be frighteningly—"

I'd had enough of this discussion and talked over her. "Are we here to invent frivolous stories, or do you think perhaps the family of the woman who is lying unconscious in hospital would like us to catch her assailant?"

Bella tried to look repentant and failed. Imelda didn't even try.

"You're absolutely right about him, Bella," she whispered, as if they were old friends. It reminded me of the conspiratorial way in which she'd spoken to her husband at lunch, and I could tell just how good she was at winning people's confidence. "I think he needs to enjoy life more. My Virgil is just the same. I doubt he's had a thought in his head for the last decade that wasn't related to pig iron or the price of lead or whatever it is he spends his days shouting into telephones. We once went on holiday to Scotland and he filled his time—"

"Penny Barker is fighting for her life!" I got to my feet to say. It was a dramatic and slightly sanctimonious moment, but the chair was really uncomfortable, and I couldn't bear to sit down any longer. In my haste, I'd got the victim's name wrong.

"You mean *Baker* not Barker," Imelda was quick to correct me.

"It was a slip of the tongue, but could you please take this more seriously?" My words came out with such force that she finally stopped smiling. Bella looked a little sorry for her and, to make sure they didn't break out laughing again, I imitated the great detective Lord Edgington in the hope that I could maintain some authority.

"The first thing we must discuss," I said as I paced before the fireplace with my hands behind my back, "is not some far-fetched and fantastical idea of illicit romances or clandestine conspiracies—"

"Although a clandestine conspiracy would have been more engaging than a fraudulent insurance claim." Imelda must have known it wasn't the right moment, as she mouthed a silent "Sorry!" to make up for her faux pas.

"We need you to tell us anything you might know about the people who were in this house when Miss Baker died."

"Barker," Bella corrected me, and then Imelda corrected her.

"No, now you've got it wrong. It's definitely Penny Baker. I've known her for years."

I stopped my pacing. It clearly hadn't done the trick. "It doesn't matter what her name was."

"Is!" they both said at the same time, and I would have sat back down again, but the chairs were like rocks.

"The point that I'm trying to make is..." I searched for my words, but I'd lost them along with any claim to competence as a detective that I might have had. "Oh, I don't know anymore. Bella, will you please take over?"

ELEVEN

It was truly impressive how quickly she changed her demeanour. It's more than possible she was relieved to make her own escape from those awkward chairs. She swapped places with Imelda, and the scene began to play out as I'd imagined before we'd entered the room. I stood by the window and watched the expert at work.

"Can you tell us about any members of staff who may know something about the robbery?" It was a perfectly simple question and elicited a simple response. Why couldn't I have done that?

"It would make me only too happy to help you, but I'm afraid I don't know enough about the servants to do so. I know that Ponsonby was present at the time, but he's been working here for a thousand years. I can't imagine he had anything to do with the crime. And if you expect me to tell you what the gardeners were up to, I simply don't know."

"Then what can you tell us about Penny Baker?"

Am I a bad person for wishing that she'd got the name wrong again?

Imelda didn't answer immediately. She looked a little sad for the first time and gazed in my direction. "I've always liked her. She has a maternal quality that I've never found in another servant. Even when I had nannies as a child, I didn't receive much love from the women who were paid to look after me. Penny always has time for people. It's an admirable quality."

We were once again confronted with the idea that everyone liked the injured woman, but then, that wasn't really what Bella wanted to know. The questions she'd asked until now were a prelude to what came next.

"Very good. Then, if we've finished with your servants, let's move on to anyone else who was in the house on Friday night."

Imelda looked back at her inquisitor, and one of her eyebrows twitched a fraction. I couldn't say for certain what it meant, but I hoped we were finally asking the right questions.

"I have nothing to hide," she said in a way that told me this was far from true.

"Then describe everything you remember."

Imelda attempted to put across the same calm, confident and endlessly welcoming disposition that she'd had when we first spoke, but it was clear that something was niggling her.

"We all had dinner together – even Virgil. He'd met my friends often enough that he was no longer too aware of their presence." She stopped then, as she evidently felt this needed explaining. "He's not as antisocial as I like to pretend. He can be quite good company when the moment takes him, but he is less interested in people than I am. Especially young people. I find this new genera-tion fascinating, whereas he'd rather have a solitary glass of cognac in his library."

Despite apparently fitting into the youthful generation to which she'd just referred, I found myself siding with her husband on this particular matter. There was no time for a *Hear, hear!* though, as Bella moved on to her next point.

"You call them your friends, but we understood you brought them here because of their work as artists."

Imelda looked hazy once more and hesitated over her answer. "That too, of course. As I hope you've come to see, I enjoy fostering the talents of those around me. Louise Thorneycroft is a particu-larly promising individual. I wouldn't like the boys to know that I have chosen a favourite, but Quentin is rather immature in his ideas, and Thomas-Richard..." A mischievous expression passed over her features as she considered the roguish gentleman. "Well, he's a different kettle of fish entirely."

"I know Quentin's family personally," Bella said, sounding every bit the daughter of a duke talking to the daughter of an earl. "But how did you come across the three artists in the first place? Can you say with any confidence that they weren't involved in the robbery?"

Imelda was more resolute this time. "Of course I can't. I've got friends I've known for decades whose surnames I've never learnt. It wouldn't surprise me in the least to discover a long-term acquaintance was a vicious killer." Before we could think too badly of her choice of friends, she added, "By which I mean that you can never truly know a person."

Bella moved away from where she was standing to block the light from one of the windows. "That doesn't explain why you selected those three people to stay at your house."

"I was just coming to that." Imelda didn't yet sound annoyed, but she clearly wasn't enjoying the experience of being interviewed as much as she had imagined. "As you already mentioned, I brought the three of them together to discuss potentially supporting one of them in their artistic endeavours. We've met regularly in London over the last year, and this is the third time they've come to Cherkley for the weekend. I hadn't expected that we'd all get along so well, but we've formed a happy little gang. I'm aware that I am old enough to be their mother, but they don't seem to mind, which is rather stimulating."

"Is that what your relationship is like then? Are you a mother figure to them?"

Imelda's perfect poise somehow improved as she delivered her icy response. "What exactly does that have to do with the attack on Penny Baker?"

"Everything is connected," I muttered somewhat opaquely, and they wisely ignored me.

Bella was never daunted, yet our hostess's firmness had successfully pushed her towards another topic of conversation. "Very well. Tell us what you were all doing at the time of the burglary."

Imelda shifted in her seat and began. "Thomas-Richard had organised something of a game for us."

"We heard it was a prank of some variety," I said, as that was the word that Nerea had used when she'd come to see me at home.

"I wouldn't say that. There were clues hidden about the house. We each had different tasks to complete. It was all rather diverting. He's got quite the brain in his head, that young man, and he always has something jolly up his sleeve."

"Jolly like theft and attempted murder?" Bella's voice was sharper than normal, and this comment drew a brief shudder from Lady Sheridan.

"Why would you think that?"

"If he organised a challenge for the three of you to complete, that would have been a very good way to ensure that you would not be in your boudoir when he wished to steal something from it. Had you ever mentioned the box that belonged to Catherine de' Medici?"

"Not that I can recall."

She kept the questions coming fast. "Had he ever visited you there?"

Three seconds passed before Imelda answered. "He may have been up there on occasion, but there's nothing in that."

For a woman who had so confidently requested that we interview her first, she no longer seemed so sure of herself. Bella had found a raw nerve and was happy to tug on it. "Keep going. Tell us exactly where you and each of the others were at the time of the attack."

Imelda's gaze dropped for the first time. I couldn't tell whether she was trying to recall the facts or she was reluctant to share them. "Maybe fifteen minutes before the bell rang for midnight, one of the clues took me to Virgil's library. There was a key hidden in a book, but I was rather distracted talking to my husband and forgot about it for some minutes."

"What did you discuss?"

She bit her lip again, and I wondered for a moment whether she was trying to protect him. "To tell you the truth, he told me that he was having trouble concentrating on his work with so many people running about the place."

"Did you argue about it?"

"Argue is a strong word. We squabbled as we always do. Our love for one another centres upon a sweetly competitive streak we both have. If I'm being honest, one of the things that appeals to me about inviting my friends here is that it makes Virgil even grumpier than usual."

"So what happened after you'd finished talking?"

"I found what I needed, and he said that anyone else looking for clues in his library would be out of luck. I believe he locked the door after me to ensure that he wouldn't be disturbed."

"Did you see anyone else after that?"

"I saw Penny, actually." That same sadness we'd heard before entered her voice once more. "She was on the terrace as I hurried towards the greenhouse. We waved to one another, and she seemed fine, but I keep wishing that I'd asked what she was doing there. I can't help feeling that it was in my power to save her, if only I'd..."

Her words faded to nothing, and Bella presumably didn't feel she could press our witness so intensely as before. "What time was that?"

Imelda looked back up at my friend. "As I said, all this happened at around a quarter to midnight. I can't tell you exactly. But I went to the greenhouse to find the final piece of Thomas-Richard's puzzle. It was a piece of cake."

"You mean that the challenge was too easy?"

She gave a sad laugh. "No, it was literally a piece of cake. That's what all the clues led to. It was sitting on a stone plinth in front of the door. I suppose Thomas-Richard decided that I should have a reward for my endeavours, as there was a small wooden box, which the key I'd found in the library unlocked. Inside it was a generous helping of chocolate cake."

"Was there anyone else about at the time?" I asked when neither of them broke the subsequent silence.

"No..." She looked over at me as though she'd forgotten I was there. "Wait! Yes, there was. I heard a noise coming from the tropical house next door. It was a squeaking sound. It could have been an animal of some kind. A fox cub, perhaps, but I believed at the time it was something more mechanical."

"Did you not enter to find out?" Bella looked concerned rather than curious.

"I would have but..." She paused then to think. "...someone rushed past behind me, and I turned to see Dennis Apps."

"Did he notice you?"

"Yes, he stopped, tipped his hat and said, 'Evenin', madam,' in his usual polite manner. Now that I think of it, I doubt I've ever heard him say much else."

"In which direction was he walking?"

She needed to consider her answer. "I would say... yes, he appeared to be walking away from the annexe where he lives. The greenhouse and tropical house are to the east of the property, and he was heading past them, up the hill towards the drive when I turned away."

"So it was presumably around midnight by then?" I hazarded, and she seemed confused by my remark.

"Yes, that sounds..." She raised one hand to stop us interrupting. "No, this was some time before midnight. Though time had passed swiftly. You may be right."

"So then you went upstairs, and that was when you discovered that Penny had been attacked?"

Looking very small in the wooden contraption in which she sat, our suspect nodded. It was obvious that she was no longer as certain of her facts as she had been. She looked like a little girl who was frightened her parents would take her in a lie.

Bella had waited long enough, and it was time to point out the first discrepancy in what we knew of Lady Sheridan's actions on the night of the crime. "Thank you for telling us your side of the story." I'm sure she chose this weighted term on purpose. "However, there's something that doesn't make sense. From what we've been told, when the footmen and nursemaid found you in the boudoir after you discovered Penny, you were dressed in a negligee."

Imelda glanced up at the mirror on the wall, though from the angle she was sitting, she would have seen nothing but the chandelier above her head. "I... Well, I suppose I'd gone to get changed in the middle of... It wasn't a negligee, as it happens. It was a chemise. I had gone to get ready for bed and been interrupted by the sound of someone running in the hall."

"Correct me if I'm wrong, but it was midnight when that happened?" I demanded.

"Yes, definitely. I've no doubt about it." She sounded relieved, and I thought perhaps she felt that she'd got through the interview unscathed.

Bella's natural blithe air had returned, and she took a step back before offering a remark in a wry tone. "You were very busy in that fifteen-minute period. It's impressive how much you got done."

"I suppose it is." Imelda had been sitting down for ten minutes by now and could presumably no longer feel her legs thanks to the curving design of the wood that supported them. She managed to push herself up to standing, and her smile remained in place.

"There's nothing else you'd like to tell us?" I asked as she pulled at the folds in her skirt to make them hang straight.

"No, I believe that's all."

"You didn't see anyone else between the end of the game and the moment you found Penny's body?" Bella asked, and Imelda stopped where she was to consider the question.

"You know, you're both very good at what you do. I came in here thinking that this would be a bit of fun, but as soon as you started asking me questions, I had the feeling come over me that I was in a terrible fix. I genuinely have no connection whatsoever to poor Penny's assault, and I certainly didn't steal from myself, but I sat there this whole time with just as much guilt as if I'd wielded the metal bar that cracked my maid's skull."

She drifted over to the door and looked set to leave, much as if this were our room and we'd invited her into it.

"So you didn't see anyone else?" I repeated Bella's question before she could go, and she only turned back for the briefest of moments to shake her head.

TWELVE

"We've rarely met a suspect who lied so obviously," Bella told me when she was sure we were alone. "At the very least, the timing of everything she told us must be distorted. I wonder if I should have pressed her more."

"No." I spoke before knowing how I truly felt on the matter, but that didn't last long. "You chose the right approach. We didn't want her to become too defensive. There's nothing to say she's the culprit, and the fact she was so eager to speak to us would seem to reinforce that idea. I think she intended to be as transparent as possible, but halfway through the conversation, a particular concern dawned on her. What if, by recalling the events of Friday night, she realised she could have incriminated someone and changed her story accordingly?"

Bella didn't say anything for a moment. Instead, she walked in my direction and perched on the sill on the other side of the French windows. It is funny how often such mundane actions remind me how much I love her. I could see that she was deep in thought as she approached. Her jet-black hair swung like a metronome, and it struck me how much that action was quintessentially hers. It was the fact that no one in the world walks quite like my Bella, and the understanding that I love this perfectly workaday detail just as much as I adore the light in her eyes when she smiles at me or the softness of her hands whenever I'm lucky enough to brush past them.

Sorry. I'm wittering on about trivialities – the most momentous of trivialities, but trivialities nonetheless – when I should be talking about the case.

Bella sat down a few feet from me, and I didn't compliment her on her walk or tell her that I remembered every time her skin had touched mine over the last year. I waited to hear what she would say.

"You may be right. I handled her with kid gloves because asking the hardest of questions would have given her the opportunity to make up easy explanations. I'd rather talk to the other suspects first."

"We know from what Lord Sheridan told us that her timing was all wrong. He said that she went to see him in the library at twenty past eleven, whereas she said it was twenty-five minutes later. I think that she started by telling the truth, but when she pushed certain times back it became apparent that she couldn't have accomplished so much in the final quarter of an hour before Penny was attacked. Let's assume for the moment that Lord Sheridan was telling the truth. In which case, the times were wrong, but perhaps the order of events Imelda told us was correct. She left her husband to his work, went to the greenhouse and saw Penny and perhaps the gardener. But she would have gone back inside far earlier than she claimed, which explains why she had time to get changed, and presumably eat the cake she'd won, as she didn't tell us anything to the contrary."

"I was thinking much the same thing. She wouldn't have simply finished the treasure trail and then gone to bed; she was abandoning her party right in the middle of it. She should at least have found Harrison and told him of her success."

"The question is why wouldn't she want us to know when she did the things she did? We'll have to talk to the others before we speak to her again. Lovebrook might know something useful, wherever he's got to."

She didn't appear to have heard me, as she was staring at a stark red-and-white painting across the room. It was part of a series which were spaced out on either side of the fireplace. Each showed the disembodied head of a tulip in a different colour. There were four in total, and the symmetry and simplicity of them was a little alarming. I found them striking, yet rather beautiful. The lack of a stem on each made them look alien somehow, but that wasn't why the closest one had caught Bella's attention.

"I believe we know the artist," she said, walking over to get a better view. "They're signed L. Thorneycroft. They're rather good."

"If only killers and burglars signed their work. It would make our job a lot easier."

She looked back at me. "Easier but duller."

"Let's go back to what we were saying. There's something that occurred to me as Imelda was speaking. Nerea told us that, when the nursemaid—"

"I believe her name is Hilary."

"That's right." I was studying a painting of a stormy sea on the opposite wall from the one she'd examined. It was far more traditional than Louise's pieces, and it looked out of place in that perfectly modern space. I did my best to read the squiggle in the bottom-right corner, and it turned out that Quentin was quite the artist. "Well, Nerea said that when Hilary found her mistress at the scene of the crime, not only was she in her chemise – as we have already discussed – one of Lady Sheridan's guests was with her."

Bella had gone walking around the room but apparently couldn't find whatever she expected to see. "There's nothing from Tom here." She pointed to the far wall where a foggy London scene was hanging. "I know that's not his because I've come across it before."

"That doesn't mean he didn't paint it."

"Maybe not, but I'm sure I saw it hanging in a gallery recently, and I'd remember the name Thomas-Richard Harrison."

I was about to explain away this discrepancy when the door opened and my dog walked in. Trust Percy to interrupt us at an important moment. He wasn't alone – as, believe it or not, four-stone basset hounds with legs far shorter than their tails aren't known for jumping and turning door handles to get into rooms. I'm not saying it's never been done, but it's certainly never been done by my lazy hound.

"I'm glad I found you," Lovebrook told us as he stepped into the (uncomfortable) sitting room.

"Have you something useful to tell us then?" I thought I'd gamble on this possibility, and Bella clearly had a similar idea.

"Have you found the very piece of evidence that will lead us to the culprit?"

"No, it's not that." He sounded nonplussed. "Once the staff in the downstairs dining room had finished spoiling him, Percy started howling for you."

I was rather pleased at this until my dog walked right past me and went to sit on Bella's feet. He looked up at her lovingly, and I couldn't really blame him for being charmed by the most exquisite woman on earth, though I sometimes wished he'd remember that I'm the one who takes him to the park most often.

It was Lovebrook's turn to be over-optimistic. "Why? Have you got something crucial to tell me?"

"Not exactly." Bella turned to communicate a few silent thoughts, and I shrugged in response.

"We have come to understand some important facts about our suspects." I thought I should at least try to sound hopeful.

The inspector attempted to sit on one of the polished wooden shapes and immediately regretted it. "My goodness, there must be comfier shards of glass I could perch on than that thing. What was it designed for? Torture?" He rubbed his back and tried to recover.

"That is one mystery we are unlikely to solve," Bella replied, and I could tell that she was eager to pick up speed. "This is Lady

Sheridan's sitting room. We spoke to her in here a few minutes ago and, while there may be an innocent explanation, she was evasive in her answers and almost certainly lied to us."

He went to sit on one of the windowsills. They were the only things in the room that deserved to be called seats. "How curious. I found her perfectly helpful when I interviewed her. She told me about the game that she and her friends had played. I didn't detect a hint of duplicity in her."

"That's probably because you're nicer than us." Bella looked at our friend with great affection. "You probably let her speak rather than badgering her until whatever simple version of reality she'd shaped for herself lost its integrity."

"You may be right. I was given strict instructions by my superior not to upset the apple cart. He implied that he'd rather I let the criminals off scot-free than in any way put the Sheridans' noses out of joint." I'd never noticed Lovebrook resorting to so many clichés, and I could only think he was quoting his chief inspector. "It's bad enough that the newspapers have already put the case on the front pages."

"Well, you needn't arrest her just yet," I reassured him, as I stood beside the French windows, "but we need to know who was at the scene immediately after the crime was discovered. Can you recall from your interviews?"

He nodded efficiently. "Lady Sheridan says that she was upstairs when she heard someone running in the corridor so went to see what was happening. She'd already finished her part of the game, but I don't believe that Quentin Urquhart had, so perhaps she thought her friends were out there. Either way, she went out to the hallway, at which point she noticed that the door to her boudoir was open and decided to inspect it. She found the scene as I previously described it to you, and then her guest, Miss Thorneycroft, was alerted by the shriek she gave. That caught the attention of the nursemaid on the floor above, and someone rang downstairs to get the attention of the footmen."

"Bother," I said... Well, actually, I used a ruder word than that, and Bella tutted at me. "I thought you would reveal something more useful."

"Why? What did you expect?"

I re-engaged my mind connection with Bella to share my now unlikely theory. Of course, it's quite possible she was thinking something else entirely, but I chose to believe that we'd both been imagining the sordid tale of Lady Sheridan shedding her clothes in the middle of the game because one of the young gentlemen was up in her bedroom. I suppose the footmen could have— On second thoughts, I should probably stop there.

"Don't worry about that," Bella replied for both of us. "We may have been mistaken, but Imelda still wasn't telling the whole truth. If you haven't been up to now, I would recommend keeping an eye on her."

Lovebrook turned a shade of grey just then that didn't suit him at all. "This job isn't easy, you know. It's not just that I have to follow more rules than you two. If I step on anyone's toes, I could lose my job. It's all very well suggesting I keep my eye on one of the incredibly rich and powerful suspects you've identified, but how should I go about it?"

I didn't like to see the inspector so disheartened, but I was distracted by something through the window, and I had to put off reassuring him that he was doing a fine job.

"Hey, you there," I shouted in the voice of the grumpy old fellow who cut the grass on the cricket pitch in my home village and never wanted a single person to step on it. "Boy, what are you doing?"

I opened the door to the garden just as the imp who was out there ducked behind a bush.

"I can still see you," I told him in a severely unimpressed tone that he deserved to hear, as he'd only moved a couple of feet lower. Before diving into the shrubbery after him, I looked across the Italianate terrace to work out why he'd been lurking there in the first place.

I hadn't been to that side of the house before. There was a long rectangular reflecting pool which was busy with marsh marigolds and water violets. In the centre, a statue of Mercury, the winged messenger, stood pretending he wasn't interested in what was happening. Further away, there were ornamental flower beds laid out and, on the far side of them, Louise Thorneycroft was standing behind an easel, presumably painting the grandest façade of Cherkley Court. I don't believe she heard the hell's delight I'd caused, as she continued gazing at her canvas.

Bella and Lovebrook joined me as I reached into the bush and grabbed hold of a collar.

"You can't do that to me," a small but furious voice insisted as I lifted up the squealing, thrashing boy. "I own this estate, and I can have you arrested."

It apparently wasn't just the lady of Cherkley Court who told the occasional half-truth. The heir to the manor was already taking after his mother.

"If you have information regarding a crime, I'm all ears," the inspector informed young Lionel, who was now suspended in the air above the privet.

"Ah, it's you, Inspector. I would tell you, of course," the brat replied as he faced up to reality, "but I've had a change of heart. If you tell this fellow to put me down, I'll let your friends off with a warning."

"That is most generous of you," I told the ten-year-old, who was as heavy as he looked. "And I will do just that, as soon as you explain why you were hiding in this bush, spying on a young lady."

Although I doubted she could hear us, our run-in with the boy had caught Louise's attention. She put her paintbrush down, and I thought she might come over. She presumably had no desire to spend time with an oik like Lionel, though, so she stayed right where she was.

"I wasn't spying," the boy claimed. "I was just..."

Bella was the next to interrogate him. "You were just what, young man? Loitering? Gawping?"

"Nothing of the sort." His voice grew squeakier as his indignance increased.

"The binoculars around your neck would suggest otherwise." I was rather pleased that I got to tell him this, but my cheer didn't last long.

"Marius!" an appalled voice called from the path around the house. "Marius, put that poor child down."

I'm glad to say that it wasn't Lady Sheridan herself, but my ex-paramour, Nerea. She hurried over to glare at me, and I finally put her student back where I'd found him.

"He was hiding in the bushes staring at Miss Thorneycroft," I said in the hope this would explain why I'd gone fishing for boy.

With all the quiet fury that I remembered from her, Nerea looked across the garden to confirm the truth of what I'd said. When she turned back to me, I could tell that she wouldn't accept my word so readily.

"He wasn't bothering anyone." She folded her arms across her chest. Back when we lived in Paris, I always knew that was a bad sign. "We were playing a game. He was hiding from me, and I had to find him."

Considering that she was neither his nursemaid nor his main governess, they spent an awful lot of time together.

"Lionel, dile!" she said, which, if I haven't forgotten every word of Spanish that she taught me, means *"Tell him!"*

Lionel looked more surprised by this than anyone. "Of course." He cleared his throat and stared at me with an arrogant mien. "It's just as she said. We were playing hide and seek, and you ruined it." Without looking at her, he leaned back against his language mistress and rested his head on her shoulder. "This man isn't nice, Nere. I don't like him."

"No te preocupes, mi amor." She patted him on the head, and her eyes flared at me as she ushered him away. "Go back to the house now, and I'll find you later. I think that Miss Tope was looking for you."

He gave me one last juvenile glare but did as he was told. Bella and Lovebrook had watched the encounter with the look of spectators in a theatre who couldn't decide whether they were enjoying themselves. When Lionel had gone, Nerea was still furious with me.

"I asked you here to find my Dennis, not terrorise a little boy. What were you thinking?"

I couldn't summon a response, which was nothing new. I can still recall feeling as if she had some indescribable power over me every time we argued – and we always argued. I've never experienced that with anyone else. She would take exception to the way I phrased a sentence or the manner in which I looked at her, and suddenly everything in the world was dark and terrible for her. I didn't know how to put it right when that happened, so I stopped trying. That was probably the beginning of the end for us; though, at the time, I believed that no other woman on earth could make me happy.

"He really did look as though he was spying on Miss Thorneycroft." Bella stepped forward to defend me, and it felt as though she'd reversed the spell my former love had cast.

Before I could speak, Nerea took control again. "Have you discovered anything?" She was a head shorter than me, but in that moment, she might have been a hundred feet tall.

"We've barely begun," I told her, at least half honestly.

She huffed out her disdain. "I don't know why I expected any better from you, Marius. You always let me down."

She turned to go, but I wouldn't let her get away with that. "We've found twenty different discrepancies in the stories that various suspects have told us. That's how it always begins. If Dennis Apps wasn't involved—"

"He wasn't!"

"If it was someone else in this house, then the process of finding the culprit has started. We'll pull at the threads we've already found until we can tell the lies from the truth and, in one moment, the whole thing will become clear."

I thought she might insult me again, but she kept her eyes dead ahead and said nothing.

"I promise, Nerea. I promise that we'll find him." I wasn't certain at that moment if I was talking about the killer or her boyfriend, but it was our job to do both.

She took a deep breath, and I could see that she was doing all she could to calm herself down. "Tell me if you learn anything... please, Marius."

All of a sudden, I remembered why I'd once loved her – or thought I had. It wasn't just because she was beautiful. It wasn't how kind and thoughtful she had been when we first met. It was that feeling whenever life went back to normal again and she didn't look at me as though I was the worst person on earth. The lows with Nerea were hard to bear, but the highs straight after were unparalleled.

She nodded to Bella, ignored Inspector Lovebrook, and marched away from the scene.

THIRTEEN

My friends chose not to comment, though I knew what they were both thinking.

"Come along then. What do you think we should do now?" I asked through somewhat gritted teeth. It wasn't their fault that I'd been outwitted, but that didn't make me feel any better about the clash I'd just endured.

"Perhaps we should take this opportunity to talk to Miss Thorneycroft since her name keeps coming up, and she's standing just over there." Bella pointed. I didn't need to look.

"What's she going to tell us?" I must admit that, with a little help from Nerea, I'd begun to lose faith in my abilities. "You've spoken to her, Lovebrook. Did you have any sense that she was hiding something from you?"

"No, I can't say that I did, but then I thought Lady Sheridan was very forthcoming in her answers, and it seems I was wrong."

I admit that it was quite irrational not to talk to Louise Thorneycroft just then. I knew that we would have to before long, but I needed a break from the disdain of yet another quick-witted, dark-haired beauty so I kept moving us along. I left the Italian garden and walked back down the slope away from the lawns.

"Tell us more about the staff here, Lovebrook," I demanded a touch insistently. "Is there even the hint of discord between them?"

"Not really," he gingerly confessed.

"Then did anyone indicate that Dennis Apps had a bad temper?" I admit that I may have become a little desperate for solid evidence by this point. "Or could he suffer from shell-shock, perhaps? You did tell us that he served in the war."

"He did indeed, but it didn't leave him with any emotional wounds that anyone has mentioned."

Bella must have decided to let me wear myself out by this point, as she kept her counsel.

"Then what about young Quentin Urquhart?" I asked her. "You know his sister. Has she ever implied that he's prone to violent impulses?"

She laughed at me then. I deserved it. "I don't think so. She used to complain that he pulled her hair when they were children, but I'm not sure that the police consider that grounds for prosecution."

The three of us fell silent, but we continued following the path away from the formal gardens to the wilder edges of the estate we had already glimpsed. The act of walking has always been a balm to me. I remember exploring London on foot to stave off loneliness after I returned from the Continent. It wasn't just the sights I saw and the neighbourhoods I got to know that helped bridge those two stages of my life. The very act of walking seemed to repair my frayed nerves, and it was on one such excursion that I decided to devote my life to writing – detective work came later.

"There's something not right about this whole thing," I declared as we approached the annexe building where Dennis Apps had his meagre lodgings. "It feels hollow somehow."

"It's different from the other crimes we've investigated," Bella was quick to comment. "Normally there's been a more substantial connection between all our suspects – a core, like my friend Cecil on our first case, who unites everyone else."

"I hadn't thought of it like that," Lovebrook remarked in that slightly amazed tone he sometimes uses, "but you're absolutely right. I knew there was something missing. Half of the suspects are employed to be here, and the rest seem to have their own motivations and interests. Admittedly, the three artists revolve around Lady Sheridan, but they are otherwise unconnected, and it's hard to see why any of them would have committed the crime in the first place."

A rush of understanding flooded my brain. "That's just it! There's a gap between what we know and what we would normally expect to find."

We had walked beyond the small brick building to the scrubby piece of land I'd seen from the upstairs window on our last visit. There was a mound of earth, heaps of cracked and discarded terra-cotta pots and a round scorch mark on the ground where the gardeners had burnt branches and the like. Lovebrook had already turned to head back towards the house, but I found myself rooted to the spot.

"What is it, Marius?" Bella asked, as though I were a famous dog in a film. I half expected her to clap her hands and call me Rin Tin Tin.

There was a spade leaning up against the side of a tumbledown shed, and I seized it before answering. "What if everything that's been put before us was a pretence? What if Dennis Apps never left the estate?"

I didn't wait for an answer and, as Lovebrook wandered closer, I ran to the mound of earth and started digging. A minute later, he had found a spade of his own and did the same. My dear Bella wasn't dressed for gardening work, but she looked for a wheel-barrow all the same and helped remove loads of loose soil to give us space. Percy, meanwhile, thought this was marvellous fun and got to digging. Sadly, his hole was some yards away and did nothing to aid our endeavours.

It was tiring, and my hands were soon sore from gripping the cracked wooden handle of the spade, but I was invigorated by the idea that we had found a new way to look at the case.

"You're saying that you think Dennis was murdered to hide what really happened?" Bella was still talking in a disbelieving, even patronising voice.

"Not quite. I think it's more likely that he was killed so that we would look in the wrong direction. That would explain why Penny was so viciously assaulted, too. The attacker wanted us to suspect Apps and focus on the violence instead of the theft. By killing the gardener and burying his body, it tied up the case in a neat bow. Any normal police officer—"

"So not like our friend Valentine here?" Bella joked, and Lovebrook was too out of breath to do more than wave his hand in appreciation.

"Precisely." I also needed a break from the work for a moment. "Any normal police officer would have accepted the idea that Apps had committed the crime and run away. The killer was counting on it. So what really happened was that the devil stole the box, knocked out Penny and then arranged to meet Apps here to kill him and shift the blame. It's a shockingly callous method, but rather an ingenious one when you think about it."

"There's only one problem," Lovebrook told us as I took up digging again.

"Yes?" I replied between heaves and sighs.

"Yes – Dennis Apps isn't buried here. The earth has been loose enough so far that it might have been feasible, but it's become far more compact the longer we've dug. There's no way that the ground beneath our feet has been disturbed recently. I'd bet my parents' estate on it."

This did support our long-held suspicion that the inspector came from money, but it also dashed my hopes that we'd made any progress. I stabbed the blade of the spade into the earth, and I realised he was right. "Oh, for the love of Mike!"

"There is one good thing, Marius." Bella no longer sounded patronising. Her voice had a mix of sympathy and relief woven into it. "Imagine how Nerea would have reacted if we'd had to tell her Apps was dead."

This wasn't as reassuring as she might have hoped. Of course I was happy that the unfortunate gardener wasn't buried there, but the case grew more slippery and diaphanous with each passing hour.

I released something akin to a lupine howl as I tossed my spade back where I'd found it. Then, muddy-shoed and with muscles aching, I marched back to the house.

FOURTEEN

"You can't rule out the possibility that he's dead on the estate somewhere." Bella was still trying to pick me up as we crossed the grand lawn on the terrace below the rear façade. It was trimmed like a bowling green, but I had forsaken the bordering footpaths (and decorum) to stomp across it.

"We could with bloodhounds," Lovebrook replied. "In fact, I believe one of the constables has a pair that he used when that politician's wife went missing near Silent Pool a few months back."

I thought Percy might take exception to being overlooked for this task, but he was busy sniffing a bush and didn't pay any attention.

"Go ahead if you think it will help," I told the inspector, "but I believe there's a more pressing task. If he isn't dead, and he didn't walk to one of the nearest towns, Apps must have had a vehicle to get away from here. He would have been spotted on foot by now otherwise."

There was too much goodness in Bella not to show compassion when it was needed. She'd been short with me for much of the day, but that didn't stop her being kind now. "You shouldn't give up on a good idea entirely. It would have all been too convenient to find Apps at the first time of asking."

"Precisely. It was lazy thinking on my part. I thought: there's a nice obvious pile of earth. There's bound to be a body buried beneath it." I wasn't about to forgive myself, no matter what rationale anyone offered. "We must be more methodical from this moment forward. The last thing we know was that Apps was walking in the opposite direction to the annexe. We need to find out where he went and how he got off the estate."

"I'll look into that," Lovebrook volunteered. "It won't be difficult to find out how many cars are normally here. There'll surely be one reserved for the gardeners."

The inspector, and Percy for some reason, had already split off at a different angle, and I had to shout. "Bear in mind that he can't have driven through the main gate. Check any other points of access."

Lovebrook waved to show that he'd heard, and Percy waddled more quickly to keep up with his fast-striding new favourite. They'd probably solve the case before we could, but I was too busy trying to forget my recent humiliations to worry about that.

"Do you know where we're going?" Bella's sympathy had apparently been replaced with concern. I must have looked like quite the cuckoo.

"I do. We're going to retrace the chain of evidence we were previously following."

I thought she might disagree or question what that meant, but I was wrong. "Good. It's time we got back to work. Imelda shared any number of interesting observations with us. There was the sound she heard coming from the tropical house – I wondered whether the attacker was in there, biding his time. To be perfectly honest, I think you were distracted by the hint of salaciousness that was implied when we heard that she was running about the house in her underclothes."

"Thank you very much. It's nice to know that you consider me to have the squalid mind of a deviant or a schoolboy."

"I couldn't have put it better!" She nudged me with her elbow then, and I had to smile.

"Well, I won't be distracted by such titillations anymore. We must concentrate on the thing that made it possible for the burglar to strike. I believe that the game the guests were playing was vital for everything else that happened."

She nodded as we quickly took the steps up to the rear terrace. "So then it's the improbably named Thomas-Richard Harrison we need."

I didn't answer. I held the door open for her and bowed like a footman. "After you, m'lady."

Finding people is far easier when there is a network of professional spies running about the place. Most people call them servants, but in every house I've visited, I find them to be excellent informers. We asked the footman Frederick, and he told us that his colleague Francis had mentioned attending Harrison a short time earlier. We found Francis in the kitchen, and he directed us to the closer of the two glasshouses. We passed Quentin on the way. He was painting in one of the downstairs salons and didn't look up.

The greenhouse provided another change of style. I don't know what Lord and Lady Sheridan had in mind when they decorated their house. Or rather, I know exactly what they had in mind, and it was a mix of several very different ideas – I wondered if this was emblematic in some ways of the contrast between the lord and lady of the manor. The interior of the house was both old and modern at the same time, and the immense crystal extension, which was built onto the far side of the house from where we'd caught Lionel spying, was something else altogether. What it offered was a chance to travel to sunny climes, just by opening the door. The heat inside was impressive, and there were electric globe lamps in multiple colours suspended from the high ceiling every few yards.

I cannot express just how massive the place was. It was at least four times the size of the house in which I grew up, and if a servant had been on hand to tell me that this and the neighbouring tropical house occupied an acre or more, I would not have been surprised. Perhaps inevitably, the real miracle was the variety of plants before us. I know nothing about the flora and fauna of countries beyond approximately Belgium, but seeing the towering cacti and ferns made me think of distant lands in Asia, America and perhaps even Africa. I kept expecting to see pith-helmeted explorers hacking through the foliage with machetes.

Instead, we found a well-dressed layabout lazing on a green metal banquette. He had a cigarette in his mouth that was somehow still smouldering as he snoozed.

"Don't wake me!" Harrison warned as we walked around the large, circular pool in the centre of the L-shaped glasshouse. "I have nothing to tell you, and I'm a terribly light sleeper."

We stopped where we were and said nothing. We really are too polite for our own good sometimes. I blame Bella for this entirely. I swear that, if I'd grown up free from her infuriatingly good influence, I'd now be blunter, ruder and more aggressive. The manners her family imparted upon me are a dastardly encumbrance.

Ten seconds later, though we didn't make a sound, Harrison gave a long, low grunt and swung his legs down to the floor. "You fiends, I was enjoying a nap, and I'll never get back to it now." To make up for his suffering, he drew on the cigarette and then pulled it from his mouth to release a lengthy puff of smoke. It goes without saying that he was not pleased to see us. "What do you want?"

Every attempt I'd made to set our suspects on edge that day – including my run-in with the infant in the garden – had ended in failure. Based on the first few words of this new interview, I didn't like our chances any better this time around. And so, instead of wanting him to think that we knew all about his crimes and that he would soon be locked up, I decided to try another technique.

"We're just looking for anyone with a brain in their heads." I walked closer and, as his cigarette appeared to have finally extinguished itself, I pulled a book of matches from my pocket and relit it for him. I don't actually smoke myself, but carrying matches is an excellent way to break the ice.

"You don't have to tell me what it's like," he replied with a shake of his head and a scratch of one thick sideburn. "I spend my life railing against the incompetents of this world!"

I'd known from the moment I'd met him that Thomas-Richard Harrison had a high opinion of himself, and my approach had been judged to perfection. "The people we've had to speak to today: I despair, I really do." I sighed so as not to have to say anything more.

"That's it in a nutshell! The world would be a wonderful place if it weren't for all the people we have to endure." He joined in with my sighing.

Bella had looked dubious at first, but she came to sit on the bench and adopted the same harried attitude. The only problem was that she wasn't very good at it. "Oh, yes. People! They're the worst, aren't they? What absolute imbeciles!"

I believe we both frowned at this, but it was my new friend who corrected her. "Go easy, madam. On the whole, people are generous and kind. As a species, I would say we are generally well meaning."

"That's it in a nutshell," I echoed him. "Humankind has done more than we had any right to achieve, but still..."

We both sighed again, our fraternal connection established, whereas Bella was trying to understand how her demeanour was any different from ours.

"Take this burglary, for example," I continued, still talking his language. "Was it really necessary to bonk the poor maid over the head with a hammer?" I knew that the burglar hadn't used a hammer, but I was curious to see what he would say.

"It's certainly not cricket!" I'd rarely heard anyone use this expression in real life.

"Or tennis," Bella tried once more and, with a wince, Harrison reluctantly accepted her point.

"There are rules to any game. That much is true." I imagine that he took a moment to consider whether the parallel between racket sports and grievous bodily harm held true. "What we can say is that an innocent maid should never be involved."

"In either, in fact." Bella sounded incredibly hopeful as she said this, but our suspect was already shaking his head.

"Really, Lady Isabella. I do not approve of that attitude. Are you saying that only the rich deserve to indulge in exercise? Should we prevent the working classes from accessing football pitches and billiard tables? It's not on. It really isn't."

"No, I suppose you're right." She looked quite crestfallen, and so I wrestled the conversation back from her.

"Of course, you couldn't have been involved in any of that nastiness," I told Harrison confidently – hoping against hope that he might accept me into his confidence and disprove this very thing. "You were busy competing in your game at the time, weren't you?"

He perched on the arm of the bench and looked at me through narrowed eyes. "Now, now. Why would you say that?"

"I just mean—"

"You've got it all wrong." I thought for a moment that he'd seen through my subterfuge, but it turned out he wasn't clever enough for that. "I was the one who devised the game. I wasn't playing it."

"So what joviality were you getting up to at the time, eh fella?" For a comparatively young person, Bella was truly hopeless when it came to doing an impersonation of a young person. She had adopted an East London accent at some point and hooked her thumbs into a pair of invisible braces.

Her attempt at camaraderie did not sit well with Harrison, but at least he answered her question. "Oh, I was just hanging about the place."

"We'd heard you were in here, as it happens." She was going too fast, and I would have liked to poke or perhaps hiss at her, but she was too far away from me. "Were you with a young lady, indulging in a spot of the old—"

It had gone on long enough, and I had to interrupt. "Harrison, tell us about this game of yours. It sounds like a complicated sort of affair. It must have taken you a dog's age to plan the thing." I was beginning to grow tired of my own voice, even though I was talking less than the others.

"Did it!" he replied, and Bella missed the nuance of this response.

"I don't know. Did it?"

"Oh, epochs! Or if I'm perfectly honest, it took epochs and epochs. Practically a lifetime I'd say."

There are clearly some people in this world who should never embark on a conversation together. Bella and Thomas-Richard Harrison were a perfect example of this.

"Really?"

"Well, no, not really. I was speaking figuratively. It took approximately a day to plan."

She put on a very false smile and did her best to look relaxed. "Oh, of course. I love speaking figuratively. I'm always doing it. Aren't I, Marius?"

Now she was roping me into her ill-conceived antics, and I was having none of it. "Yes, Bella. You are *literally* always doing it." I gave her a hard stare, and when that didn't work, I went to stand on the other side of Harrison so that he would turn to me – and away from Bella. "As I was saying, it can't have been easy. Did you come up with different clues for each of your friends?"

"Not just my friends!" Harrison emitted a laugh that reminded me of a ship leaving port. It was loud and unpleasant. "We got the butler to join in too. I made up all sorts of ridiculous things for him, and as for Quentin..." I thought he would guffaw again, but he grew unexpectedly circumspect and sniffed instead.

"What sort of things did you have them doing?"

His good humour returned. "Old Ponsonby was the best of them! I thought he'd turn his nose up at fishing in the outside pond for ceramic toads, but he must have had a brandy or two as he grabbed a net, rolled up his trousers and climbed straight in! If only I'd had a camera!" Something in this last comment made him lose his good cheer once more.

"It sounds like a lot of fun." I spoke quickly as Bella was edging back around to talk to him. She must have known what a mess she was making, but she never gives up on a challenge. "It's a shame we missed it, but maybe you could tell us how you went about organising the whole thing. Was it a surprise or had you told everyone in advance?"

"I'll tell you all about it." He put his hand on my back to show how willing he was. I'd had a feeling over lunch that Harrison could be the slipperiest character at Cherkley Court, but I'd apparently overestimated him. "I conceived of different clues and different tasks for each of my four competitors. I set the whole thing in motion when I arrived here on Thursday, but I didn't tell the competitors about it until Friday night. It wasn't easy convincing the kitchen staff to make me a chocolate cake with a silver coin baked into each quarter – or tying a wedding ring to a frog for that matter – but it was worth every moment! I swore the servants to secrecy, and I believe they obliged."

"Fascinating!" She was back. "Did Ponsonby have to kiss the frog?"

"Is that how you treat your servants, madam?" Harrison actually tutted this time. "I wasn't trying to embarrass the man. In fact, I'd planned the whole thing for Lord Sheridan, but he made it clear that he wasn't interested." He tipped his head to one side to have a bit of a think. "To be fair to the fella, I should have seen that coming. He was a good sport letting us rampage around his house, and he didn't have a problem with the thing in principle, but he's not exactly a party hound and preferred to devote his time to his work."

"So it was just Quentin, Louise, Lady Sheridan and Ponsonby taking part, is that correct?" Bella couldn't go wrong with this simple question, and yet it somehow still drew a frown from our suspect.

"That was the idea, but Louise wasn't keen from the beginning. She completed the first clue, was unhappy about having to walk to the woods to find the second and gave up there and then."

"What time would that have been?" I was finally asking straightforward questions.

"Let me think." He had another puff on his now far shorter cigarette. "The proceedings commenced at dead on eleven o'clock.

I know because that was when I started my chronograph." He took out a slightly dented silver watch from his pocket and, pressing the crown on top, the second hand began to move around the dial.

"I've been meaning to ask, are you one of the Winchester Harrisons?" Bella was focusing on all the wrong things.

"Close enough. They're my cousins. Do you know Sarah and Charlie?"

She folded her arms, as though she'd come over all cold, despite being in a hothouse. "No, I can't say I do."

"Oh, they're wonderful people. It would be my pleasure to introduce you one day."

I maintained my pretence of bonhomie. "So what were you doing while the competitors were dashing about the house and gardens?"

"I followed them. I was peeking through the library window when Imelda went in there to find the key, and then I was down to the tropical house for... Well, I was everywhere, really." His evasiveness had returned. He was trying to pass it off as indecision, but it was clear he didn't want to tell us whatever had happened next. Everyone we'd spoken to so far had something to hide – even the butler, it turned out. Ponsonby had said nothing of his involvement in the elaborate game. "I took particular care not to miss Ponsonby's dip in the moonlit pool outside."

Just to make things abundantly clear, Cherkley Court had three large ponds, one in each glasshouse and one outside where we'd caught Lionel lurking. My own lavish family estate has a bucket for catching rainwater, but it's not quite the same thing.

"Come along then, tell us who the winner was!" I urged him.

"Actually, it might surprise you." I know that I was encouraging him to do so, but it was impressive just how gaily he could discuss the events of a night on which a terrible crime had been committed.

"Was it Imelda?" Bella hurried to guess, thus disappointing Harrison yet again. If I'd been closer, I'd have poked her until she stopped talking.

"Yes... yes, it was."

"Who would have thought?" I tried to maintain my cheery disposition, but it wasn't easy. I even took out my matches, but he'd crushed his cigarette underfoot and apparently had no desire for another. "Did you happen to notice how long it took her?"

He looked at his watch again, as though this would help him remember. "She needed thirty-two minutes and fifteen seconds. Ponsonby was very disappointed not to finish first, and Quentin..." He cleared his throat and it was clear that, if we wanted to know anything about the final competitor, we would have to talk to him ourselves. "As it went, Imelda was a woman possessed. She rushed through every challenge."

"She told us that she'd spent some minutes in the library with her husband." Bella had given up trying to be one of the boys. Her voice had become sterner, and she had a troubled expression to match. "She said they squabbled before she looked for the clue."

He pursed his lips and glanced across at the Hellenic sculpture of a woman with an urn in the middle of the pond. A steady flow of water gushed out of it to splash down over her. "That's all true, but I'd say it was a matter of seconds, not minutes. He asked for peace and quiet, she was in a hurry looking for the key and barely listened, and then he locked her out when she'd gone. I don't think either of them saw me, but Lord Sheridan looked quite amused by his wife's interruption."

"Did you see him again that night?"

"Not that I recall." He raised one finger to correct himself. "Wait, yes. After they discovered the injured maid, a footman came to fetch the butler, so I went with him. We were in the garden, and Lord Sheridan was still locked away with his work." His sombre manner didn't last long, and he was soon grinning. "You should have seen old Ponsonby's face when he had to go into his master's library with his socks and shoes squelching."

It was my turn to ask a question. "Did you notice anyone else between the time Lady Sheridan left the library and the time you were called upstairs?"

He leaned back against the metal bench and closed his eyes for a moment or two, as if he wished he could return to his nap. "No, but I heard someone. I wandered over here, and as I did, I heard a door open and someone running along the gravel path that spans the length of the house."

"Could it have been the gardener who's gone missing?"

"I wouldn't know. I don't believe I've ever seen the man."

"Did you notice where the person went?" I tried again.

"No, I only heard him. But from the sound of the receding footsteps, he ran right along the path and down the hill."

"Would that fit with the clues you provided?" Bella finally contributed something useful to the interview. "You said that Louise was supposed to go to the woods."

"No, that was in quite the other direction, and besides, she'd given up and gone to bed. I ate her chocolate cake and greatly enjoyed it."

Harrison was something of a pseudo. He was brash and arrogant, and I didn't particularly like him, but he was the first person who'd given us a clear picture of what had occurred on Friday night. I had one last significant question to ask him before we could talk to someone more pleasant.

"We know that Imelda's final clue led her outside. What about Quentin and Ponsonby's?"

He smiled to himself, clearly proud of what he'd done. "That was rather clever, actually. Everyone started back where they had begun, but I'd swapped the first clue for the chocolate cake each time. Ponsonby ended up on the other side of the house, and Quentin... well, Quentin never actually finished, but after the tropical house he was supposed to go to the kitchen."

FIFTEEN

"Really, Bella?" I asked once we had escaped the humidity of the greenhouse. I should probably have adopted a friendlier manner. "First you sounded like a music hall comedian and then you asked him about his family as though you'd only trust him if he were one of the *Winchester* Harrisons as opposed to those pesky Shrewsbury or Beaulieu Harrisons. What were you thinking?"

"What was *I* thinking? Why didn't you push him whenever he was reluctant to reveal the truth?" I didn't know how to answer this, and so *she* pushed *me*! "You were enjoying being his friend too much to find out what we needed to know. Every time he mentioned Quentin or the tropical house, he looked somewhere between heartbroken and appalled, but you just changed the topic as though it were of no significance."

"You did the same thing with Lady Sheridan. We can interrogate him properly once we've got everyone's initial account. We're only here because Lovebrook requested our assistance. If we upset the wrong people, Lord and Lady Sheridan could banish us from the house, and then the culprit might never be caught."

She clearly didn't accept my answer, but she chose not to contradict me. "Fine, then what did you make of Harrison? There's something smarmy about him. I don't understand why Lady

Sheridan would invite a man like that here. I can't put my finger on it, but I don't trust him."

"I'm not suggesting you marry the man, Bella. And I can see why he wouldn't be your type of person, but he answered our questions accurately enough."

"Yes, he told us what he wanted us to know, but nothing he said cast the faintest shadow upon him."

"That might be because he had nothing to do with the burglary."

She remained unconvinced by all I'd said, so I didn't expect this to have much impact either.

"Don't be such a dope, Marius. He was the one who planned the game for Friday night. He kept it a secret to surprise the others."

"Yes, but the staff knew what he was up to – to an extent, at least. He went round the house planting clues and asking favours."

"Fine, but he chose the time and was best prepared to make use of the distraction. He gave us no sense of what he did in the half hour between Lady Sheridan finishing the treasure trail and the attack."

"Whereas Lady Sheridan herself stretched time, reorganised the order of events and outright lied to us, yet it's Harrison you suspect."

She exhaled her frustration. "I suspect everyone!"

"Which, as we both know, is the right attitude to have." I'd adopted a conciliatory tone, mainly because I knew that she wouldn't agree with what I was about to say. "However, I think you took exception to young Harrison for another reason altogether."

We had stopped to argue in a neat, formal garden close to the main terrace. Apps and his colleagues had done their best to brighten the area with rows of planted flowers, but if the bad weather we'd been having continued, their fragile petals wouldn't last. As Bella showed her anger, I felt some empathy for those withering pansies.

"I beg your pardon?"

"Oh, come along, Bella. I don't like to cast aspersions, but it certainly seemed as though you were asking about his family to check that he was the right sort of Harrison. If that was the case, it was pure snobbishness, and I don't approve."

Her jaw dropped open, and a barely audible sound emerged from the back of her throat to demonstrate her disbelief. "How can you think so poorly of me?"

I didn't dare answer.

"Admit that you've been taken in by a swindler, Marius. He made you feel like an old pal, and you failed to do your job." A new possibility occurred to her then. "Perhaps his supposed reluctance to talk about whatever happened to Quentin in the tropical house was a way to distract us from darker secrets he was hiding."

"It seems we'll never know..." I paused to make her think I would say no more. "...until we walk up to Quentin and ask him about it."

"Sir. Madam," a voice called from the nearest door into the house, and there stood Ponsonby, looking paler of face and more uncomfortable than we'd seen him. "I'm sorry to interrupt, but there's been... Well, I don't know how to say it, but your presence is required inside. Inspector Lovebrook has called everyone together in the hall."

It was strange to see him loitering in the doorway like that, and even stranger that he would call to us rather than coming over to speak in the discreet murmur that was characteristic of his profession. He didn't even wait for our response but bustled back into the house. His disquiet fed into mine. Even though I was happy to cut short the argument I'd been having with Bella, I had a feeling that whatever was to come would be tougher to endure.

We hurried after him, passing the billiard table in the games room before reaching the small passage leading to the centre of the house. It appeared that we were two of the last people to arrive. Thomas-Richard Harrison and the other artists had already been rounded up, and the gardeners, John and Jack, or James and Jerry or whatever their names were, strolled in a moment after we did.

They were out of place in their overalls and muddy hobnail boots, but they weren't the only ones looking sheepish.

Harrison emerged from a room on the upper gallery, and, on the ground floor, I noticed Quentin Urquhart standing separately from the main group. He held one hand to the back of his neck and appeared to be muttering nervously to himself. The man had looked panicked all day, but by this point he seemed to be on the brink of exploding. Lady Sheridan wasn't a great deal more relaxed, either. She stood at the bottom of the stairs – in what might be considered the prime position to witness the drama that was about to unfold – and I could see through the crowd that her fingers never stopped fidgeting in the pockets of her loose, batwing gown. Her eyes occasionally strayed across to Louise Thorneycroft, who was one of the calmest people present. She leaned languidly against the wall and even smiled when Lovebrook raised one hand to get everyone's attention.

"If we're all here, then I'll begin." The inspector was halfway up the stairs to address the hastily assembled congregation. Sitting at his side, looking every bit the policeman's dog, was Percy, and there were more than a few nervous faces staring back at them.

Nerea and the governess were there, but Lionel had clearly been left out of the proceedings – presumably because his mother felt he was too young to be included. This had not prevented the boy from lurking upstairs to hear. I could see his chubby face peering through a crack in one of the doors on the floor above us.

"Ladies and gentlemen," Lovebrook pronounced in a wonderfully authoritative voice that he rarely used. "I regret to interrupt your day like this. I had hoped that the next time I spoke to you all it would be to share good news, but I'm afraid that isn't the case." He paused then, and I could see that his job was not a happy one. "Ponsonby has just received word from my man at Horsham Hospital. Penny Baker has died from the injuries she sustained here on Friday night."

He paused to allow the shock to pass over the staff and residents of Cherkley Court. I didn't hear a single word uttered, but there were a fair few intakes of breath. I swallowed silently, as even though I'd never met the woman, I had a real sense of how much she'd meant to people in the house. No one had said a word against her – except for the brat who was blinking down from the gallery. His mother's face had gone white when she heard the news, but she distracted herself by going to comfort another of the maids. In fact, one of the people who looked most upset was Quentin. His eyes were glistening, and he had to grip hold of the doorframe to support himself.

Lovebrook cleared his throat before continuing. "This means that we are now investigating a murder. And I think I should tell you that, if one of you here was involved in the theft from Lady Sheridan's boudoir or the attack on poor Penny, then I promise you now, we will find you, and you *will* be punished."

SIXTEEN

The house felt very different after that. Everyone we saw looked haunted by the news of the maid's death. I don't know about them, but I found myself viewing her as an unwitting victim – caught in someone else's plot. We'd investigated the murders of a film star, a diplomat, a police officer and various well-to-do folk, but they had been the protagonists of their own stories. There was nothing to suggest that Penny had been anything more than unlucky to have gone upstairs when she did, and it made the case all the sadder.

From the stunned expressions of Penny's colleagues, I could see just how hard they would find it to accept this new reality. Perhaps some of them were relieved they hadn't crossed paths with a killer, but the fear still remained that it could happen again and, next time, they could be the victims. It was hard to ignore the realisation that we were sharing the refined space with that lowest of creatures – a murderer. It was stamped on every word we uttered and present in every thought.

A woman has been killed. This gorgeous house will forever be tainted by that wicked crime.

I read these words on every face as we went through the formality of interviewing the staff with whom we were yet to speak. There were tears in the kitchen, but none of the other maids could tell us why Penny had gone upstairs at such an hour. The footmen and the hall boy were astonished by the news of her death, but only Francis had something significant to tell us.

"I saw Penny in the garden before she died. It wasn't unusual for her to be awake at such a time," the older of the two footmen explained in an accent I took to be Liverpudlian. "Though her shift was over, she was something of a night owl. Sometimes she'd stay in the kitchen reading in case Lord and Lady Sheridan needed something. And sometimes she'd walk about the grounds to wear herself out."

"Where exactly did you see her?" Bella asked him, and I thought perhaps that the same numbness I felt slowed down Francis's answer too.

"I believe it was just outside the two glasshouses. In fact, yes, she was sitting beside the tropical house when we arrived."

This fitted with what Lady Sheridan had told us, but there was something else I needed to know. "And what time was that?"

He looked up at the ceiling of the servants' dining room where we'd found them polishing silver. "Oh, I'd say that were half past eleven, proximately. I had been instructed by Mr Harrison to stay with Lady Sheridan as she completed her challenges. There were some things she had to do which required me to get my hands dirty. I didn't mind, though."

"Did you see anyone else on your trip about the place?"

He was an open, friendly sort, and sounded as if he genuinely wished to help us. "I can't say that I did. Except for the other people playing the game, of course. Lord Sheridan was in his library throughout. I know because I brought him a drink before we started and then had to wait outside while Lady Sheridan spoke to him."

"Am I right in saying that was around twenty minutes after the game began?" Bella inquired and Francis nodded.

"Did you notice where Ponsonby or Quentin Urquhart were from then until midnight?" I asked as an idea popped into my head.

He took his time to think once more. "Now, did I see Mr Urquhart going into the dining room just after we finished outside? Yes, I think I did. Apart from that, I didn't see anyone. And when I'd completed my duties helping Lady Sheridan to win the competition, I retired to the kitchen where Frederick and I were when the bell rang to call us upstairs." He grew a little grimmer then. "Just think, it had felt like such an achievement to finish first. And thirty minutes later, that savage attacked our Penny. Perhaps she was too good for this world."

His fellow footman Frederick was on hand to console him, so then we asked a few more questions, thanked them both for their time and headed off to find the next member of staff we needed to interview.

"Why did you ask about Ponsonby?" Bella asked as we wound our way upstairs. "You don't really think that the butler could have done it, do you?"

Percy was asleep on the landing, so clearly his brief working shift had left him dog tired. Either way, he wouldn't have answered this question, but I could. "We shouldn't ignore the possibility just because Mr Ponsonby's getting on in life and looks the least likely killer imaginable. His name keeps coming up in the events of Friday night, and yet, when we spoke to him, he shared nothing of his starring role."

"Yes, but we only asked him about Penny Baker and Dennis Apps. We never mentioned the game to him. It's not his fault we failed to ask the right questions."

"Nevertheless, he didn't volunteer any relevant information, and Lovebrook doesn't appear to know much about what the butler was up to at the time. We'll have to interview him again."

We'd reached a second staircase that, unlike the grand one at the centre of the house, was hidden behind a small, unremarkable door. It took us up to a landing with three more rooms coming off it. One door said NURSERY. One said CLASSROOM and the other was blank. Inevitably, I couldn't resist trying this mysterious portal, but it was locked. So then we went into the nursery instead, where we found the nursemaid of whom Nerea had spoken. There was no sign of Lionel, and from the occasional muffled complaint that travelled through the wall, I assumed he was receiving classes next door.

"Afternoon, sir, m'lady," the rosy-cheeked young woman said with a curtsey. She was busy folding bedsheets into a small airing cupboard and looked flustered to receive visitors.

"We're sorry to bother you, Hilary," Bella began because, aside from her clash with Thomas-Richard Harrison, she is best at setting people at ease, and I am perfectly competent at setting them on edge again. "We'd like to talk to you about what happened on Friday night. We heard from Nerea that you were one of the first to see Penny after the attack."

Her pleasant face immediately crumpled with sadness. "That's right, m'lady. It was a horrible thing, and I'll never forget it." She looked around the nursery as though searching for hope.

The room was decorated in a light pastel blue, as one might expect. It had surely been the same ever since Lionel was born ten years earlier. It still had an obligatory rocking horse in one corner and a vast selection of bears, dogs, cats and other stuffed beasts arranged at the end of the bed. Having briefly made the tyke's acquaintance, it was hard for me to imagine him playing with any such toys, unless he required something to blow up or burn with a magnifying glass.

"Would you mind telling us exactly what happened that night from your perspective?" Bella asked when Hilary offered no more.

The nursemaid curtseyed again, out of nervous instinct rather than necessity. "Very well, m'lady. I'll do the best I can." She took a moment to breathe in deeply before beginning but then continued in just as small and cautious a voice as before. "I suppose the part of things that might interest you began when Lionel, love him though I do, started playing up. He's never the easiest child around bedtime, but he was particularly difficult that night."

I had to look away out of fear that I might mutter a rude

comment. I must admit that I hadn't formed the highest opinion of the Sheridans' heir.

"I can't really blame him," she continued. "He was excited because of the party and the young visitors, and he couldn't fall asleep. I tried lying down next to him, but that did no good, and I tried leaving him alone with just one candle burning in the corner, but that was when he sneaked downstairs. It wasn't long before midnight... Not long before they found poor Penny."

"And where were you at this point?"

The sound of my voice rising unexpectedly must have surprised her, but she regained her composure and pointed to a door standing ajar in the far wall. "I have my bedroom in there, sir. I was reading and must have nodded off. When I woke up, I went to check on Lionel. I had a feeling he had more mischief in him that night. I should have known not to leave him alone."

"Just how badly behaved a child is he?" I should probably have phrased this in a less critical manner, but it didn't matter as Bella was there to speak for me.

"I believe my friend is curious as to what Lionel got up to downstairs."

She is a wonder at reassuring our witnesses. I should probably give up talking altogether.

"I think he just wanted to see what was happening. He isn't such a bad lad. I know he says some curious things at times, and he can be quite cold to his governess, but he's perfectly nice to Nerea and me."

"And that night?"

"It took me a while to find him, as I assumed at first he'd be downstairs. In the end, he was hiding in his parents' bedroom. He wouldn't tell me what he'd been up to, but he had a knowing smile on his face." She paused then, and a contemplative look sparkled in her eyes. "I must admit that it's often best to let him think he has the upper hand. I could spend my life going back and forth to the mistress to tell her all that Lionel's done, but it would do neither of us any good."

This was a far cry from what she'd said moments earlier about him being a decent sort, but we weren't there for a report on his behaviour, and Bella swiftly moved things forward.

"Nerea told us you heard a noise?"

Hilary seemed to come back to herself then, as though the thoughts she'd been having had been swatted away like a cloud of gnats. "That's right, though it was only the next day that I realised what it must have been. I was downstairs looking for Lionel. I thought perhaps he'd gone to see his father, but the library was locked as usual, and I was about to try the dining room when I heard a thud from upstairs, and I thought he must be playing up there after all."

"So you think that was Penny falling?" I asked, having already forgotten my lesson.

"Yes, sir. Or perhaps it was whatever that monster used to kill her as he dropped it on the carpet. But that couldn't have been further from my thoughts just then. I went back upstairs, calling out Lionel's name this time, and when I was halfway up, I heard giggling and knew he was in his parents' room. I pulled him out from under the bed, even if he didn't want to come. He kept complaining that I'd spoilt his fun, and I was having none of it."

Though she couldn't have been much more than twenty, Hilary had a toughness to her that I wouldn't have expected. I could imagine her impish infant ward bending to her will despite himself. I suppose that children like Lionel need such a presence in their lives, especially when, from what I'd seen at least, his parents had little to do with him. All we'd heard about was his mother pursuing her own interests and his father's obsession with money.

"Was that the end of it?" Bella had been sitting on a small chair at a small table but got up to communicate just how important she thought this question was. "Did you see or hear anyone else after that?"

When Hilary realised that there was something more, a look of horror crossed her features. "Oh my goodness, I heard him. I heard the killer. I know I did. There was someone breathing heavily as if they'd been running or what have you."

"Do you know from which room the sound came?" For a moment, I thought this might tell us everything we needed to know, but I had overlooked the obvious.

"It must have been the boudoir where Penny was attacked. That's the only thing that makes sense, and it certainly came from that general direction." Hilary looked so pale then that Bella began to rub her arms, afraid she might faint. "I was talking to Lionel and didn't think about it, but I'm sure that's what happened." She'd been holding back the emotion well enough, but it was all too much for her and tears now appeared in the corners of her eyes. "I don't like to say this considering how Penny ended up, but it could have been us too. We came this close to seeing the killer."

SEVENTEEN

"One of the worst things about being a detective – or at least playing at being one, as you and I do – is the feeling that we might finally be able to see through the fog of the case, only to discover that everything is just as murky and confusing as it was at the beginning."

I said my grumpy piece and then stood where I was on the bright gallery, holding on to the cast-iron railing and looking down on the floor below as various members of staff buzzed about there. I found it sad to think that they still had to complete their afternoon tasks even as the reality of their friend's death settled in for them.

"I don't know about that, Marius," Bella responded. "I thought Hilary was very helpful."

There was a white marble pillar just next to me, and I considered giving it a frustrated punch but decided that I preferred my knuckles unbroken. "Helpful in the sense of solidifying the idea that the man we're chasing is some kind of phantom. All the chess pieces were darting here and there across the board, but no one saw who entered or exited Lady Sheridan's boudoir. It could still be any one of our suspects. It could be Lord Sheridan himself, though it's hard to imagine why he would have let us poke around here if that were the case. It's more likely to be a member of staff." I almost said that it could still be Dennis Apps, but I resisted.

"I thought you'd already dismissed that idea for the simple lack of motive."

I shook my head because I didn't know what else to do. "I'm aware that we've both contradicted ourselves five times today, but motive doesn't prove a suspect's guilt. Just as a lack of obvious motive doesn't make him innocent."

She laughed at me – she generally does when I'm feeling glum. "I stand corrected. Now can you please stop moping and do your job?"

I didn't reply. I was too lethargic for that. All my excitement about Hilary's account of the neighbouring room (well, hallway) to where Penny was attacked in the very moments that it occurred had drained away to be replaced by nothing of any value.

Luckily, the same couldn't be said for Bella. She walked towards the scene of the crime, and Percy roused himself to follow her. The pair of them stood in the doorway to the boudoir and glanced inside. He'd probably do a better job than me anyway. I left them to it and went back to watching the tops of people's heads. Ponsonby wandered by, calling instructions to an unseen colleague in a surprisingly commanding tone of voice. Lady Sheridan stood for a moment looking lost and then put on a sunny expression when a maid walked past. She eventually disappeared again to make way for Quentin, who rushed into view with his easel under one arm and a clutch of paints and brushes under the other. The moment I saw him, I knew that the nervy, clumsy fellow would drop them and drop them he did.

We still hadn't heard his version of what had happened on Friday night. The problem was that, whilst I'd previously hoped that everyone knew more than they were willing to reveal, I was coming around to the idea that no one knew anything at all, and the obvious culprit truly was the killer. I'd held onto the idea that Apps was innocent for Nerea's sake more than anything else, but no one had seen anything suspicious upstairs, and though I'd hinted otherwise, I didn't actually believe that the killer was a ghost.

I confess that I was tempted to call down to Quentin, both to get his attention and to see whether he would drop his materials again, but then a door opened just beyond where Bella was still doing our job.

"Oh, hello," Louise Thorneycroft said, retreating a step as she took in my friend and my dog. "Were you waiting to see me?"

Bella looked just as surprised to see her but responded directly. "That's right. We'd heard you were up here."

I would probably have told the truth, but then I couldn't see what possible insight a young artist who seemed largely unconnected to both the victim and the owners of the house might offer us. We lacked a common link between the suspects. Lady Sheridan was connected to the three artists, but did not seem particularly involved in the lives of the staff, whereas her husband was cut off from almost everyone else in the house. If he'd at least sent some hungry glances in Louise's direction, we might have been able to imagine a tantalising tryst between them, but he'd taken no interest in anyone but his wife since we'd arrived there.

She and Bella (and Percy) loitered for a few moments as Louise peeked into Lady Sheridan's boudoir and gave a silent shudder.

"We can talk in my room if you wish," she said, so as not to have to look at the neighbouring room any longer. Of course, I couldn't promise that the conversation we were about to have would set her at ease. We would have to at least raise the possibility that she was the killer, after all.

Bella nodded, Percy scampered ahead of us, and Louise laughed to suggest that she didn't mind dogs in her already messy room – even if she hadn't issued him a formal invitation.

"How can I help you?" she asked as she sat down on a cushioned wooden box beside the semicircular bay window that gave views over the forest on one side and the gardens on the other. The room was rather homely compared to many we'd seen. There were plain white curtains, the walls were a pleasant shade of pastel grey, and the furniture was a little less ostentatious than in the other bedrooms.

Bella had the same good-humoured expression she'd worn out in the hall, and I knew that she wanted me to ask the questions for some reason. Perhaps she simply wished the division of labour to be more equitable, which was fair enough.

She sat down on the side of the bed, and I walked closer to our suspect to begin the interview.

"I suppose you should start by telling us how you came to know Lady Sheridan in the first place." I probably sounded a touch indifferent, but it occurred to me for the first time that we had been remiss in not finding out the precise details from any of the others.

"Very well." She leaned back a fraction, and the light behind her made her expression harder to read. "I studied at the Royal Academy. One of my paintings went on display in an exhibition at a small gallery off Trafalgar Square, and Imelda bought it on the very first day. She said she fell in love with the picture and asked the gallery owner for the address of my studio in Bloomsbury. She's since bought three more of my paintings."

"We saw them hanging downstairs," I said, intentionally not passing judgement on them as I didn't want her becoming too comfortable. If painters are anything like authors, she would spend the rest of the conversation wondering what we thought of them... had Bella not told her.

"They're excellent," she exclaimed with just a hint of animation in her voice, as if she secretly wished to celebrate the works more fervently. "Really. They're unlike anything I've seen before."

Percy was lying on his side in a patch of light and released a long, unimpressed yawn at this moment to compensate for Bella's enthusiasm.

"Yes, they're quite good," I said to do the same, "but that doesn't explain how you and the other two ended up spending time here at Cherkley Court. We know that there is some element of patronage on offer, but why the three of you, and why now?"

Louise was not afraid of us, and not just because Bella hadn't gone along with my plan. She was a confident, capable person. It was clear from the way she spoke and even sat. She pushed her hair from her eyes with the authority of a woman who knew not to fear those around her. "I suppose that Imelda decided that we were good enough artists to be worthy of her support. As for the timing, we initially came here a few months ago to have the opportunity to discuss our plans. I believe she enjoys our company so much that she keeps inviting us back. Is there anything sinister in that?"

A frisson of excitement passed through me as I realised that I had, if not underestimated her, then at least overlooked certain possibilities. She was a worthy adversary in a way which the others simply were not. I could definitely imagine a woman like Louise Thorneycroft plotting to achieve her ambitions, whatever they might be.

"No, no," I said with just as much self-assuredness as she possessed. "Although, having met the two idiots downstairs who claim to be artists, I found myself wondering what someone like you thinks of them."

It was already apparent that she was enjoying herself. "I don't think I'd use the word 'idiot'."

"Really?" I replied, and Bella's head swivelled back to look at me. "From what I saw this morning, you were struggling to tolerate their antics. Is it very tiring watching Tom and Quentin compete for Lady Sheridan's attention?"

She leaned forward once more, and the line of her mouth was firmer than it had been. "The best response I can offer is that I let my paintings talk for me. I don't believe in one-upmanship."

I tried not to give away that, while I knew I'd touched a nerve, I couldn't explain why that might be. "And what do you think of them as artists? When they're not wagging their tails to get your patron to rub their bellies at least."

Percy raised his head to look at me before realising that this comment was not for his benefit and collapsing once more.

"I don't," she responded in as curt a manner as possible. "Quentin and Thomas-Richard are perfectly pleasant company when they act their age, but I don't consider them competition in any respect."

So that told me, but we were only just getting started. "Very well, is that why you refused to be a part of the game on Friday night?"

She pursed her lips and held back whatever her first response would have been. "Not at all. I simply found it childish. I didn't come here to run about the grounds, jumping in ponds or climbing trees for Tom's pleasure."

"Is that how it worked then? Did he organise the whole affair for his own enjoyment?" I really must learn not to be sullen. A few minutes earlier, I'd felt like giving up, and now the faintest glimmer of interest had pulled me back to my senses.

Louise looked at Bella, perhaps feeling that she might get more sense out of her. "You should ask Thomas-Richard. I don't like putting words in other people's mouths."

She was excellent at deflecting any point I might raise, and it wasn't easy to respond to her. That just made me more eager to do so. "What did you do whilst the others were jumping into ponds?"

"I came up here and got into bed with a book about Peter Paul Rubens. I fell asleep reading it."

I looked around the room to see whether she had invented her reading material, but there was a thick and very worthy-looking cloth-bound book on her bedside table that fitted the description.

"It doesn't sound as though it was particularly interesting," I told her. "Have you considered switching to mystery novels?"

"Have you considered writing something with more artistic merit?"

"No. No, I have not." I was having a wonderful time. "Now, at what point exactly did you wake up?"

"It must have been when... I think it was just after I heard the chimes for midnight."

"From which clock?"

"I don't know..." Her confidence was ebbing, her answers no longer so clear. "I suppose it was the one on the landing."

"The one on the landing which presumably makes a noise for every passing hour? Do you wake up every time it chimes?"

"No, but... Well, I hadn't intended to fall asleep, so it wasn't as deep as it might have been. And when I heard that it was midnight, I realised that I should wake up again." Her brown eyes seemed to darken as the questions piled up, and she struggled to make sense of her memories – or perhaps the tales she was weaving.

"So you counted the twelve chimes in your sleep, is that what you mean?"

"No... I just thought that... Or perhaps it was the sound of Imelda screaming that brought me back to consciousness."

I held my hands out in apparent acceptance. "That must have been it. You left the treasure trail because it was childish, came up here to read, fell asleep and then woke up to the sound of your friend discovering that her maid had been attacked."

I could hear her breathing more loudly through her nostrils. "That's exactly what happened, so why are you speaking as though everything I just said sounds ludicrous?" She batted her hair from her eyes out of anger for once.

"I'm not trying to upset you, Louise." I spoke in the calmest and most understanding voice I could muster. "We simply want to know what really happened on Friday night."

She was panicking more with every comment I made, but that didn't mean I'd landed a winning blow. Her reaction was completely out of proportion. "What do you mean 'really'? I just told you what *really* happened."

"Yes, but I'm afraid I don't believe you. I came in here with no preconceptions of how you might be involved in the murder of Penny Baker. I had no reason whatsoever to think that you knew anything about it, but you're beginning to act suspiciously."

She looked at Bella then, whose silence was deafening. In return, she gave an apologetic tilt of her head, and Louise looked even more guilty.

"Perhaps I'm just one of those people who can't handle being interrogated." She tipped her chin back in an attempt to assert herself. I don't believe it worked.

"Or perhaps you're one of those people who aren't as good at hiding their involvement in a crime as they'd hoped."

She was an attractive young woman. Lithe and dark-skinned, she was just the kind who could have stolen my heart, had I not been in love with the person who had forced me to become a detective in the first place. However, as she writhed and reacted to my fairly reasonable questions, I found something about her quite unpleasant.

"You're twisting my words," was the next defence she attempted.

"No, I'm not." I had been standing beside the fireplace for some time, but the light behind her was getting on my nerves, so I walked across the room to look at a bookshelf beside the bed.

"You're taking what I've said and making it sound as if I'm capable of killing an innocent woman when the truth is that I would gain nothing from the maid's death."

"You're free to say that, of course, but it isn't true. For one thing, I haven't done anything with your words. All I've said is that your nervousness is out of proportion with the trajectory of this interview. To me, that suggests that there is a topic you wish to avoid and that I've inadvertently raised it. As for not gaining from the murder, that would seem to overlook the theft of a certain historically significant silver box."

"You're talking absolute—" She cut herself short. I don't know whether she had come around to my argument, or she realised that answering back would only make us think worse of her.

I'd been leafing through a book on conifers but now clapped it shut. "Let's just imagine for a moment that you aren't a killer and you really are getting hot and bothered over something which will not lead to your imprisonment and possible hanging."

This did not put her at ease. She swallowed so hard and abruptly that I could hear it several feet away. She raised her hand to soothe the pain of this involuntary gesture, and I kept talking.

"Let's further imagine that this conversation will do nothing to help us identify the culprit. Even if that is the case, you must realise how it looks at this moment. You were perfectly happy to talk to us at the beginning. I haven't come across such a clear-minded person all day as the woman who invited us in here, so perhaps you'd care to reveal what has changed."

I didn't think she had it in her to answer, and when this turned out to be the case, Bella spoke again.

"There are crumbs on your bedside table."

Louise looked at her with a dismissive mien. "The maids were told not to clean the bedrooms after the burglary. I'm sorry it doesn't meet your high standards, *m'lady*."

Bella really was in a strange mood. It was true that there was a small pile of dark brown crumbs resting beside the book Louise had been reading, but we hadn't gone in there to check that she was keeping her room tidy.

"You do realise that you're more likely to find yourself in trouble if you don't tell us what you know than if you do?" I tried again, as I thought I'd seen a flicker of acceptance a few moments earlier.

Still nothing came back to us, and so I kept talking. "Are you frightened because you don't want the killer to know that you know something? Is that it?"

Bella changed her approach and decided to speak in a friendlier manner. "Lionel's nursemaid heard a thud on the floor around midnight, and then there was someone breathing heavily in one of the rooms shortly after that. Is that what woke you? Imelda's boudoir is right next door. You surely heard something if you were already awake."

"That's enough!" The volume of her voice surprised us both. The look of fear on her face was even more alarming. "I have nothing to tell you. Do you hear me? I was asleep, and that's all there is to it. I only left this room when I heard Imelda scream."

EIGHTEEN

I walked away from Louise Thorneycroft's bedroom with several loud thoughts hammering in my head. "I feel a fool for dismissing the very idea that she could know something."

"They all know something, Marius," Bella replied, taking me a touch too literally. "The question is whether she knows anything that's relevant to the killing. I'm not denying that she was rattled. She clearly thought she could get through an interview without incriminating herself, but your remarkable power of interrogation overwhelmed her."

Walking between us, Percy wheezed a little louder than normal. He apparently found Bella quite hilarious.

"Very droll, I'm sure." It was hard to know what to say after this. She had a remarkable ability to make me feel like a dunce. "Whatever you might think, what I told her was true. I touched a nerve, and either she was involved in the attack, she's protecting someone who was or she's hiding something else entirely."

"I agree, Marius."

I replied with a disbelieving expression as we reached the top of the stairs.

"I do!" she insisted. "But I think it's far more likely to be the third option. Perhaps she was in there with Tom or Quentin, and she couldn't tell the truth because her patron wouldn't approve." A new possibility entered her mind, and she added to this conjecture. "Perhaps she was in there with one of the servants! That would be a real scandal."

"I'd pity the poor footman who loses his job for her." I realised this sounded cattish, so had to add a brief footnote. "Not that a woman like Louise wouldn't be worth losing one's job over, but…"

"Oh, so she's good looking enough for you to make such a sacrifice, is she?" Bella was back to being offended by everything I said.

"I didn't mean that, and you know it. I simply wished to say that it would be the footman or hall boy – or perhaps even a gardener – who would ultimately suffer. Tom, Quentin and Louise are hardly struggling artists in the traditional sense. It seems to me that they're from just as well-to-do families as their would-be patron is. I bet they're mainly after her money to say that they've won the game."

I must have delivered my defence with a wounded look, as she relented – that was something else she did a lot of that day. "I'm sorry for being facetious, Marius." She squeezed my arm affectionately. "I can see you meant nothing by it. I must stop being so sensitive."

We'd descended the stairs by now, and we were about to find the room where we'd previously seen Quentin painting, when we heard some kind of disagreement at the front of the house.

"It's not true!" a voice I instantly recognised loudly declared.

"Señorita Barriuso," Lovebrook responded as we reached the open door to what I took to be a morning room, "you must believe that I am sympathetic to your situation—"

"That's not true. It's not. If you were in any way sympathetic, you would not say these terrible things. My Dennis is a good man. I know he is, and I won't listen to any more of your lies!"

In the far corner of the room from where we stood, there was a tall birdcage made of rounded white bars. Inside was a lone grey parrot that looked out at us mournfully. In that moment, he rather reminded me of my ex-love. They had both been taken away from their homelands to an often damp and occasionally cold corner of a foreign country and, as Nerea sat on the chenille sofa that sank too far to be comfortable, I could see that she was just as trapped there as the poor bird.

"Is there anything we can do to help?" Bella took a few steps into the duck-egg green room to ask.

It wasn't just the walls and the sofa that were in matching shades. Even the bookcases had been painted that colour, and it was a good thing none of us had opted for verdant tones that morning, or we would have blended into the background.

Nerea had turned away to sob into a handkerchief, and Lovebrook looked reluctant to explain himself, but he eventually answered her question.

"I don't believe you can. In fact, I feel I must apologise for wasting your time." Standing on the pale green carpet in the centre of the room, the inspector rocked on his heels. "I was just telling your friend here that we have some new information on Dennis Apps."

Nerea spun around in her seat. The whites of her eyes had taken on a pinkish hue, but her brown irises were as deep and mesmeric as they ever had been. "Marius, it isn't true. You must believe me."

Lovebrook intervened once more. "I've been trying to tell Señorita Barriuso that there's no longer any doubt. I did as we discussed and spoke to the staff about the vehicles here. There are two vans used by the grounds staff, and one of them is missing. They hadn't been used for the last two days, so no one noticed that it wasn't in the garage. I feel responsible for not thinking to check earlier, but it's clear now that Apps stole the vehicle to make his getaway."

"Then how did he get off the estate without anyone noticing?" I took up Nerea's cause, as it seemed that no one else would.

Lovebrook folded his arms, clearly embarrassed by what had happened. "There's an old gate along one of the paths that leads through the woods. According to the gardeners, it's rarely used, but my men have inspected it and there are signs that it's recently been opened. It was locked, but Dennis would have had a key."

"That doesn't mean that he's a killer..." Nerea had lost some of her fight, and her voice had fallen quieter, but she was no less vehement in what she was saying.

"I accept that, in principle. I really do." Lovebrook grimaced for a moment before coming closer to the Spaniard and perching on the coffee table in front of her. "But that isn't all we've discovered. As soon as we knew about the van, we shared a description of it with the local and Metropolitan police. Within an hour, a bobby had found the vehicle abandoned near King's Cross Station."

"That doesn't prove anything!" Nerea tried once more. Even though Lovebrook was speaking to her in a gentle manner, she couldn't bring herself to look at him.

It was Bella's turn to help the distraught woman. "You know, there's nothing to say for certain that he killed Penny."

"You can think that if you like, but when an inspector went to the station with a photograph of Apps, he tracked down the man who'd been on duty early on Saturday morning. The guard distinctly remembered the gardener boarding the *Flying Scotsman* to Edinburgh. He said he stood out as he had no suitcase but carried his possessions in a paper bag, and yet he paid for a third-class fare with a five-pound note."

Nerea let out a cry of quiet anguish and held her hand out for me to take. "Please, Marius. Do something. I promise that whatever they think they know about Dennis isn't true. If he was on the train, there's nothing strange about him travelling without luggage, as he doesn't own any. He has two suits to wear when he isn't working and one good pair of shoes. If he really did take a van and hurry off in the dead of night, then there must be an explanation." She turned to plead with Bella. "There was probably some kind of emergency which called him away. Perhaps he has relatives in Scotland."

"Has he ever mentioned any family up there?" Lovebrook

asked. To give him his due, he was willing to listen to what Nerea had to say.

Sadly for her, she could think of nothing more to defend the man. "No, but that doesn't mean..." Her words faded away, and she dropped her head.

"If any other solution had presented itself, I would keep an open mind," the inspector told her as I continued to hold her hand. "As things stand, it's hard for me to imagine any other scenario than that Dennis Apps stole the silver box and bludgeoned Penny Baker. You must remember that it happened late at night. The staff were asleep or busy with the game that Mr Harrison had arranged. Dennis could have crept into the house through one of the back doors that lead off the terrace. He would have had to time it carefully, but it wouldn't have been difficult to sneak upstairs, seize the box and, before he was interrupted by the maid, hide behind the door to hit her over the head as she came inside."

Nerea didn't look up or make a sound. Her world was falling apart.

"Unless you can think of any information which could definitively point to another suspect, I will instruct the constabulary in Edinburgh to search for Dennis Apps."

He glanced at us then, but the truth was that we had nothing to give him. We'd uncovered plenty of uncertainty and witnessed some decidedly circumspect behaviour, but nothing that day had led us to believe that another of the inmates of Cherkley Court was to blame for Penny Baker's murder.

So what could we do? Nerea was just as distressed as she had been when we'd entered the room. Lovebrook was just as sure in his conviction that, despite all we'd said that morning, Dennis Apps was the culprit, and I had no way of rebutting this theory.

The three of them looked at me for an answer, but there was only one I could give. "I'm sorry, Nerea. We've learnt nothing that could prove his innocence."

NINETEEN

It didn't take us long to prepare to leave. We thanked Lady Sheridan for her hospitality, and I said goodbye to Quentin and Thomas-Richard, but Louise stayed in her room. I must admit that the question of what she'd been so desperate to hide would vex me for some time. When we'd thanked the staff and wished them all well, Lovebrook came to see us outside.

"It still doesn't sit right with me," Bella told him as Caxton emerged from the Sunbeam to open the door for his mistress. He'd be waiting some time. "Every interview we conducted made me feel we were getting closer to uncovering what really happened here. And that's without mentioning the strange behaviour we encountered."

The inspector looked back over his shoulder to make sure that no one was listening. "If you ask me, they're all rather queer. *The fish stinks first at the head*, they say, and Lord Sheridan takes so little interest in what goes on in his own house that something like this was bound to happen."

"'Something like this'?" I echoed him in a more cynical tone, and I think he realised how his words sounded.

"Well, maybe not quite like this, but having spent two days

here, I can say without hesitation that I would not invite those three artists into my house."

This made me reflect that we didn't even know where Lovebrook lived. I really should have made more effort to get to know him when we first met. Any questions I could ask of him now would just sound rude.

"People are strange wherever we go," I told Bella, as if the daughter of a duke needed any such reminder. "More often than not, it's for a perfectly innocent – though still quite curious – reason. I think that, this time, we took them all too seriously."

I shook hands with our dear friend, and he turned sombre as we walked to the car.

"Please keep us informed of what happens next," Bella told him, and Lovebrook nodded and headed back into the house.

I noticed that Nerea had remained in the morning room. She was still sitting where we'd left her – still looking forlorn as she peered out of the window at us. I'd told her that she could contact me for any eventuality, but I very much doubted that she would. I can't deny that I felt great sadness for her. Life rarely turns out as we hope it will, but to lose the person you love in such a swift and terrible fashion would be hard for anyone to endure.

Considering how dejected the whole affair had made me, I could only imagine what she was feeling. I didn't even notice Caxton seething or looking daggers in my direction. Although Nerea's situation reminded me of the way she'd made me feel when she left me all those years earlier, there was no longer any malice left in me. I wouldn't have wished that pain on her.

We pulled away from the house, and Caxton accelerated up the hill to lead us off the estate. I hadn't realised until we crested the slope just how much of the day had gone – or that we'd left Percy inside and had to go back down the hill to get the grumblesome pup. He took it most personally, but then we set off once more. The light was already dying, and this knowledge sparked a feeling of insatiable hunger in me. I doubt it was a lack of food that did it. All my emotions were muddled up and mixed together, with my sadness at the events at Cherkley Court pre-eminent amongst them.

For whatever reason, Dennis Apps had decided that the only solution to the problems in his life was to rob and kill. An innocent woman was dead. A family home was tainted with blood and, if he were lucky, the killer would spend his remaining years in gaol. Hopping on the train to Edinburgh was just about the most obvious (and least likely to succeed) plan imaginable. At least if he'd crossed the Channel there would have been less chance of the police finding him, but I had no doubt that, by the following weekend, he'd be residing in a cell somewhere in Scotland. People like Apps aren't lucky enough to disappear entirely. I felt quite sure that he had left a trail behind him, and the police would have no trouble following it.

We drove out of Cherkley Court and back to the winding country lanes of Surrey. I thought we would keep our thoughts to ourselves, but Bella was in a more gregarious mood than I, and she offered some reflections on our unusual day.

"All things considered, I think we did rather well. We managed to uncover any number of delicate matters even without there being a killer present for us to catch."

I smiled, as she had a wonderful way of unearthing nuggets of positivity in the darkest of mines. "We surely outdid ourselves."

"We did!" she insisted, batting at my arm with her hand. "I'm just disappointed we'll never know what the arrangement was with Lady Sheridan and her little gang of followers."

"Bella, where's your discretion? It was a perfectly normal arrangement in which an older, married woman dangled the promise of riches over three attractive young artists."

She laughed silently and looked out of the window at the trees flashing past. "Our visit resembled two overly optimistic people sticking their heads into a wasps' nest and pulling them out again before they could get stung."

"Let's just hope the wasps don't follow us home. I would hate to wake up to find Harrison buzzing about my bedroom, or Quentin desperately trying to escape through solid glass."

Percy was already fast asleep between us. He'd had a busy day, too.

"Poor Quentin," Bella said with a sigh. "I thought he was rather sweet. His sister always said that he was a hopeless case. I could just imagine him taking up his hobby, desperate to prove to his family that he could make something of himself, no matter how little they might think of him."

"I wouldn't want to be part of a family like that."

"Maybe not..." Her sudden silence seemed to suggest that she had more to tell me that she would hold back for a suitable time.

And so the conversation dried up, but the atmosphere in the car had changed. Bella could brighten my mood without even trying. She was the source of all that was light and bright and brilliant in my life. The only problem was that the scowling lump in the front seat, who hadn't stopped grunting under his breath at every word I'd said since we climbed into the car, was taking me to my family home, and the journey was a short one.

We passed through the tunnel of trees that leads to Hurtwood Village, and I felt my heart tighten again. The leaves of the new season had grown back since I'd last been home, but the night was almost upon us, and little light broke through. Before I knew it, the car slowed down, we turned into my road, and the time to say goodbye had arrived.

I opened the door for Percy to lumber over me, but he just sat there looking at his Bella. A moment's silence passed before I accepted that I would have to get out of the car before he would agree to move.

"Wait just a moment," Bella called after us as we walked up the steps to my childhood home, where my aunt and uncle had been living for the last year and where I would spend the night. Percy looked back at her from the top step with an expression that suggested he thought she might finally confess her undying love for him. "Marius, I have to ask you something."

She'd presumably told Caxton not to get out of the car, as he wasn't gawking at me.

"Feel free," I said, as I glanced back to see whether my Uncle Stan had spotted us and was watching through the window. It looked as though we were in the clear for the moment, though I doubted it would last. That man had ears like a bat crossed with an elephant.

"Why did things end between you and Nerea? You haven't told me."

She'd asked this question so casually that I answered without realising it was a difficult topic to discuss. "She left me for a richer and presumably more handsome man, then somehow made me believe it was my fault for neglecting her. She said that I couldn't love her because I was still in love with you, but that was just an excuse when she saw the chance to move up in the world."

I waited for her to show her usual sympathy, but it didn't come, and so I added more to the story.

"I spent the next six months thinking how stupid I'd been to let such an exquisite human being slip through my hands." I almost added *for the second time*, but I wasn't feeling brave. "Even though our courtship largely consisted of arguing and making up again, I honestly once believed that I would marry her and spend my life in France. It took me all those months to come back to my senses."

"And then what happened?" She delivered these words with great care, as though afraid of the impact they would have.

"I spent a lot of that time just walking around Paris. One day, I was standing at the highest point on Montmartre, with the city stretching out in front of me into infinity, when I finally realised how much of myself I'd lost as I tried to be the person that Nerea wanted. After today, I can see that I was just as much to blame as she was, but we should never have come together in the first place. I didn't like the people that we were back then."

Of course, what I didn't tell Bella was that, standing in front of Sacré-Cœur de Montmartre that day, I also came to see that I'd fallen in love with Nerea in an attempt to forget the girl I'd left behind at home. The girl whom, rather than asking her to marry me, I had abandoned and couldn't face seeing again.

I expected Bella to say something simple and hollow like *That must have been hard* or *How did you recover?* But she just stood before me on the step, waiting to see whether I wanted to tell her anything more.

"If it hadn't been for that moment in Paris, I might never have recovered from my ill-chosen love. Nerea and I weren't fashioned from the stars for one another. We weren't destined to come together despite being born a thousand miles apart. We were two lonely people who happened to cross paths at the wrong time, and I could finally see that. So I left Paris to go to Berlin, then travelled around the Continent for as long as it seemed like a good idea. When that was no longer the case, I came back home."

Now I was the one waiting. I wanted to know what she made of everything I'd just told her, but she wouldn't give anything away.

"I'm glad that you did," she said, and she offered me her hand.

At first, I found this a rather formal gesture, but I wasn't about to turn down the opportunity to feel her fingers in mine. And when they connected, she squeezed with such affection that Percy became jealous and gave a short, grumpy growl. I suppose he might also have been hungry for his dinner but, either way, Bella and I laughed as she released my hand.

Percy went to scratch at the door, and I watched Bella descend the path to her car. Once she was inside, Caxton released the brake, and the Sunbeam went dawdling up the hill towards Hurtwood Manor, but some tiny part of Bella remained. I could still feel her warm fingers on mine, and I realised that they had erased any memory of my contact with Nerea, not just in the moments before we left Cherkley Court, but during my time in Paris, too.

"Who would have thought it, eh, boy?" I said as the door swung open. "Maybe she can tolerate me after all."

TWENTY

I woke the next morning conscious of something niggling at me. It was both obvious and hard to fathom at the same time, much as if someone had hammered a nail into my head but I couldn't tell what had caused the pain.

I turned over and looked at the faint light coming in through the curtains of my childhood bedroom. I didn't need to squint at the clock to know that the sun would soon be rising, but that didn't make my conundrum any easier to solve. As the waking world made itself known to me once more, I knew that there was something about Penny Baker's death that still didn't feel right. It was all well and good saying that Dennis Apps had to be the killer because everything pointed in his direction, but that didn't actually make him guilty.

I knew that there was something obvious we were missing, but it wouldn't come to me. It was a bit like that sensation when you feel as if you've lived a moment of your life before and, if you could just get your thoughts in order, you'd be able to say what happens next. For me at least, the moment always passes and I come to doubt my own memory, but I wouldn't let it happen this time. There was still a puzzle to solve, and though the grand revelation that I felt was only just out of reach never materialised, I had realised something significant.

I got dressed and ran downstairs. Auntie Elle was presumably still asleep, and Uncle Stan had already gone to the bakery, leaving plenty of yesterday's bread in the larder for my breakfast. I stuck my last piece of toast in my mouth and pulled open the front door only to come face-to-face with Bella.

"Something doesn't make sense," we both said at the same time. Well, perhaps the words weren't identical, but the meaning was as close as could be.

"It was what you said yesterday," I told her, before realising I was being rude. "Actually, you should go first."

She didn't hesitate to do so. "I think that Harrison has been lying to Lady Sheridan. I remember where I saw the painting in her sitting room. I'm certain that it's by a young French artist who had an exhibition of her work in Chelsea recently. Harrison must be passing it off as his own."

"That sounds quite likely, as I realised something else about him. It was what you mentioned yesterday about his name. You said it was impossible or improbable."

"That's right. I said he was improbably named, what of it?"

Percy nosed his way around my legs, then rolled onto his back for attention and got it. "It took me until this morning to realise what you meant. Thomas-Richard Harrison is not so different from Tom, Dick and Harry."

"Oh, I realised that straight away," she said matter-of-factly. "It's rare enough to meet someone with a double-barrel first name that I mulled it over in my brain."

My first thought was to ask, *Then why didn't you say anything?* But I calmed myself and, most diplomatically, asked, "And what do you think that says about him?"

"That his parents are terribly upper-crust and perhaps the tiniest bit pretentious."

"So it didn't strike you that Harrison could have invented the name and be hiding his true identity?"

Judging by the reaction, she did not see this as any kind of a failure.

"Have a nice day, Percy," I told my dog, and he actually barked at me, which is a rare occurrence indeed.

Perhaps it's no wonder that he likes Bella more than me. She's the one who always makes sure he's included. "How could you be so cruel as to leave him behind?" she asked as she helped him onto the back seat of the Sunbeam.

"I have a heart of stone," I told her, knowing that there was no sense in arguing.

I'm happy to say that Bella had driven down the hill herself that morning, and I would not be subjected to her chauffeur's glowering. I got into the passenger seat, and Bella started the engine. A few moments later, we'd left the village behind on the journey out of the Hurtwood and through the Mole Valley to Cherkley Court. If you don't know Surrey well, it probably sounds like I made up those places – much as I'm certain there is no one on earth called Tom-Dick Harry – but look them up on a map and you'll find that they're all there.

It had gone seven by the time we were admitted to Lord Sheridan's estate. Bella didn't spare her car as we shot along the undulating driveway and down the hill to the main house. There was no sign of Lovebrook's little brown car, and I wondered whether he'd moved on to another case.

Ponsonby was already at the door, so he must have been informed of our arrival by the guards at the gatehouse. I can't say he looked particularly pleased to see us, though.

"Sir, m'lady..." he began, but then he hesitated over what to say next. "I don't have the words to explain it. You must follow me immediately."

He turned in his usual fashion and led us through the house to the dining room, but we didn't stop there. He kept walking through the tall doors that gave on to the tropical house and there, stretched out on one of the giant lily pads, looking every bit the tragic heroine, was Lady Imelda Sheridan. There was blood below her nose.

Her eyes were open but motionless, and I knew in an instant that we were too late to save her.

TWENTY-ONE

The two footmen were standing on either side of the immense circular pond, the twin of which we'd seen in the greenhouse the day before. They didn't move; they didn't appear to know how. They stood sentry over their dead mistress, and I must say that the scene before us was just like an image one might see on the cover of a gruesome novel. The exotic plants that I might normally have found appealing looked predatory and marauding. I noticed the sharp spines of various cacti, and the creeping influence of the vines that covered every once-white beam and surface.

Lady Sheridan herself looked beautiful in her red cotton chemise with a white silk foulard tied around her neck. One of her slender arms was trapped beneath her on the immense floating leaf, and the other was extended towards the side entrance of the glass-and-metal building. Her skin was as pale as Snow White's, and the red of her outfit reminded me of the apple which that unfortunate character had eaten. But there would be no second chance for Imelda – no dashing prince who could bring her back to life. Her stillness was reflected in the scene around her, and it continued as I addressed her staff.

"Have you called the police? Is Lovebrook on his way?"

The ineffective guards looked at Ponsonby for direction before the butler answered. "Yes, sir. One of the gardeners found our dear mistress here not fifteen minutes ago, and I immediately called Lord Sheridan and Scotland Yard. I couldn't speak to his lordship directly, but a message was left with his housekeeper, Mrs Batty. I gave her the responsibility of waking him up and breaking the bad news." I could tell that this was a task he was glad not to undertake himself. "She told me that he had been working until the early hours in his office at the property in Maida Vale. She let his secretary out at two in the morning, and Lord Sheridan was still up when Mrs Batty retired shortly afterwards."

I had more questions to ask him, but Bella had gone to the stone edge of the pool and crouched down beside it to look at the victim more closely.

"You know that I'm not so experienced in these matters," she began, surely doing herself an injustice, "but the colour of her skin would suggest she's been dead for some time, wouldn't you say?"

I considered the fact that one foot was in contact with the cold water of the pond. Any cooling effect would have been limited by the warm air in the tropical house, and I could only agree. "We'll wait for the police surgeon to give us a clearer picture, but it would seem that way. It certainly wasn't in the last few hours."

I bent to lean out over the water and feel the tension in her wrist. It was almost rigid, and though rigor mortis can set in as early as an hour after death, it wouldn't have reached the extremities so quickly. If anyone had asked me to guess, I would have said she couldn't have died much later than two in the morning.

"Were there more games played last night?" I asked the butler.

"No, sir. It was a quiet evening by anyone's standards. An early dinner was eaten at Lady Sheridan's request. I believe that the staff were all in bed by midnight. There's a nightman who sits in the front porch in case anyone should need to be granted admittance, but he didn't see anything unusual. Another man was stationed at the front gate, of course, but here inside the house, there was no one on duty."

I couldn't think of a single other thing to say. I turned back to the body and put one hand on Bella's shoulder, as I could see she was shocked by the turn of events. I'm sure that, just like me, she was already struggling to understand how this fitted with anything we'd discovered the day before.

"It's just awful," she whispered, and I hadn't seen her so affected by a death since her aunt had been killed a few months earlier. "I rather liked her. I didn't say it yesterday because she was still a suspect, but I genuinely enjoyed her company. She was one of those mischievous types who may take a different approach to life from you or me, but to whom one can't help but being drawn. It's just..." I believe she stopped this sentence short so as not to repeat herself.

"She was certainly an appealing sort of person. I know she gave us some dubious answers when we interviewed her, but I never thought of her as the likely culprit."

"Sir?" Ponsonby was still lurking behind us and took the lull in the conversation as an opportunity to interrupt. "I beg your pardon, sir, but I was wondering whether you thought we should wake up Lady Sheridan's guests."

If the truth be told, I didn't know what to think, but I could see that the butler desperately wanted something to do, and in the absence of his master or the police, it fell to us to assign his duties. "I think that we should wait, for the moment. For one thing, there's a chance that one of them is responsible for the murders."

This drew a gasp from the footman Francis, whereas his colleague gave a Percy-like growl from the base of his throat. I decided that I should probably not let them get carried away before we knew what had happened, so I spoke again. "We can't say anything for certain, of course, but it will be easier for us to do our job without too many people moving about the place."

"Very good, sir." Ponsonby was still lingering expectantly, so I gave him something to do.

"You can tell your staff what has happened. Obviously, if anyone knows anything, send them to us. Oh, and please ensure that they suspend any cleaning until further notice."

"They only just went back to it last night, sir," he explained in a sorry voice, and it occurred to me that, on our cases in grand houses like Cherkley Court, the suspension and recommencement of such mundane work served to mark the start and now (hopefully) the end of any killings.

The butler wandered away, taking Francis with him for support.

"What I can't see is what killed her," Bella whispered to me once they'd left.

I pointed to the silk scarf around her neck. "I would imagine that the damage is hidden by that. Judging by the dry blood beneath her nose and the red spots in her eyes, I'd say she was strangled."

I didn't know whether it was the scarf itself that had been used to kill her. It did seem odd that she would have worn it to bed. I studied her for a few moments longer before my mind jumped back to the present, and I turned to the remaining footman.

"Frederick, do you have any sense of what has been happening in this house?"

He showed the same look of disgust I'd previously seen. It was as if, by addressing him directly, I'd given him permission to share his true feelings. "I don't, sir. All I know is that there is true evil here. That anyone could hurt two such good-hearted people as Penny and our mistress just to steal something from the house... Well, it doesn't bear imagining, but two women are dead and, as far as I can see, the police will have their work cut out to put the pieces together."

"Why would you say that?" The emotion was plain in Bella's voice.

He paused before speaking, perhaps to remind himself that he was still talking to his employers' guests. "Because he killed Penny and got away with it. I don't know what his game was, but he obviously thought he was clever enough to do it again without being caught."

Something in what he'd said made me rise to show my appreciation. "Thank you, Frederick, that may be very helpful. I would suggest you remain here until the police arrive."

I began to drift away, and Bella came with me. She waited until we'd passed back into the dining room before speaking. "What did he say that was so enlightening?"

"Just that he thinks the killer has got away with more than just murder. It's fair to assume there are few personal motives that would require the extermination of both Lady Sheridan and her maid. That makes me think that the killer tried to steal something last night that he'd failed to obtain on his first attempt. We must now work out what that was."

"Yes..." She spoke dreamily and needed a few moments before she could say what she was thinking. "I suppose there must be more than the pretty tableau that was left for us in the tropical house."

"You noticed the elegance of the scene then, did you? It is just like a composition for a great artist to paint. It makes me think for some reason of *Las Meninas* by Velázquez; a carefully arranged moment captured in time."

"Or a seedy postcard from some shabby seaside parlour," Bella said, thus reversing our usual high and low cultural references. Who'd have thought that I would come across as the sophisticated one for once? "Did you notice the camera tripod that was hidden by the plants on the far side of the pond?"

"No," I said, surprised that I could miss such an unusual detail, but then I had been concentrating as much as possible on the dead woman. "You don't think that there is some element of..." I didn't know a polite word for whatever I was trying to describe. "I mean to say, it couldn't be one of those terrible cases you read about in the paper but hope never to encounter. You don't think the killer's sole motivation was a photograph of the dead woman?"

"Are you saying that everything that came before was just a distraction?"

I didn't have an answer for her, and she shivered a little at the very idea, so I decided not to pursue it further. The house was still quiet for the moment. We passed the hall boy carrying a box of polish and brushes towards the kitchen, but otherwise we had the place to ourselves. We curved up that grand staircase and all the way to the landing where I'd despaired of our chances of finding the killer the day before. Everything had been turned upside down since then, yet in a way, I'd been proved right. The case we were investigating was incomplete and perhaps impossible to solve without this new instalment. I had to hope that, if the killer had achieved his goal on the second time of asking, we would come to understand his motive.

The doors to every bedroom but one were closed. Lord and Lady Sheridan's room was located at the furthest point around the gallery, and I could see as soon as we reached the top of the stairs that something wasn't right in there. There were cushions visible on the floor and, as we got closer, I could see that sheets had been ripped from the bed.

"Should we wait for the police?" Bella asked when we stopped for a moment in the doorway.

"We could," I said, stretching out the word as I stepped into the room, "or we could try to get ahead of the killer and solve this case before any more terrible things happen."

She didn't need persuading and followed me inside. The place looked as if a family of boars had been encouraged to go snuffling through it in search of truffles. Nothing was where it should have been. Imelda's clothes had been emptied out of the two large wardrobes and a chest of drawers. Books had been pulled down from the shelves near the bed, and a pile of papers had been scattered here and there. I examined a few in case they were connected to Lord Sheridan's business, and the killer's initial sortie into the dead woman's boudoir had been a mistake, but they were mainly letters from friends and relatives which didn't appear to relate to the crime.

"Her jewellery box has been upended," Bella said, focusing on more likely avenues of investigation, "but it's hard to imagine the culprit ignoring so many emeralds and rubies if that was what he wanted to steal."

"Yes, it's looking increasingly likely that he had something specific in mind. He evidently didn't find it on Friday, so he stole the silver box to confuse things. He was interrupted in his task by Penny Baker, but he didn't give up. He had a second go last night, but I believe he must have killed Imelda first. He needed time alone here to find whatever he was after."

"Do you think he got it?" Bella stood in a small circle of space, surrounded by piles of the victim's possessions. She looked out of place amidst such disorder.

I studied the room for a few moments before coming to a decision, more or less. "I think it is impossible to say. He presumably had reason to believe that what he wanted was here somewhere, but perhaps it had nothing to do with Imelda. Perhaps whatever he was happy to kill to obtain belonged to her husband. It will be the first question I ask Lord Sheridan when he arrives."

Bella couldn't take the disappointment. We had not discovered the answer to the thirty or so minor mysteries we'd failed to solve the day before, or the ten new ones that had sprung up overnight. She went to sit down on the bed and, when she found her voice again, it was smaller and more pitiful than usual.

"This changes everything, doesn't it? All that we thought we knew yesterday will have to be re-examined in the light of the second killing."

"I'm afraid so," I said just as sombrely, but I wouldn't let her be so pessimistic. For one thing, that was normally my job, but for another, I needed her help. "But trust me, Bella: he won't get away with it."

TWENTY-TWO

It was at this point that I realised we'd lost Percy. I felt quite confident that some gullible maid with more time on her hands than usual had fallen for his charms and was ensuring that he remained as heavy as ever. Had I known I would one day be a detective, I believe that I would have opted for a smaller and less ravenous dog than my current canine companion. Having said that, I didn't choose Percy in the first place, and I'd rarely elected to bring him along on a case with us. Such decisions had been taken out of my hands.

Wherever he was, Percy wasn't our most pressing concern. We had a decision to make.

"It's fair to assume that Harrison isn't the amiable toff that he's made himself out to be," Bella reminded me. "Should we start with him?"

I didn't answer her question directly as I was thinking of other things. "I'm trying to fit together what we learnt yesterday with the events of this morning. We know that several of the suspects became nervous when we spoke to them. Last night, it was easy enough to dismiss that phenomenon as innocent people reacting to the pressure of an interview, but now that Lady Sheridan has been killed, we must look again at what was said."

"Imelda herself was one of those who became skittish."

I walked to the window to look down at the terrace. Lionel was already out there, running his governess ragged. She yelled at him to stop being such a naughty boy, and he chose to ignore her.

"She contradicted herself, didn't she?" I looked back at her across the room. "Imelda pretended that she was busy with the game until just before midnight when, in actual fact, she had already finished a half hour earlier."

"Does that mean she was protecting herself or someone else?"

"Maybe she thought she knew who the killer was and didn't wish to see him punished." It turns out that I'm good at not answering questions. I should do it more often.

"Would she really have protected him after he robbed her and killed Penny? Isn't it more likely that she was protecting someone who wasn't related to the crime but could have got in trouble for another reason?"

"That's what I normally do to build intrigue when a character in my books isn't the killer but must appear somewhat guilty, so why not?"

She ignored this and continued to lay out her thoughts. "It's still possible that Imelda was having an affair. Her offer of patronage – which lasted an awfully long time without actually providing one of the artists with a prize – could have been a ruse in order to spend time with her beau."

"That also sounds like something I would make up for one of my stories."

"Marius," she tutted at me then; I'm sure I deserved it, "could you please concentrate on reality instead of fiction? Unless you know of a way to skip ahead in the story to reveal the name of the killer, nothing you are saying is particularly helpful."

I loosened my tie before replying. "You are right, as always, Bella. However, I do like to think that, for all their easy delights, my books contain a certain level of..." I searched for the right word. "... psychological realism. Well, not the new book that's coming out any day now. That has as much sense in it as a bag full of—"

"Marius!" she barked again, and I tried to behave myself.

"Yes, good. Right. I was about to say that, if your theory regarding Lady Sheridan's infidelity is true..." I became aware of just what a salacious sentence this was and dropped my voice. "... who do you think the likely lover was?"

"It's not just the timing," she said, as she had also learnt how to avoid answering questions. *Touché, Bella, mon amor. Touché!* "She was in her chemise when Penny was killed. And the noise of heavy breathing, which the nursemaid assumed was coming from the scene of the crime, might actually have been coming from right here. We still don't know where Quentin was at midnight."

"Quentin?" I asked with no lack of cynicism in my voice. "Weedy, nervous Quentin, who looks approximately twelve?"

She hopped off her island in the middle of the clutter and came to issue a stern reply. "Yes, Marius. That Quentin. And as for how attractive a woman might find him, he's perfectly handsome."

"For a child," I said under my breath, though plenty loud enough for her to hear.

"Then perhaps Imelda enjoyed mothering him. That would fit with her role as his patron. Of course, it's tragic to think of her actual son who will suffer her death more than anyone." Bella bashed her palm against her forehead in irritation. "Oh, we are stupid. Imelda can't have been in here up to no good when Penny was killed because Lionel was. His nursemaid told us that she found him hiding in here."

"So does that mean we need to re-examine everything we thought we knew for a second time? Or is it a third time now? I've lost track."

Bella was close enough to the cushions by the door to pick one up and throw it at me. She missed.

"Isn't it more likely," I said, as I'd had a few minutes to think about it, "that the man here under a false identity is the one who wormed his way into Imelda's affections? On Friday night, he made sure that Lord Sheridan was locked away in his library and that everyone else was busy with the game he'd devised – going so far as to include the aging butler. He went upstairs for a tryst with his lover before sneaking away to steal some item of great value he believed he would find in the boudoir. Penny interrupted him, so he killed her. And then, with the box he took as a consolation prize, he returned to his slumbering lover in his own bedroom – hiding his bloodstained clothes up the chimney on the way. In the small hours of this morning, he had his second bite of the substantial cherry but waited until everyone was in bed to kill the woman he was robbing and ensure that he had all the time he needed here in the bedroom."

She pouted. I always feel oddly proud when I make her pout.

"I suppose you may be right, but that's still a lot to get done in a short time. We know that Imelda finished her challenges at half past eleven and that Mr Tom, Dick or Harry was still involved in other things that happened downstairs – he was there with Ponsonby for the pond dipping, for example, and he did something he didn't wish to mention in the tropical house – so that would have restricted the time he had up here."

I felt she was being pernickety now, but I adjusted my workings by a reasonable margin nevertheless. "Fine, then Imelda came upstairs on the half hour, and Harrison followed twenty minutes later to avoid suspicion. They enjoyed their intimate moment in his bedroom. He waited for Lionel and the nursemaid to return to their rooms and then sneaked out to the boudoir."

"So that's how long intimate moments take," Bella said with a mischievous smile that showed her pretty white teeth. "I must admit I've often wondered."

I decided to ignore her innuendo. "He could have hidden the stolen box easily enough and then returned to see Imelda. When she was talking to us yesterday, she realised that he had been out of the room at the time Penny was killed, which is why she attempted to shift around the order of events and tried to pretend she was downstairs later than she was." I was tempted to raise my hands in mock celebration. I didn't know for certain that I'd solved the case, but I'd made a good fist of it.

Bella wasn't quite so jubilant. She thought about this for a moment and said, "It's undeniable. You are very good at plotting fiction, but do we have any evidence that any of what you just said actually happened?"

I had no desire to continue our spiralling conversation, so I grabbed her by the hand. "Come with me, and we might find some."

I pulled her out to the corridor, then past Louise's bedroom and the boudoir. The only problem was that I didn't actually know where Harrison was staying. Luckily, there were only two rooms there which we hadn't entered, and I'd seen our top suspect coming out of one of them the day before.

"We'll storm in there and terrify him," I said, already anticipating our task.

Bella and I looked at one another. Throwing herself into the adventure I'd envisioned, she counted backwards from three, and we rushed into the room.

TWENTY-THREE

"Hello, old bean. How's tricks?" I asked at the top of my voice as we came to a stop at the end of the large bed that dominated the even larger room.

There was only one problem with my plan. The man known as Thomas-Richard Harrison was a phenomenally deep sleeper. The day before, he'd told us the opposite. So that was another of his lies.

"I say, fella," I tried again, "is everything fine and dandy?"

"Why are you talking like that?" Bella asked in a crisp whisper.

"I had a whole skit planned, but he's not waking up."

She frowned and her eyebrows drew together. "You don't think he's..."

I didn't, but it's always best to check. Inching forward, I approached the bed with my hand out.

"Be careful, Marius," Bella stayed way back to tell me.

I stopped and turned to look at her. "Why? Are you expecting him to wake up and bite me?"

I kept going, and just as I was about to pull the thick Welsh quilt off his body, he sat up.

"Ahhh!" This was Bella jumping out of her skin, not me.

"What are you doing in here?" Harrison demanded in a hazy tone.

"Hello, old bean. How's tricks?" I asked for the second time.

He regarded me suspiciously with the thick blanket pulled up to his chest.

"Come along, my dear chap. Let's talk brass tacks, shall we? What will it be?"

He looked at Bella, then at me, before returning to the safer option. "What's happened to him? Why is he talking like that?"

She didn't have the answer, but she smiled as though it were quite the most normal thing in the world – even if she secretly thought I'd lost my marbles.

"This is how folk like you and I bally talk, isn't it, *amigo*?" I don't know why I'd dipped into my limited Spanish there.

His confusion had turned to apprehension, but he rubbed his eyes and pretended not to be worried. "Well, yes, I suppose you may be right." He still sounded posher than I did, and I was really trying.

"Hang it all, man! Use your loaf. We seem to be in something of an imbroglio here, and you're resolutely sang-froidical about the whole thing."

"Well, I suppose I would be, as I haven't the faintest idea what's happened."

I raised my eyebrows to show him that the game was over. "Oh, haven't you, Thomas-Richard?" My voice was back to normal, and there would be no more *old sticks* or *tally-hos* until we'd picked apart the matter we'd come to discuss. "Or do you prefer Tom-Dick?"

"Don't look at me," Bella told him when he did just that. "I'm not going to let you get away with any more lies."

He opened his mouth and would presumably have tried to string us along for some time, but then his shoulders sank, and he seemed to accept that there was no sense in it.

"You must be in possession of an unhealthy dose of arrogance to use such a playful alias as that," Bella told him.

I was busy glaring in the hope that he might crack. "It's lucky the police aren't here yet, or you'd already be locked up." I didn't hold out any great hope that he would view the pair of us as toughs, but we'd managed to unsettle him.

"What are you saying?" he demanded, the panic beginning to show. "Why would anyone arrest me when I haven't done anything?"

I exchanged amused glances with my once-and-hopefully-future love, then motioned for her to continue.

"You haven't done anything?" She laughed that enchanting laugh of hers. "So you're just an innocent man with a false name who came here to pass himself off as an artist."

"I *am* an artist." His voice rose in tone and volume, and he was clearly annoyed by the insinuation.

"Is the painting of the foggy London scene in the sitting room one of yours then?" I put to him as I sat down in the armchair beside his bed.

"Yes, as it happens. Lady Sheridan bought it from my studio." Feeling that he was on firmer ground now, he indulged in a yawn.

"Another lie!" Bella exclaimed. "I saw that very piece in an exhibition not six months ago. I have no doubt that it was the same one."

"It was the same one," he complained. "I submitted it to the gallery, and they put it up with the wrong label. I complained when I saw it, and they soon rectified the problem."

My heart beat faster – or I was at least more aware of the sound in my ears. "How convenient. And did you sign it Thomas-Richard Harrison?"

"I... Well maybe not back then, no. But if you look, you'll see my name hidden in the bottom left corner."

I wanted to say *How convenient*, but I'd already said that.

Bella was wracking her memory for something that might prove he was making all this up, but nothing would come.

I wasn't doing much better myself. "Do you admit that you're here under a false name?"

"No, I..." He swallowed his response, and I saw a chink in his defences.

"So you really are related to the Windsor Harrisons?"

Bella was about to correct me, so I tapped her foot with mine before she could.

"Yes, Charlie and..."

"Sarah," she replied, realising what I'd done.

He forced himself all the way up to sitting now. "That's right. They're my cousins."

"And if we were to telephone them in Windsor, they'd vouch for you, would they?" Her words came out in a steady stream to beat Harrison backwards, and I knew we'd almost got him.

"It's hard to say. After all, we're only third cousins. They might not know anything of my branch of the family."

Bella released the faintest breath through her nose. "That's funny, as yesterday you told us what lovely people they are."

"Well, that was—"

She leapt on this and wouldn't let him speak. "The famous family, with whom you claimed a connection, come from Winchester, not Windsor. And you, whatever your name is, are a liar."

TWENTY-FOUR

I would quite like to have shaken my wonderful Bella's hand at that moment, although I accept it would have looked arrogant on our part, and we still hadn't confirmed that he was the killer.

"You're no artist. I knew it when I saw you," she continued, and Harrison calmly and quietly swung his legs out of bed.

He was wearing a pair of quarter-length undergarments, and Bella had to look away so as not to see too much of his very hairy legs. I wasn't desperate to see them myself, I should add, but it would have looked prudish if I'd averted my gaze.

"That was why I found it so hard to talk to you yesterday." She kept talking as she took a sudden interest in the plain wooden ceiling. "You're a fake."

"You're wrong on one account, Lady Bella," he said assuredly, having dropped his upper-crust diction. "I *am* an artist; I am a *con* artist, and a very good one."

She was speechless, but she'd fallen into the trap of thinking that he was confessing to the murders when I was certain that wasn't the case. It would take something more to get us that far.

"They're coming for you now," I said with something of a snarl. "You realise that, don't you? The police, when they arrive, will treat you like the savage that you are and send you away in shackles. But whatever they do to you, it won't be nearly so bad as what happens when you get to prison. I imagine you've heard of honour among thieves. In my experience, the honourable ones don't like cowards who kill defenceless, unarmed women."

He was putting on a long cotton dressing gown and made no sign of having heard me.

"And as for what you did to Quentin during the game on Friday? Well, that really was below the belt."

"I didn't mean to take things so far!" he immediately responded, and I knew I'd got through to him. "I admit that I should have thought more carefully about it. It was supposed to be a bit of fun. I certainly never meant to humiliate him when—" He stopped himself to size me up. "You don't know what happened, do you? You're just fishing for clues."

"Who are you really, Tom?" Bella tried in a softer tone. "And what did you come here to steal?"

He huffed then and searched in the drawers of his night table for... well, I didn't know what at the time, but he soon found a cigarette case and a box of matches. I must say that I respected him at that moment. He was young, and I had expected to be able to intimidate him, but he did something that most of our suspects fail to do: he took his time.

"You know," he said as one of the matches erupted into life to lend an orange glow to his skin, "when I was a child, I really did want to be a painter or what have you." His voice wasn't so posh now, but it had only descended one social bracket, not all the way down. "My father told me I was wasting my time. He wished for me to become a doctor or some such nonsense, but all I wanted was an easy life. I wanted to live without needing to strive and toil as he had. And so rather than entering a trade, I learnt how to get what I desired with as little effort as possible."

"It sounds to me as if you learnt to steal." Bella was suitably disgusted. "What was your scheme here? Did you hope to pass off another artist's work as your own in order to win Lady Sheridan's patronage?"

He sucked long and hard on his cigarette, as though he needed the smoke to survive. Even when he let it pipe back out again after several seconds, he did so reluctantly.

"Something like that, yes. But have you noticed that there's nothing inherently illegal in what you just described?"

I was about to contradict him, but I wasn't certain that I knew how.

Bella did better than I could. "The artist whose work you daubed your name over might have something to say about that. And I'm sure the police could find some obscure charge for you, if they don't arrest you for more serious offences first."

With the cigarette hanging from his lips, he raised his hands. "Let's all just calm down, shall we?" Neither of us disagreed, and so he picked a strand of tobacco from his mouth and tried to fashion a defence for his immorality. "I know you're thinking that, because I'm something of a swindler, I must have stolen the silver box and killed the maid."

I put on my most innocent voice. "I thought you said that the police would only bother themselves with the little people. Surely you couldn't be a suspect in any of that?"

He ignored me. "I may look like the obvious choice, but I'm not a violent person. I would never have hurt that poor woman."

"Which poor woman?" Bella asked loudly enough for her words to rattle some glasses on the dressing table.

"The maid, of course," he answered in a light, frivolous tone that reminded me of the one he'd been putting on until now.

My friend's gaze hardened. "So you don't deny killing Lady Sheridan?"

"Lady Sheridan?" His cigarette fell from his mouth to scatter its embers across the carpet. He desperately seized it, then stamped out the remaining traces with one foot. He looked back up at us with real intensity. "What's happened to her?"

"Is exactly what you would say if you'd murdered her in the tropical house and wanted to imply you knew nothing about it," I countered.

"And it's also what I'd say if I knew nothing about it."

I must admit, his buffoonish act had been so convincing the day before that it was hard to imagine him summoning such a reply. It made me question how much we'd fallen for his tricks when we'd spoken in the greenhouse.

He collapsed back onto the bed and sat there staring at nothing. "Are you really telling me Imelda's dead?"

I didn't have it in me to keep pushing him. The obvious response of a police officer would have been, *You know she is!* But it sounded so forced and artificial that I simply answered his question. "Yes. The staff found her less than an hour ago. We think she's been strangled."

He looked at us for a moment then opened his mouth as wide as it would go to scream a silent scream. He rolled onto his side and pulled his legs up to his chest. "You're right. I'll be blamed for everything, but you must believe that I didn't do any of this."

"Why should we believe you?" Bella began. "We don't even know your name."

It was hard to decide whether to feel for the man or take his reaction as the overblown hysterics of a desperate criminal.

"It really is Thomas. Thomas Richard Smith. That's why I chose to call myself Thomas-Richard Harrison. I thought I was so anonymous as plain old Tom Smith, I'd try to make something of it. I might have been born any old Tom, Dick or Harry, but I knew I could be more. With the dash of a hyphen, I transformed myself into one of your lot."

He seemed to include me in this group, which was Bella's fault again. My parents were from working-class stock, and I was just as proud of my heritage as the duke's daughter standing next to me was of hers. Now that I think about it, I should probably have offered her the chair.

Tom Smith had started crying, and it was too much for Bella to accept. "Why are you suddenly acting so emotional when two minutes ago you were the picture of self-confidence?"

"You don't understand!" he practically screeched. "Imelda could have spoken up for me."

"I doubt she would have when she found out that she'd been hoodwinked," I said more as an aside to Bella than a retort, but he answered all the same.

"Yes, she would. She would have told the truth. You see, she knew all about me. My ruse wasn't as sophisticated as I'd hoped. I thought I could buy up a few paintings by a lesser-known artist and put my name on them. I thought that would be enough to trick her, but she saw through my plan."

We'd been haunted by bad art over the last few months. I had to wonder what that said about the kind of company we kept.

"Are you saying that Lady Sheridan knew you were a fake?" Bella couldn't hide her disbelief.

"Exactly."

"Then why did she invite you to stay here? Why did she tolerate your lies?"

He took a deep breath and pushed himself upright once more. "She said I was worth it for the entertainment I could provide."

My always-suspicious mind was only ever going to conclude one thing. "So the two of you were lovers?"

He looked quite shocked. "No! Why would you think that?"

"Perhaps because you carried on the whole time as though you were." I thought back to their playfulness at lunch the day before, even after a woman had already been murdered in the house. "That must have been your intention at some point. You were up against two other artists in the competition for her patronage. You couldn't paint for her, so you imagined yourself winning her favour in another way."

Perhaps I was jumping to conclusions, but the man was a chancer. Aside from his good looks and charm, he didn't have a great deal more at his disposal.

"No, that's not how it is. Or at least, that's not how it turned out." See, I was right! "I might have seen her as easy game when we'd first met, but Imelda was smarter than most people. She saw what I was in an instant."

The room fell quiet as we considered the possibility that he was telling the truth. I can only assume that Tom took this time to contemplate his fate.

"You'll forgive me for not believing you," I told him. "It's just all a bit too convenient. The one person who can save you is the person who was murdered in the night. I can't yet say for certain that you're to blame, but the evidence is building up against you. You planned that treasure trail of yours to draw as many people as possible away from Lady Sheridan's rooms. So tell us what it was you wanted to steal!"

His face was creased, his teeth gritted. "You're not listening to me. I may not be the most scrupulous of individuals, but I didn't come here to steal anything. I devised that game to continue to be of value to Imelda. I was trying to be the life of the party that she obviously wanted. Why else do you think I would carry on like that in front of her husband?"

I'd expected Bella to at least consider his explanation, but that was evidently not the case. She cleared her throat rather formally and, in a cold, compassionless voice, said, "That will be one of the questions that the police attempt to answer. Just be aware that Inspector Lovebrook may come across as a kind, forgiving sort of person, but you haven't seen him when he gets on a scent." Peering down her perfectly straight nose at our main suspect, she spoke her parting words. "If I were you, I would tell us all you know before he gets here."

TWENTY-FIVE

"My goodness, Bella," I told her once we were out of the room. "You're a more skilful liar than he is. If I hadn't known better, I would have believed that Lovebrook was the furious thug you made him out to be."

"For all the good it did us. That charlatan still didn't give himself away. Do you actually think he's the killer?"

I looked back along the corridor to see whether any of the other doors had opened since we'd entered Tom Smith's room. "It's hard to say. He's a rotter of sorts. He admitted to being lazy and wanting an easy life no matter who loses out. And we know that he wished to hoodwink Imelda when they first met."

"And as you told him, plenty of circumstantial evidence points towards his involvement in the crime. But does any of that mean he would murder two people?"

"I was about to ask the same thing." We descended the stairs, and another thought occurred to me. "Of course, now that I think about it, it's still not impossible that Lady Sheridan worked out who was to blame for killing Penny. She knew her pet ruffian was the likely culprit and so she tried to make it seem as if she – and thus Tom – were downstairs later than they really were."

We'd come to a stop at the bottom of the stairs in that bright and cheerful light-well in the centre of the house.

Bella was smiling for the first time in a while. "Wonderful, we'll tell Lovebrook to arrest him just as soon as he turns up."

"Who do you want me to arrest?" the inspector asked as, evidently, he'd already arrived.

"Bella was being facetious," I explained. "She often is."

I got a thwack around the back of my head for my trouble, and she changed the topic. "How did you get here so quickly? I assumed you'd returned to London."

He put his hand to his apparently stiff neck, and I knew his answer in advance. "No, it was too far to go. I slept in my car a few miles from here."

"You are an odd fellow, Lovebrook," I politely informed him. "You could have had a spare room at Bella's house. She has at least forty of them."

Bella rolled her eyes. "We do not have forty spare bedrooms at Hurtwood Manor, Marius. There are thirty at most."

"Have you heard the bad news?" I asked the inspector.

"Yes." He was still rubbing his neck. "I rang Scotland Yard as soon as I woke up, and they told me to hurry back here. I was planning to drive to London to interview Dennis Apps, but in light of recent events, they're sending him here instead."

"You've arrested Apps?" I asked in amazement. "How did that happen?"

Lovebrook's eyebrows waggled to show that he knew something that we didn't. "He was staying in the very first place we looked. The receptionist at the North British Hotel beside the station in Edinburgh knew him as soon as a constable went there with a description. He'd been staying at the hotel since he stepped off the train on Saturday. From what I hear, he'd been eating in the restaurant and drinking in the bar without the slightest fear of arrest."

"Did he have the silver box with him?" Bella asked before I could.

"No, there was no sign of it. He claims that he was up there running an errand for Lord Sheridan, though our host certainly hasn't mentioned any such thing. An inspector from Edinburgh escorted Apps back on last night's sleeper service. The *Night Scotsman* left Edinburgh at ten o'clock and arrived in London just after six. A man from Scotland Yard is driving him here now. He should be with us before you know it."

"The wonders of modern transportation!" I commented, admittedly distracted from more important topics. I'm sure that the idea of a train service from Edinburgh that took a mere eight hours would have sounded like pure fantasy to my grandparents.

Bella continued to take the matter seriously. "Does this mean he's innocent after all?"

"Why would you say that?" Lovebrook looked unusually dour. "All it means is that he had an accomplice and raced away from the house to confuse things when the maid was killed. What have you discovered since you got here? And now that I come to think of it, how did you know to come?"

We gave a brief summary of our morning at Cherkley Court before taking him to see Lady Sheridan's body. As we talked, the coroner, a police surgeon and a number of local constables arrived and were despatched about the place to interview the staff, gather evidence and generally make their presence felt.

Nerea must have heard about Dennis Apps as she whispered, "I told you so!" as she hurried past us with the governess. Ponsonby was still on hand looking distressed, but Lionel and his nursemaid made no appearance. I suddenly felt great sympathy for the boy. I hadn't taken a liking to him, but he'd lost his mother, and that was a hard thing to overcome at such a tender age. I supposed that it would fall to Lovebrook to break the bad news if Lord Sheridan didn't appear first. Whoever had to do it, I didn't envy them one bit.

"You should send someone to talk to the nursemaid. You don't want the boy coming down here and getting wind of what's happened."

"He's already been taken up to the nursery, sir," Ponsonby eagerly informed me, and I once again had to wonder whether we should have considered his role in the affair more carefully.

"This way, Inspector," Bella said once the butler had left, and the three of us went back to the tropical house.

The police surgeon was already inspecting the body. He was kneeling beside the pond just as we had, examining Lady Sheridan's ever-more rigid corpse in various ways.

"Was she strangled?" I asked, and the taciturn, grey-suited defender of the dead nodded wordlessly.

"But not with the scarf, I think," I guessed again. "It would have to be something finer than that for the wound to be hidden. Some sort of wire, perhaps?"

He frowned, apparently impressed by my conclusion.

"Time of death was around two in the morning, I'd say."

He finally stopped what he was doing and looked at me. "If you already know all that, why did you call me? Are you trained in pathology or the law?"

"Marius is trained in making things up," Bella answered on my behalf. "But he's exceedingly good at it."

The expert would say no more. He went back to his task, and we continued talking to the inspector, who looked moved by the terrible scene there.

"That poor woman. I found her rather charming. She was quite different from her husband, at least."

I was distracted once again by the strength of the immense lily pad. I had to wonder how great a load one could hold, as it didn't even dip beneath the water where Imelda was lying, and it was nearly wide enough to support her whole body.

"We said much the same," Bella agreed. "It's a tragedy, and I'm sorry to say that all the simple solutions seem redundant."

"Yes, but someone must have killed her!" Lovebrook looked as though he wished to groan in anguish, but he maintained his composure.

I noticed Quentin Urquhart lingering in the dining room

behind him. He must have been told what had happened, as he stood there with a face that was approximately as cheerful as a rainy Wednesday morning. He didn't come any closer, and he did nothing to communicate with us, but I could see that he was trying to make sense of the violence that had occurred – just as we all were.

His pain was nothing compared to the suffering of the woman who now rushed past him. Louise Thorneycroft was in tears before she reached us. She fell to her knees between the door and the pond where her friend's body had been left. Or at least, I assumed that she had been killed somewhere else and moved onto the lily pad. It would have been difficult to do it any other way.

The workmanlike coroner took a brief look over his shoulder and presumably considered continuing with his work, but Louise's cries were so shrill and intense that he and the police surgeon finally stepped aside to let her mourn. The artist reached her hand out towards the artfully arranged body but went no closer.

Bella went to put her hand on Louise's shoulder, and I was just beginning to think that Louise's reaction was excessive – or perhaps even performative – when she explained why the discovery cut so deeply.

"I may have been the last person to see her alive. We shared a bottle of wine last night and talked about perfectly normal things. I don't understand who would have hurt her. She was so..." She couldn't find the appropriate word, and it fell to Lovebrook to ask a basic question.

"Can you tell us what time that was?"

Louise looked up at him. I believe she was still wearing mascara from the night before, as her eyes were a mess of black smudges. "I... I suppose it was past midnight. The boys had drunk too much and gone to bed. We'd been celebrating after you told us that ..." She kept stopping to stifle a cry or catch her breath. "...after you told us that Apps was the killer. I really thought the nightmare was over."

Her sadness overwhelmed her once more. She looked up at us

with such pain that I felt guilty for being the heartless cynic that I am. There were any number of questions we still had to answer, but it was beyond doubt that Louise felt the loss of her friend. I've met incredibly talented actors, and few could have put on a display of sorrow that she had.

Few, but admittedly not none.

TWENTY-SIX

It was hard to know what to do next. Lovebrook was busy with his duties. We could hardly interrogate Louise when she was in such a state, and none of the staff present had emerged as genuine suspects. We were waiting for two vital people to arrive, but it would take Lord Sheridan some time to drive from the city, and no one knew exactly when Dennis Apps had left London.

"It'll have to be Quentin," Bella said, not quite out of the blue, as I'm certain she'd followed a similar chain of thought to my own.

"Poor Quentin," I said, aware that I'd described almost every person in that house as "poor" at some point over the last two days. "I feel he will spend his life being a stopgap. We don't know who else to interview, but we've been putting it off for long enough, so it might as well be him."

Bella probably didn't want to agree with me, but it was hard to think otherwise. Quentin Urquhart had the demeanour of one of life's also-rans. Even a pair of detectives in a murder investigation couldn't muster the interest to consider him anything more than a bystander. Of course, that would be the perfect disguise for a killer, but it was hard to imagine it for the moment.

One thing we could say about Quentin was that he was somewhat elusive. We didn't find him in any of the downstairs salons, though we couldn't check the library, which remained locked as it had been since Lord Sheridan had left the day before. I was tempted to ask Ponsonby for a key just to be able to nose around, but I doubted he would agree to it. Since the very beginning, we had felt limited in what we could do there. We were in Lord Sheridan's house. This was Inspector Lovebrook's case, and we had barely reached the level of welcome guests.

Percy was the only one who was truly free to stroll about the place as he liked. To prove this point, we found him having a sniff around the parrot's cage in the morning room. The parrot watched him suspiciously, but Percy acted as though this was all perfectly normal. He accompanied us out of the room as though we hadn't noticed he'd been sneaking about the house without us.

He led us up the stairs to the only door in the gallery through which we were yet to pass. Just as I was coming to believe that my dog had developed a detective's instinct, he continued walking.

"Come in," Quentin called when I knocked.

Percy scampered along to Louise's room and slipped inside.

"Did you just see that?" I asked, pointing after him.

"Marius, we're not here to solve the mystery of what Percy gets up to when we're not watching." Bella pulled me into the room before us, and I tried to concentrate on our task.

The bedroom was almost identical to Tom's but in a shade of cream rather than brown. There was a similarly sized four-poster bed, and the same French furniture was scattered about the room, but unlike the space next door, there was no one inside it. Bella realised something before I did. She cut a path to a pair of doors that opened onto a large stone balcony.

"Oh, it's you," Quentin said by way of a greeting. It wasn't the warmest welcome but, given the circumstances, I thought it fitting.

He was standing before a tall easel, looking out across the wooded landscape in the valley at the rear of the house. The view really was remarkable. The natural amphitheatre of trees which filled than one hundred and eighty degrees of our vision was complemented by the semicircular arboretum closer to the house.

Species from all over the world had been planted there to add contrast and colour. If I'd lived at Cherkley Court, I would have spent every evening up there watching the sunset over the downs.

"You're rather good, Quentin," Bella told him as she examined the simulacrum of the view on the canvas.

"You sound surprised, Lady Bella." He, on the other hand, sounded wary, tired and perhaps a touch defensive.

"I shouldn't be," she replied. "I have every reason to believe you have the skills required to be a great artist. Your sister always spoke so highly of you."

"Now I know you're lying." He didn't let out an exasperated groan at this moment, though I felt he would have liked to.

She watched him prod his brush into the grey mess on his palette before applying it to the painting.

"We thought you'd like to share your thoughts on what has happened to Lady Sheridan."

"Imelda," he replied, not taking his eyes off his work. "She always wanted to be called Imelda. She wasn't one of these aloof, cold aristocrats we both know so well, Bella. She was my friend."

He almost smiled then, but the memory of what he'd seen from the dining room must have come back to him, and he continued his work with the same sullen expression in place.

"You seemed quite happy when we arrived here yesterday, but we know that something unpleasant occurred to you on Friday night." Bella had judged her tone to perfection, and I knew that I wouldn't have much to do for the duration of the interview. They were of the same ilk. They even knew a lot of the same people, and I was an outsider.

"It was not as bad as what happened to the maid," he said with a touch of bitterness. "Or to Imelda last night."

If I'd been interviewing him, I'd have insisted he told me how he knew when Lady Sheridan had died. Had someone informed him that she'd been killed in the night, or did he know because he was there?

Bella adopted a different approach. She took a step closer to him and, still in that gentle, understanding manner, said, "Tom upset you during the game he planned, didn't he? I'm sure you'll feel better if you tell us what happened."

His eyes shifted to look at her for a few short moments, but they soon moved back to his painting. "I doubt that I would."

Bella looked past him to where I stood, but there was nothing I could say to change his mind. Now, had she wished for me to discuss the best ways to murder someone without a house full of people being woken, I could have listed any number of options, but convincing a suspect that we were only there to help him was very much her department. And I'd like to point out that this was nothing to do with her being a woman and me a man. This was a Bella and Marius problem. She was softly spoken and diplomatic, and I spent too much time alone in my flat reading about gruesome killings before planning a few of my own.

"He humiliated you, didn't he?" Bella continued. "That's his word, not mine. Of course, I don't believe he would have told us about it if he didn't feel regret for what he'd done."

This caused Quentin to hit his canvas a little more roughly than before. He evidently hadn't forgiven Tom, and I wondered how much more it would take to make him talk. I was impressed that, as he moved the brush more violently, the painting still benefited from it. The scene was slowly taking shape, and the boy really knew what he was doing. He didn't even look quite so juvenile as I'd previously found him.

"Fine." Bella pulled her hand away and walked to the edge of the balcony to peer down at the terrace below. "I understand that you might not want to discuss exactly what happened. But you can at least tell us why he did it."

Quentin stared at the horizon for a moment and, far from avoiding the topic as I had expected, he went back to the part he'd already declined to discuss. "He did humiliate me; that's just the word for it. He made sure that each of my stops on the treasure trail was more embarrassing than the last. He used me as a source of fun, hoping to win points with Imelda."

He paused then, and I could see the anger flowing through him. "First, I had to put my face in a pail of mud to extract a key with my teeth for no other reason than that he wanted to see me suffer. Later, I had to take all my clothes off and wade into the pond in the tropical house to find the next clue. What I didn't know was that Ponsonby's task at that moment was to wait until I was in my inexpressibles and take a photo. I don't blame him. He was just following orders. Tom was the one pulling the strings."

This explained the tripod we'd seen, but there was something that didn't make sense.

"Why didn't you just say no?" Oh, gosh. I'd finally asked a question.

He looked at me as though I were an immense and unusual fungus that had suddenly sprouted from the room beneath us. "Because he has a very clever way with people. He's exceptional at getting others to do what he thinks we should, and even better at making us feel as though we are boring old stick-in-the-muds if we complain."

"We aren't here to tell you he's a good person. If anything, he's the suspect we've come to trust least over the last day. That's why we need you to explain why he singled you out for mistreatment."

With the hardest part of his confession over, Quentin returned to his painting. "It's as I said, he was always trying to entertain Imelda. I couldn't understand it."

"Do you think it's possible that she and Thomas were having an affair?" Bella asked, and another story began to unfold in my mind.

Quentin really struggled to answer this time. "I believe... I think that Tom would very much like that to have been the case. I'd never met him until a few months ago, but it's become clear in that time that he is not what you might call a scrupulous person. He sees the people around him as... well, perhaps expendable is too harsh a word. But I believe he would seduce any married woman and wreck any home if he thought it would serve him well."

Bella grimaced for a moment, perhaps weighing in her mind

whether to reveal what we knew about Tom Smith's subterfuge. When she didn't respond, Quentin continued.

"Our arrival at lunch yesterday is a perfect example of his showmanship and manipulation. Imelda's husband was at home, and yet he picked her up on his shoulder without even asking whether she wanted him to, and he made me support her on the other side. I felt such shame when I realised that Lord Sheridan was there. He'd been most kind to tolerate our presence, and I didn't want him to get the wrong idea about..."

This was something he couldn't say, but we didn't need him to finish the sentence to understand its meaning.

"I suppose that's beside the point," he continued. "I'm really only describing my own insecurities – whereas Thomas-Richard Harrison doesn't possess any such weaknesses." He needed a break from this sad topic and added some more paint to his brush. "We rubbed along together well enough at first, but then on Thursday, soon after we arrived here, I had a dig at him because he'd described the chair he was on as a 'settee'. To which I replied, 'Careful, old man. A *settee* is a type of ship!'"

Quentin had a bit of a laugh at this, and Bella shyly joined in, but it took me a moment to realise what he meant. "That's not something posh people say then, is it? I suppose you call settees *thrones* or *sitting benches* or some such nonsense."

"We call them sofas, Marius." Bella couldn't turn down another chance to look disappointed in me. "As well you know."

"Fine, but what has that got to do with Friday night?"

We both turned back to Quentin, and any amusement he'd felt had faded away.

"This was clearly a topic which Tom didn't wish to discuss. I feel he probably got teased at school for not coming from the very highest echelon of the very highest echelon."

We knew that there was more to it than that, but Bella must have decided that it wasn't the time or perhaps our job to tell Quentin.

"I should have been more gracious, but it was only supposed to be a joke. I really didn't expect him to get so upset."

"Or seek revenge," I muttered.

"Well, precisely. He made sure to be there at the moment of my great shame in the tropical house. He popped out of the foliage just after Ponsonby took the photo. I'm really very glad that there were no young ladies about at the time. My embarrassment would have turned to mortification."

"And what happened after that?"

"Well, I shouted at him, of course. I shouted and I quite possibly screamed, and I definitely ended up with tears in my eyes." This was all that Quentin could take, and in a gesture of sudden, rising violence, he snapped his brush in two and threw the pieces as far as they would go off the balcony. "I acted like the silly little boy that everyone in my family has always said I am. I took it far too personally, told him that he was the worst person I'd ever met, and promised that I would dedicate the rest of my days to getting even with him."

These words came out in one long burst, and he looked quite out of breath now that they'd been said. His normally perfectly coiffed brown hair had become a fraction messier at some point. He set his loose fringe back in place and pushed his tortoiseshell glasses up his nose.

I kept quiet in the hope that he would continue to reveal potentially damaging information about himself and our other suspects. He soon obliged. "He said that it was all a joke, and I must admit that he looked a little shamefaced, but he didn't apologise as he left me there. I was quite distraught, and I'm sure I would have continued like that if Penny hadn't appeared."

"The maid came to see you before she was killed?" I asked in amazement.

"Only for a minute, but she was very nice to me. I must have been making a terrible racket, as she heard me from out in the garden and felt that she couldn't just let someone suffer. She came inside despite her training never to interfere with matters above stairs. She put her arm around my shoulder and sat next to me on the bench by the pond. She gave me the loveliest hug I think I've ever received, and I couldn't help wondering whether I'd be a more worthwhile human if I'd been brought up by someone like her rather than the bitter, emotionless husks I have for parents."

His anger had mounted again, and he was really shouting. His words carried off across the landscape, and I was torn between feeling terribly sorry for him and wondering whether any of this could have pushed him to kill.

"At what time did this occur?"

He looked at the floor as though he were still ashamed of all that had gone on in the tropical house. "I suppose she left me at around a quarter to midnight."

"What happened after that, Quentin?" Bella asked with some insistence in her voice. "Where did Penny go?"

His mouth protruded so that he looked a little houndlike. "She offered to bring me a hot drink, and I never saw her again."

"She didn't even send someone with a cup of tea?" Perhaps I was concentrating on the wrong thing, but I hoped it could direct us to the last person who'd seen the maid alive.

"No. I sat waiting for her to return, and she never did. I assumed she'd been waylaid with other duties." Quentin looked pensive, and I could tell he was still trying to make sense of Penny's death. "I eventually gave up and went to bed, which is when I discovered that she hadn't come back to see me because she was lying bloodied on the floor of the boudoir."

TWENTY-SEVEN

"We really have made a mare's nest of this whole thing." Back out on the landing, Bella was pessimistic in my stead.

"It's true that we've gone about everything in a less than straightforward manner, but the fact that we know where Penny was minutes before she was killed doesn't greatly alter our perception of the case. We'd already learnt that she went for a walk in the garden, and now we know that she went into the tropical house to see Quentin."

"And judging by the time that Tom Smith says Lady Sheridan finished the game, the squeaking sound that she heard was most likely Ponsonby setting up the tripod. She mentioned that it sounded mechanical rather than organic."

I turned my head to look at her. "That's possible, but it won't help us understand where Penny went afterwards, or why she failed to bring Quentin the drink she'd promised him."

"I think there's someone who might be able to answer that, though." She didn't wait for me to ask who this might be. She must have heard something outside as she hurried down the stairs and all the way to the grand, pillared porch.

Sure enough, as we arrived, two men were getting out of an unremarkable black car. One was a police constable and the other,

I could only assume, was the head gardener of Cherkley Court. This impression was confirmed when a beautiful young Spanish woman came rushing out of the house behind us to embrace him.

"Oh, Dennis! My Dennis! I'm so happy you've come back to us." She covered his cheek with kisses, and the fellow looked terribly shy. "I told everyone that you couldn't be to blame."

"'S very kind of you, Miss Nerea. 'S very nice to know you were thinkin' of me."

He was evidently a humble, reserved sort of person. He barely had the confidence to return her hug, even as she pulled him closer. I suppose it didn't help that his hands were still cuffed.

"Señorita Barriuso, please stand back," Lovebrook came alongside us to declare. "There will be plenty of time for the pair of you to become reacquainted later. For the moment, Mr Apps is under arrest and will need to explain himself."

Looking as though even this level of separation tore at her heart, Nerea pulled away from him. Before the pair could embrace again, the constable seized the gardener and pushed him by the shoulder towards the house.

"Where should we...?" Lovebrook began once we'd followed our detainee inside.

I suppose he must have recalled that one of the owners of Cherkley Court was absent and the other was dead, as he responded to his own unfinished question by leading us to the grand salon at the back of the house. I'd been a touch disappointed that our investigation hadn't taken us to the room where I'd noticed the fluted brass bar the day before. It was as long as a snooker table and stocked with bottles from all over the world. I was tempted to mix everyone a cocktail but decided that it wasn't the right moment.

The room itself was, to say the least, unconventional in its design. The heavily patterned Victorian wallpaper – complete with all the hallmarks you might expect, from paisley patterns to vines, and small finches to foliage – had been partially covered with five brightly coloured paintings of faceless people in dramatic poses. It was stark, unusual and spoke to the dead woman's eclectic tastes.

I'm sure I was the only one who noticed it, though, as Lovebrook directed Apps to sit on one of the settees... sorry, sofas, and the inspector placed a chair in front of the suspect to begin the interview. Well, he was about to start when he realised there was a problem.

"Señorita, I'm afraid you can't be in here. This is a police matter, and you must wait outside."

Nerea looked like a petulant child just then. She glanced at Bella and me as though to say, *But they're in here, and they're not even in love with him!* The constable who'd driven the wanted man to the house had taken him to his destination and now saw the impassioned Spaniard from the room.

Lovebrook waited until the door was closed and the room was quiet before beginning. "Now, Mr Apps, I'm sure you understand that we have a lot of questions for you."

"Yes, sir. And I'm terrible sorry if my actions have caused any trouble." It was at this moment he realised he was still wearing his flat cap and hurried to pull it from his head. "It certainly weren't my intention to make a nasty situation worse."

He was not a well-spoken man, but he had a quiet dignity about him, and I already believed that he was telling the truth. Whether I still would when we came to discuss the crime was another question, but I found him an appealing sort. He had a thick, dark beard and black eyes. He couldn't have been more than thirty, and it was easy to understand why Nerea had come to like him in the first place. He was tall and handsome without being in any way showy – unlike that charmer Tom Smith up in his room. There was a faint scar on his cheek and, from the way he carried himself, I imagined that this was more likely to have been caused by a German sniper's mercifully wide bullet than his work in the gardens.

"If we could begin on the evening of the fifteenth. Am I right in thinking that you retired to your quarters early that night?"

Apps looked up at Bella and me. We were standing on either side of Lovebrook eagerly awaiting his answer. I believe that his confusion over our presence combined with his uncertainty over the date, as he asked, "Sorry, is it Friday night you're meanin'?"

Lovebrook smiled. "That's right. Tell us all you can about Friday night."

Clutching his tweed cap in his manacled hands, he had a think before answering. "Now then... I went to m' room at nine. The others usually stay up late on a Friday, but Nerea were out at her cousin's house, so I decided t' have an early night." He had a broad but pleasant country accent. "I was prob'ly fast asleep by ten o'clock, if I'm honest."

The gardener had answered the first question and nothing more, so Lovebrook prompted him. "I appreciate your clarity. Thank you. Now, would you mind telling me how you went from being asleep at ten o'clock to boarding a train to Edinburgh some hours later?"

"You must think it all looks so suspect," he commented with a shake of the head, as if even he couldn't believe what had happened. "Well, at ten minutes to midnight, a knock came at m' door. It took me a minute or two to rouse m'self, but I made my way over and pulled it open, only to see Penny standin' before me."

"Penny Baker?" Bella asked in surprise, which was a touch silly as we hadn't heard of any other Pennys.

"The very same." His smile turned sad then. "She said, 'Sorry to bother you, Dennis. But I've been asked to bring you this.'"

He put his cap down in his lap to hold his hand out in front of him as though he were offering us something.

"What was it?" I asked when he just sat there.

He laughed a single *Ha* of laughter and then fell quiet for a moment. "The master had sent me a fiver— Sorry, sir, that is to say, it was an envelope with a five-pound note inside. There was a written message and all, tellin' me to leave the house that instant, drive to London and take the first train to Edinburgh."

TWENTY-EIGHT

"Valentine, perhaps you could unshackle poor Dennis here." Bella was once more putting our suspects at ease, and no doubt making a friend in the process.

The inspector immediately did as she'd suggested, and Apps nodded his thanks and rubbed his sore wrists.

"That's awfully good of you, ma'am. And I feel I should tell you that I'm not likely to run away. Where would I go if I did?"

I considered answering, *Edinburgh*, but it was no time for quips.

"I'd like to be sure that I've understood you correctly, Dennis," Lovebrook said in the slow, clear manner he'd adopted. Perhaps we were all gullible and Apps really was the mastermind behind the first robbery and murder. It was impossible to ignore how much we all wanted him to be innocent. "What you're saying is that you received a note giving you instructions on where to go and what to do."

He grinned his friendly grin once more. "That's right. And being the idiot I am, I didn't question whether it were really from the master or not. I thought, because Penny had brought the message, it must be from him. But when the police found me in the hotel, I showed them it, and they said it looked like it was written by a seven-year-old, not some bigwig lord. I believe it was passed to Scotland Yard."

It was my turn to chivvy him along. "What exactly did the message say?"

"It's like I told you; it said that I was to get the train to Edinburgh to collect a package for his lordship. It said I should get into m' van immediately and drive off the estate through the woods without talking to no one. Now that's somethin' that really should have made me think somethin' was wrong, but I s'pose I were so proud that Lord Sheridan had chosen me of all people to carry out the task for him that I didn't stop to think."

"So you got dressed, packed a change of clothes, and headed to the train station."

"That's it." Dennis looked phenomenally happy every time he could agree with something one of us said. "Of course, what I hadn't considered was that there are no trains at that time o' night. I napped in my van by the station and went to buy my ticket as soon as it opened. Before I knew it, I was in Scotland. I'd never been no further north than Oxford b'fore, so you can imagine how excited I was."

Bella was perhaps the most mystified by the story we were hearing. "And then, when you arrived, you simply walked across the station concourse and asked for a room at the nearest hotel."

"Well, not quite, ma'am. I had to cross the road to get to the hotel, but the rest of what you said was right enough. I did exactly what the note what Penny brought instructed. I stayed at the hotel, waiting for a man who would give me an important package for his lordship. Course, I realise now what was really happenin'."

Lovebrook leaned forward, clearly hoping that we'd got to the essential part of the interview. "Oh, yes?"

"Well, yes, Inspector. I was only sent up there to distract from what were goin' on down here. I woulda' thought you could work that out yourself, seeing as you're a policeman and all."

Other officers would have been offended by this, but Lovebrook took it in the spirit in which it had been said. "You're quite right, Dennis. I should have thought."

"I do feel a fool for wastin' so many people's time," the sincere chap insisted. "I didn't even step out o' the hotel to get a newspaper, so I didn't know nothin' about what was happenin' down here. If I'd thought for a second that Penny—" A note of sadness had entered his voice, but I could see that he was not the type to discuss his feelings. "You do believe me, don't you?"

He looked at Bella as he asked this question. She glanced at the two of us before answering, but I think we all knew what she would say. "I don't believe we have any reason not to. Everything you've told us fits with what other witnesses told us, including Lady Sheridan."

He looked sombre again at the mention of this name and sat up straighter in his chair. "The constable what picked me up in London told me about her. Is it true, ma'am? Is the mistress really dead like our Penny?"

There was something charmingly innocent about his manner. I would not say he was in any way simple-minded – in fact there was a brightness behind his eyes that suggested he had a good head on his shoulders – but he seemed somehow pure and trustworthy in a way that was rare in men my age.

"I'm afraid so, Dennis. So if there is anything you might know that could help us find the person responsible, we would be very grateful."

He fiddled with his cap again and struggled to answer. "I wish there was, ma'am. I really do. But I've told you all I saw."

"You didn't notice anyone on the terrace as you went to your van, for example?" I tried.

"No, there was no one there. I saw his lordship in his library as I passed the window. He were hard at work, though."

"You didn't see Penny?" Bella asked hopefully.

"Yes, I saw Penny," he replied as if she'd said something foolish. "I overtook her on the path by the house. I'd been quick to pack, and she wasn't so fast a walker as me, but there was no one on the terrace just after I passed her."

"Lady Sheridan told us she saw you there." The details of the interview we'd conducted with her ran through my head. "She said that you'd spoken."

"Yes, but she weren't on the terrace. She were sittin' on the windowsill of her bedroom, smokin' a cigarette."

TWENTY-NINE

It felt odd to release the man back to his ordinary life after he'd been transported across the country in shackles, but no one truly believed he was to blame for any of the contemptible crimes that had been committed. He thanked us all earnestly and, when I opened the door for him to leave, Nerea was there waiting. She threw her arms around him and, this time, he returned the gesture with all his heart and no small amount of relief.

I saw Bella smiling at the two of them and, as they walked away, hand in hand, Nerea looked back over her shoulder and mouthed, "Thank you, Marius. Thank you so much."

I found myself flooded with unexpected delight on seeing the two of them together. It was mixed with the sorrow of the morning, but Apps seemed like a good man, and perhaps I'd always been too hard on my former paramour. I could only imagine what they'd both suffered through their separation and Dennis's arrest. They deserved some happiness.

Of course, once the door was closed behind us, we still had a murderer to catch.

"Can we just take a moment to make sense of Lady Sheridan's movements on the night that her maid was killed?" Lovebrook asked, walking back and forth anxiously before the bar. I had a far better solution for anxiety and went to stand behind it.

"Without a doubt, old friend. But first, what can I make you?"

A few minutes later, we were all sipping Corpse Reviver Number Ones, which I'd drunk a few times at the Savoy. With the stimulating concoction running through me, the case didn't seem nearly so complicated as it otherwise might have.

"There's really no surprise in what he said," I told the others. "We know that Imelda lied about her timing on Friday night. We should have realised that she couldn't have seen Dennis, as she'd already gone upstairs. She completed the task that Tom had set her at just after half past eleven. She claimed to have gone straight to bed, but she wasn't in her bedroom when her son escaped from the nursemaid before midnight."

"What if that was because Imelda was busy killing Penny?" Bella's words were so stark that they knocked my concentration for a moment. "Maybe someone killed her in revenge."

"But why would she have murdered Penny? What would she gain from robbing herself?" She had no answers, and so I continued. "It is possible that she was romantically entangled with one of the gentlemen she entertained. However, I get the feeling that she mainly liked having them here to pique her husband. Why else would she have continued to invite Tom when she knew he wasn't a real artist? He was good value for money. A rogue, but an entertaining one."

"I've got a question for you," Lovebrook declared as he dabbed his lips dry on a napkin I hadn't thought to give him. "Are we actually any closer to finding the killer?"

I shrugged, Bella looked disheartened, and Lovebrook came to a resolution.

"Right, that's what I thought." He slammed his empty glass down and marched towards the door. "We've conducted this investigation far too politely since the very beginning. It's time to break some eggshells."

So that was my career as a barman over – though I wondered

whether I could squeeze a bar of my own into my London flat somehow. Either way, I'd rarely seen Lovebrook so animated before. He positively rocketed from the room to round up his constables, and they convened in the hall to receive their orders.

"You are to go through every room upstairs to look for anything out of place. In particular, we are searching for an antique silver box. But you should report any valuables that you find hidden."

"But, sir," the youngest and squeakiest-voiced of the constables put his hand up to say, "we looked through the bedrooms on Saturday morning when we first came here."

"No, we peeked around them respectfully, without wishing to disturb anyone. I want you to empty every drawer, pull out every book from every shelf and generally make certain that nothing has been overlooked. I'll call for more men from London to go through the rest of the house if necessary, and then we'll go out to the gardens and do the same thing. But start with the main bedrooms. Leave no crevice unsearched!"

I could see that the officers were surprised, excited and perhaps a little daunted by the work ahead of them.

"Inspector Lovebrook," Ponsonby came to say in a quiet voice, "you asked me to tell you when Lord Sheridan arrived. Well, he got here a few minutes ago and is currently in his library."

"Excellent." Lovebrook was a man transformed. He spun on the spot, and I half expected him to roll up his sleeves and clench his fists. Sadly, the butler had more to say.

"But he's in there with his son, and he has asked to be left alone."

"Ah, I see." Lovebrook was a man transformed back to how he had previously been. "Thank you for telling me." He hesitated for a moment, then stomped up the stairs.

"Come along, Marius," Bella urged me. "We don't want to miss anything."

So we hurried after him towards the ruckus that the constables were making. There were six of them in all. They had split into pairs and wisely started with the bedrooms of Lady Sheridan's three guests. In the first room we came to, Quentin looked on placidly as his room was torn to pieces. After a few moments, he returned to his painting on the balcony, and we moved on to the next room. There was no sign of Tom, but Louise was out in the hall complaining about the treatment she had received.

"I'm very sorry, miss." Lovebrook adopted a tougher tone than he would normally have used. "This won't take long, but we must get to the bottom of what has been happening here."

She still looked distressed from her time in the tropical house. She opened her mouth to complain, then accepted defeat and clung to the doorframe as the constables within rifled through drawers and emptied cases.

I decided to look for the swindler, and when I couldn't find him hiding anywhere in his bedroom, I tried the adjoining bathroom.

"What in the name of heaven are you doing?" I asked when I found him in there, kneeling on the floor.

He rolled his eyes as though the answer were obvious. "He wandered into my room and gave me the definite impression that he fancied a wash."

My dog was standing in the bathtub, covered in soap, which Tom was about to rinse off with a bowl of water.

"Really, I thought better of you!" I believe I may have tutted.

"I'm sorry, Mr Quin, but I believed that—"

"I was talking to the dog!"

Percy shook his jowls at me, and I was about to find a towel to dry off the silly beast – well, both of them – when one of the constables in the room behind me shouted something.

"Sir!" the young officer who had spoken downstairs called. "Sir, I think I've found what we need."

I got there just as Bella and Lovebrook did.

"What is it, Watson?" This wasn't an allusion to Sherlock Holmes. I believe the constable's name really was Watson.

"I found it wrapped up just under the bed, sir." He held out the parcel he'd found, and his superior officer pulled away the red silk handkerchief to reveal an ornate silver box. It was remarkable for its filigree and complicated engravings. It reminded me of some of the exquisitely designed monstrances I'd seen in Catholic churches on the Continent.

It was just then that the self-proclaimed con artist came out to us. His hands dangled before him, still covered in soap, and he had a few bubbles in his hair.

"What's that?" he asked with the innocence of a cherub.

"You tell us, *Mr Smith*," Lovebrook demanded, putting plenty of emphasis on the fraud's real name. "I believe it matches the description of the box that was stolen on Friday night. Would you care to tell us how it found its way into your room?"

"I've never seen it before in my life." Tom looked scared again. We'd seen that same expression on his face when we'd confronted him that morning, but this time the situation was even blacker. "If I were the thief, why would I have left it here in my room for anyone to stumble across it? I like my neck too much the way it is to risk paying a visit to the hangman."

"Sir, I don't mean to interrupt," Watson began, "and I can't tell you for certain that he isn't the so-and-so we're after, but I do know that there was nothing under the bed when we came in here on Saturday."

Lovebrook couldn't have looked more discouraged just then. He turned to stare at the door he'd just come through and finally decided to tramp back through it. I pulled Bella after me as the inspector entered the neighbouring room. We had to step around piles of bedclothes to reach the balcony.

"Urquhart," Lovebrook began once more, "did you plant this in your friend Thomas's bedroom?"

He hesitated for half a second too long.

"Don't lie, Quentin," Bella told him, in the same voice that she used whenever she argued with her brothers. "We'll know if you lie."

"Fine, yes, I did. But only because I found it in my room when

I went in there an hour ago. I assumed Tom was trying to get me in trouble."

"And you didn't think of telling the police about the vital piece of evidence you'd discovered?" Lovebrook was fairly close to the end of his tether.

Quentin pointed his brush at the inspector in acknowledgement. "Now that you say it, that would have been a better idea."

Lovebrook closed his eyes and sighed. "Do not leave this spot. If you do, one of my men will arrest you. Do you hear me?"

The meek artist promptly nodded, and we hurried off to our final stop.

"Clear out of here, men. I think we've found what we need."

The two constables in Louise's room exchanged confused glances but complied with the command. For her part, Louise Thorneycroft was sitting on the windowsill with her legs dangling outside and her back to us. She turned to see what was happening and no longer appeared quite so afflicted as she had.

"Miss Thorneycroft," Lovebrook called, desperately trying to summon the energy to ask the question for a third time, "did you put this box in Mr Urquhart's room?"

She closed her eyes. I thought perhaps she was wishing that she could wake up somewhere far away, in a world without murders or burglaries or obnoxious imposters. If that were the case, it didn't work. When she opened them again, we were still there.

"I suppose there's not much point in lying." She swung her bare legs back inside before pulling her black cotton skirt down over them. "I put the box there because, when I woke up this morning, it was sitting on my bookshelf. To be perfectly honest, I'd meant to leave it in Tom's room. He's much more of a snake than little Quentin, but Quentin's door was open, and I saw that he was downstairs, so I put it in the closest place I could that wouldn't point to me."

"You've interfered with an official investigation!" Lovebrook barked at her, still not calming down as the maelstrom of the case spiralled around us. "I could arrest the three of you for this."

"Oh, please. Go ahead!" Louise spat the words back at him. She wasn't so much angry as racked with sadness after everything that had happened. "I will happily do whatever I can to escape this place."

Bella ignored the argument to consider the facts. "Assuming that whoever put the box in here hadn't already found it in his own room, and you weren't passing the thing around like the proverbial hot cross bun..." She meant hot potato, but I didn't correct her. "...why you?"

"What do you mean?"

Bella didn't answer. She looked first at the window where Louise had been sitting, and then at the bedside table before turning to Lovebrook and me. "I'm sorry, gentlemen, you'll have to leave the room for a moment."

THIRTY

We obliged, of course, though neither of us could imagine why it was necessary. Fortunately, two minutes after we'd left, the door opened once more, and we were readmitted.

"Louise has something to tell us, but I will conduct the interview," Bella announced before waving us through.

There was a small round table with two chairs in the corner of the room and, sitting on the bed herself, Louise motioned us over to them. Bella remained on her feet to ask questions. I can't deny that I found her assertive manner appealing. It also meant I could sit back and enjoy the interview, knowing that I wouldn't be called upon to do too much.

"Tell them what happened after you left the game on Friday night," she commanded, and Louise began her tale.

"I'm sorry that I didn't say anything before." She swept the hair from her eyes, and I wondered whether she used her long fringe as a veil at times – to hide in plain sight. "The truth is that, after I abandoned Tom's childish pursuit on Friday, I opened a bottle of wine. Imelda joined me half an hour later. We sat right where you are and..." She hesitated and looked at Bella as though she needed permission. "We talked about all sorts of things, as we often did when the boys weren't around to bring down the level of conversation."

"But why—" Lovebrook began. Bella wouldn't let him speak.

"There were crumbs on the bedside table when we spoke to Louise here yesterday," Bella told us a little abstrusely. "It was only natural, as the maids hadn't been able to clean after the first murder, but I noticed that they were dark brown, almost black. It was only just now that I realised they were from a chocolate cake. We knew that neither Louise nor Quentin finished the game, and that Thomas-Richard ate her prize. So unless Ponsonby had been up here enjoying his cake, that only left Lady Sheridan."

"Yes, but—"

"And then I remembered that Dennis Apps had been able to talk to Imelda as he passed the house. He said he'd seen her sitting in her bedroom window, but he wasn't to know that her bedroom was to the front of the building. It was only when I saw Louise sitting there that it all came together."

"That was around midnight. Before that—" Lovebrook tried again, and Bella interrupted (again).

"Before that, they spent a half hour talking and drinking. They didn't notice anything from the boudoir next door because they were having such a pleasant time." I knew there was more to it than Bella was admitting. That was obvious from the moment she let us back into the room.

Louise continued the story in a solemn tone. "It was only when we finished our drinks and Imelda slipped out to the gallery that she noticed the door to the boudoir was ajar. She looked inside, and that was when she let out a shriek that brought the nursemaid running down from upstairs. I'd already rung the bell for the footmen by then."

"And you didn't hear anything else all that time?" Bella asked quickly so that the inspector wouldn't try.

Louise shook her head. "We didn't. I believe that some other people in the house heard a thud, but we were obviously chattering so loudly together that we didn't notice anything."

"What about Penny arriving or the killer making his escape?"

Louise released an audible stream of air before answering. "I think that Imelda mentioned hearing footsteps at one point, but we thought nothing of it. We were in a world of our own. Whenever we were together, we forgot about everything else and just enjoyed one another's company. That's why I was so destroyed when I went downstairs to breakfast this morning and discovered that she was..." She couldn't utter the obvious word, so she abandoned the sentence. "Imelda was an incredible person. It wasn't just for professional reasons that I appreciated the interest she showed in me. I've never had another friend like her."

"And last night before she died?" Bella spoke so compassionately when she knew it was necessary. "Do you remember anything unusual occurring?"

"Nothing. We all dined together. We raised a glass to Penny, and I believe that every one of us was relieved that Apps had been identified as the killer – and that he was far away from Cherkley Court." I saw her chest rise as she breathed in slowly. "I wish there were something I could tell you. I keep going over the same thoughts, trying to remember something that might have seemed innocuous at the time that actually meant a lot more. I don't particularly like Tom, but then there are plenty of people I don't like, and that doesn't make them killers."

Lovebrook wanted to ask a question every time she spoke, but he remembered not to this time.

"So there's nothing else you can tell us?" Bella asked on his behalf.

Louise leaned back on her elbows and looked disheartened. "Only that it feels as if two good, kind women have been spirited away from us." Her voice cracked, and she had to sit forward again to raise a hand to her face.

Bella went to kneel down beside her. "It will be all right. No one else will die here. You will leave and find a way to get back on with your life. You'll become a great artist whose work will be adored across the world. You'll always look back on your time here with sadness, but life will eventually get brighter again."

This was too much for Louise. Her tears poured forth. They'd been queuing up for some time and couldn't wait to run free. Bella silently put her arms around the sobbing woman.

"We appreciate your time, Miss Thorneycroft," Lovebrook told her before coming to worry that he'd spoken out of turn. "If you don't mind my saying that."

He looked as though he would very much like to leave the room, and so I escorted him out to the gallery.

"Do you understand anything that just happened?" he asked, looking profoundly mystified.

I remembered the noises that the nursemaid had overheard, Lionel laughing when he hid in his parents' bedroom, and what he'd been doing out in the garden, so I answered, "Yes. Yes, I think I do."

THIRTY-ONE

"We'll have to confirm Lord Sheridan's alibi," I told Lovebrook, but he was often more organised than I might have expected and had already taken that step.

"I sent a constable from Scotland Yard as soon as I heard about the death. The husband is so often to blame in such cases that I thought it necessary."

"That's just the word for it. And what did you discover?"

"We know that he was working with his secretary until the early hours of the morning and went to bed in his townhouse soon after. He was in his room when his housekeeper brought him the bad news first thing. It's just about feasible that he could have driven here and back in that time, but my man checked on Sheridan's car, and it was locked up in a local garage. Besides that, there was a nightman on the front door here who didn't see anything, and it would have been a great risk for his lordship to appear on the estate when he was supposed to be in London. All it would have taken was one sighting and his plan to kill his wife would have fallen apart."

As we waited for Bella to emerge, we heard the sound of a crowd talking downstairs and went to investigate. The servants had formed two long lines between the central staircase and the library. Some were dressed in black. Others wore a band of cloth around their arms out of respect for their slain mistress and colleague. Ponsonby was directing them to stay in line when a couple of the younger members of staff leaned forward to talk to one another.

We had arrived at an opportune moment. As we came into view of the library door, it opened and out stepped the unimposing figure of Lord Sheridan. His hair somehow looked whiter than it had the day before, and his skin was sickly pale. He was not alone. He walked with his hand on his son's shoulder, and I noticed for the first time just how alike they were. I believe that they had both been crying; they had the same bloodshot eyes and troubled features.

Although Lord Sheridan nodded to his staff in gratitude for their sombre observance, little Lionel couldn't raise his eyes from the royal blue carpet runner. We stood back from the others, not wishing to interrupt the occasion, but when father and son got to the staircase, they continued up it, and I knew we would need to speak to the sole remaining owner of Cherkley Court.

Lovebrook waited until we got to the top of the stairs to speak to him. "I'm very sorry, Lord Sheridan, but we will need your help for a short time."

He didn't reply directly but bent down to talk to his son. "You'll remember what I said, Lionel?"

The boy still didn't look up but nodded to his father.

"I am here whenever you need me." He was clearly full of good intentions, but I imagine that he realised just how businesslike this sounded, as he squeezed the boy's shoulder and tried to communicate his emotion more directly. "I mean it, Lionel. We are united in our grief, and I will do whatever I can to make this tragedy less terrible for you."

Even the steely industrialist had to stifle a note of deeper, rawer emotion then. He straightened up once more and gestured for his son to leave us. Lionel glanced briefly at his father to be certain that he was allowed to go, then hurried over to the stairs that led up to the nursery. I suppose it was partly down to the feelings I retain from my own father's disappearance – admittedly I was eighteen at the time and almost a grown man – but I felt a pang of sorrow as I watched Lionel vanish through the door. He was surely the person who would suffer most from the events of that week; nothing would make up for the loss of his mother.

"What can I do?" Sheridan asked in a far weaker voice than the one he'd just used, and I could tell that he had managed to hold his nerve just long enough to see his son through that torturous revelation.

Had I been leading the investigation, I would have put him in a room with two chairs and a bottle of whisky and not left until he'd told us every scrap of information that could help us catch his wife's killer. Lovebrook had a more conventional idea.

"I'd like you to come to your bedroom and tell us whether anything is missing."

Lord Sheridan breathed out noisily, as if it hurt to do so. "Very well."

Lovebrook pointed the way, and we followed our host towards the furthest bedroom around the gallery. The normally bright space had dimmed out of respect for that terrible day. The clouds visible through the domed glass above the stairs had turned as black as mourning attire.

When Lord Sheridan saw the state of his bedroom, a deep, tormented groan escaped from him. "Did you really have to make such a mess of the place?"

"We believe that was the work of the killer, sir. It seems he didn't get what he wanted on the first night and tried again. It would be a great help if you could look through your possessions."

Sheridan wandered into the room and looked around as though he had never seen the place before. He clearly didn't know where to start, and so I made a suggestion. "Perhaps you could look for any valuables that are normally here."

He stared straight at me, his gaze so haunted that, for a

moment, he resembled several of the corpses I'd seen. "All my stocks and significant papers and the like are down in my library, which I keep locked at all times."

For a moment, I wondered whether this would be significant. I would have to suggest to Lovebrook that it was the key that the killer was after. He could have stolen the box as a distraction, knowing that Apps would take the blame for the first killing.

"Then what about your wife's things?"

He still looked dazed as he glanced around the upturned room. "Very well."

He walked over to Lady Sheridan's dressing table. There was a tilting mirror that had been knocked back so that it was parallel to the floor. The contents of the jewellery box had spilt out, and there were a few books strewn about the place too.

"She had a diamond ring. We bought it together when we were first married, and it cost a small fortune. She often wore it on special occasions, so someone could have seen her with it and—" He'd been rifling through the jewellery with his eyes alone and came to a sudden stop. "No, my apologies. It's there. It wasn't taken. What kind of—"

He had to swallow down his pain then; he couldn't express the anger he felt.

"You're doing very well, Lord Sheridan," Lovebrook assured him, but the man was having none of it.

"Don't talk rot! She was my wife, for goodness' sake. She was my wife, and I don't even know what she kept in the bedroom we shared together!" The rage and infuriation poured out of him. "I should have known everything about her, but all I've ever cared about is making money. I locked myself away from the world in my library or in the city. I don't even remember the last time we fell asleep at the same time in the same bed. Imelda and our son should have been the most important things in my life, but I barely knew they existed."

There were more questions I could have asked him. I wanted to know whether Lady Sheridan had ever fallen out with an important friend. I needed to ask him who would inherit her family fortune and whether there was anyone with a vendetta against either of them, but it was impossible now. He was a broken man, and it was apparent that he wouldn't be able to tell us anything more for some time.

THIRTY-TWO

The constables who had been assigned to go through the bedrooms were now guarding our three main suspects. Just three – not ten or a thousand. If the staff weren't to blame, we had to choose between three possible suspects, and this was apparently beyond us.

We needed to put some space between ourselves and that mess of a case, so I suggested that we go for a walk in the grounds – not least because we hadn't actually inspected the most impressive part of them. I'd heard talk of a mock-Grecian temple and a rose garden – and who doesn't love a rose garden?

We walked down the steep stone steps between the terraced lawns to the well-pruned display and, by the time we got there, we all had ideas to share. "They were lovers, weren't they!" Lovebrook declared to break the pensive silence. "It's just come to me. Lady Sheridan and Louise Thorneycroft weren't just having cake, wine and conversation. They were in the throes of..." He was so shocked by this that he couldn't utter the scandalous word *passion*.

I doubt I'd have done much better, and it turned out that Bella was more worldly in these taboo matters than either of us. "Don't be so surprised. It takes all sorts to make a world. My father has some close friends who, though they have never told us explicitly, have spent their adult lives living together. Auntie Sheila and

Auntie Usha are dear old things, and I've never known two people who are so well suited to one another."

"That's all well and good," I said, as occasionally I like to be the one to keep the conversation on track. "But does it change anything? I mean, it explains why they both lied to us – they obviously didn't want anyone to find out. But might not this whole thing have been caused by a lovers' tiff? Perhaps Penny overheard them, and they dealt with her accordingly. They took the box to suggest it was a burglary, but the knowledge of their crime drove them apart, and then Louise ended up killing Imelda so that she wouldn't go to the police."

Lovebrook was more decisive now. "No, that's simply not possible. Don't forget the part that Apps was made to play in all of this. It was not some spontaneous decision to rob and kill. It was all planned in advance. Planned, no doubt, to coincide with Tom Smith's game."

So that ruled out my fabulous theory.

Lovebrook and I sat down on a bench beside the circular stone temple and stretched our legs out as we considered other potential solutions. The Grecian structure was as picturesque as I had imagined the Sheridans' very own personal temple would be. It looked more like something you would find in the illustrations of a fairy tale than the ruins of a once-powerful city in the hills of Athens or where have you, but they'd certainly found an attractive spot for it. Behind us, the sloping bank of the lawn was covered with the first, brave wildflowers of the nascent season.

Luckily, Bella had another idea to keep us going. "I think we've been too trusting throughout. I can't deny that I find Quentin terribly sweet, but he was clearly angry with Tom for the way he'd been humiliated. Perhaps he had time to write out a note and give it to Penny to take to whichever of the gardeners she chose. Knowing his family, he would have no trouble producing the necessary sum of money in a hurry. He may have killed Penny so that she wouldn't tell anyone, and then taken the box to hide it in Tom's bedroom."

"Remind me, Bella. What did you say about making up stories?"

"I couldn't possibly tell you," she lied.

"Well, unless you have some evidence to support this tale of revenge, I'm afraid I can't accept it. Why would Quentin have chosen Dennis? How would he even have known his name?"

"Besides, you didn't explain why he killed Lady Sheridan," Lovebrook added.

Bella raised a hand and looked as though she would do just that. Then she immediately put it down again, and we were back to where we started.

"Fine. What about Tom?" I asked, seeing as we'd already considered the others.

Lovebrook looked at Bella, who subsequently looked at me, and none of us knew what to say.

"I suppose I'll have to do it myself then." I cleared my throat and began. "On paper, he is the obvious suspect. He was here under false pretences. He can't prove that Lady Sheridan knew about his true identity. He admits to being a swindler, and I'm sure that if you look hard enough, you'll find some record of him in a police station's files."

Lovebrook hit his forehead and made a grumpy sort of humming sound. "The file! I've been so busy that I didn't have time to tell you. If he's the same twenty-six-year-old Tom Smith whose file my man in the Scotland Yard records room located, then yes, he has quite some history. According to the telephone call I just received, Smith has never spent any time in gaol, but he was certainly nearby when some valuable items went missing. There have also been several complaints about him worming his way into some overly trusting individuals' lives to benefit from their kindness."

"There we go then, a criminal through and through."

"But does he have any convictions for violence?" Bella's tone suggested that she already knew this would not be the case.

"No," Lovebrook confirmed. "Not even a drunken brawl in a pub."

"He's too clever for that," Bella told us with the very same degree of confidence. "But is he clever enough to get away with murder?"

As I couldn't answer this question, I continued to list the evidence against him. "He organised the game – and apparently hadn't told anyone but the staff about it in advance – so he was best placed to use it as a distraction."

It was Lovebrook's turn to mention a flaw in our thinking. "That's true but, according to the interviews I conducted, the game finished before midnight. It might have provided a diversion when he sent Penny to take his message to Dennis in the annexe, but it wouldn't have done much to distract from the crime itself."

Bella sat down on the bench next to us and, one by one, we let out a dispirited sigh. It was hard to imagine where we might go from here.

"There's still Ponsonby," Bella tried a little half-heartedly. "He was at least present for both crimes."

"Not a chance," Lovebrook disagreed. "For a start, as soon as the game was over, the butler went down to the kitchen to eat his chocolate cake. He was there when the bell rang and the two footmen dashed upstairs. Did you not ask him?"

"We really should have," Bella said in a tone which meant, *Marius really should have.*

"In all honesty," I said in apparent defence, "we carefully examined the possibility that he might be our culprit before deciding he was too stiff and rusty to go running about the place killing people."

"Lord Sheridan could have killed his maid," Lovebrook spoke up in a sudden harsh tone, as though he were readying himself to throw the cuffs on our host. "But there does not appear to be any reason to do so, and he was away when his wife was killed."

"It seems that no one had a real reason to kill Penny, though," I contested. "Unless the motive really was theft, and except for the box, we still haven't determined what anyone would want to steal. Lord Sheridan made it clear that the real valuables are kept in his library, and I would assume that they are stored in some kind of locked box or safe."

Bella had another suggestion. "Isn't it possible that Thomas Smith used his game to poke about the house before stealing whatever he'd come to steal?"

"It's more than possible," the inspector replied. "But how can we prove it? He might have sent Penny to give Apps the message to clear out, and he might have then gone to steal the box, but how would Penny have ended up there to catch him in the act?"

There was an unexpected flash of light in the deep, dark caverns of my brain. "Maybe there was something inside the box. Maybe we've been so fixated on the container that we didn't consider the contents."

I looked hopefully at the others, but they were unconvinced.

Bella even looked away from me to enjoy the pretty garden. "Why wouldn't Imelda have told us what was in it when she was still alive?"

Lovebrook wouldn't give up. "Then what about another member of staff?"

"Nerea wasn't present for the first murder," I answered, "but she could have done it in league with her boyfriend, invented the story about the note and killed Lady Imelda to throw us off the scent."

Bella still wasn't happy with me. "Haven't you given up on casting that poor couple as criminals?" Her frown made me feel guilty. "What would they have gained from it, seeing as the box has since been recovered? And for that matter, why wouldn't Apps have taken the box and gone to ground? And why do you persist with the idea that Nerea is an evil witch just because she left you?"

"You know it's more complicated than that," I began, but before I could say anything else, Lovebrook had diplomatically interrupted.

"The footmen were both in the kitchen with Ponsonby at

around the time Penny was killed. I suppose it's theoretically possible that one of them dashed upstairs and back, but they would have had to be in cahoots, and the butler too. I don't see it happening, and the rest of the servants say they were asleep or in their quarters at the time."

"The gardeners were in a shed, playing cards," I helpfully pointed out, realising as I said it that this did not help one bit.

We'd hit another dead end. In fact, they'd become a feature of the case. A dejected groan escaped me, but it sounded so pessimistic that I had to do something about it. I got up from the bench and walked over to the stone temple as though I were about to make a speech. Which is more or less what I did.

"We'll go over the events from the beginning for the hundredth time," I told them, though neither looked too excited by the suggestion. "Everyone was together at eleven o'clock when the game began. Louise tired of it after she found the first clue and went upstairs to her bedroom. That would suggest that she had more time than anyone else to plan the crime. She could have written the note for Dennis and even thrown it down to Penny from her window. We know it was sloppily written, so perhaps Louise wrote it with her weak hand to disguise her handwriting but signed Lord Sheridan's name to get Dennis to follow the orders there within."

Lovebrook already had a correction to make. "I believe that the planning was done well before then. Don't forget the metal gardening stake with Dennis's fingerprints on it. That was presumably taken knowing that he had touched it. Which suggests that the killer arranged everything in advance. The envelope with Dennis's name on it that we found in his room confirms that he wasn't chosen willy-nilly either."

"All true," I conceded. "So maybe that isn't a point against Louise after all. In the meantime, Ponsonby had to climb into the pond. Lady Sheridan dashed about the place at record speed to complete her tasks and earn some time alone with her secret love—"

"The existence of whom might provide Lord Sheridan with a

reason to want his wife dead," Bella interrupted, and I pointed at her to accept this before continuing with what I was saying.

"Quentin was doing all he could to obtain his chocolatey prize, to the extent that he stripped down to his knickerbockers and, like Ponsonby, had to take a dip in yet another pond to retrieve one of his clues. At which point the butler himself took a photograph of the young aesthete in a compromising position."

"Will this help us identify the killer?" Lovebrook asked, and I wished people would have more faith in me.

"Perhaps not, but hear me out. That was the point at which things became more interesting. Quentin put on his clothes, and the emotion of the situation got too much for him. Penny, who was known to go for a late-night walk in the grounds before bed, heard his cries from the tropical house and went to comfort him. By this time Lady Sheridan had won her piece of cake and gone upstairs to enjoy it with Louise."

The movement and flow of the narrative had worked its way into my body, and I swayed a little as I told it. "Penny left Quentin, promising to return with something to drink, but she was not seen in the kitchen, and we know that she brought a note to Dennis Apps in the annexe. The question is, who gave it to her?"

"It couldn't have been Louise and Imelda." Bella spoke as though the words were coming to her one at a time, and she wasn't sure that what she was saying was actually true. "Unless they were the killers and lied about what happened."

"By which you mean, it could have been them," I replied, remembering a hypothesis we'd already considered. "Which might make sense if they were so desperate to hide their love from the others. But then they were running about like naughty children, even when Lady Sheridan's husband was in the house, so that seems an odd way to go about maintaining a secret."

"We're reliant on the word of Quentin that Penny was ever in the tropical house and that she left to get him a drink." Lovebrook put his hands through his light brown hair as he told us this. "It's equally possible that *he* gave her the note. He's offered us no alibi for the time of the attack."

I didn't think it needed pointing out that this still didn't provide him with a motive for the crimes, especially as Quentin's main objective appeared to be the procurement of Lady Sheridan's patronage. *Unless...* Thoughts of his desire for revenge when he discovered that Imelda would award the money to Louise registered in my brain. Imelda had told us that she had chosen her favourite, but I stored this theory away for later and answered Lovebrook's point.

"As it tends to in these situations, our understanding of events comes from witnesses with every reason to lie to us. With that caveat, we can be fairly confident that Penny went to the annexe and returned to the house. She was overtaken by Apps as she approached the upper terrace. He took one of the gardeners' vans and drove off the estate through an unwatched gate which was normally kept locked. If Lady Sheridan's information was accurate, he walked around the house and would have been driving off at the time Penny was murdered – once again reducing the likelihood of Apps being a killer."

"Is it wrong of me to admit that I find that reassuring?" Bella became a little bashful as she asked this, and both Lovebrook and I replied with fond looks.

"Not at all. I feel the same way." I didn't mind being interrupted when she did it in such a sweet fashion. "Apps left. Penny returned to the house and then, for some reason, went upstairs to her mistress's boudoir."

"Imelda could have called down to her!" Lovebrook's whole demeanour switched in an instant. "Don't forget that she saw Apps outside because she was sitting in Louise's bedroom, looking out of the window after they'd finished their... conversation." It was apparently his turn to be coy.

"Yes, you're right." I hadn't considered this before, and it threw me a little. "My gosh, that could make sense. Except that Imelda never mentioned it to anyone. And once again, if she weren't the killer, it's unlikely she would have lied."

"Continue, Marius," Bella prompted me when I'd fallen quiet for too long.

"Very well. Penny went upstairs for whatever reason. She went into the boudoir and was knocked unconscious, then beaten on the floor." Another small burst of light illuminated my thoughts, and I realised something we'd overlooked. "Which now makes sense, as it was presumably the killer who had sent her to see Dennis. He'd worked hard to incriminate the gardener and couldn't have her telling the police that he'd sent her on an errand."

"So he followed her upstairs with the metal stake that he'd previously obtained." Bella was joining in with my storytelling. "As soon as she stepped into the boudoir, he brought the bar down on her skull, and she fell to the floor."

We both fell silent, and Lovebrook asked the inevitable, terrible question. "And then what happened?"

"The killer hid himself away. Imelda found the injured maid, and we still don't know anything more." I clapped my hands together in chagrin, struggling to believe we could get so far and still have nothing.

"Should we consider the second killing?" Bella's voice had fallen lower.

"It's harder, as everyone was supposed to be asleep at the time. There are no alibis to examine or timings to consider. What can we actually say?"

Lovebrook folded his arms, Bella's shoulders sank, and I sat back down beside them.

"The way I see it," the inspector began, but then the wind went out of him. "The way I see it, the item that the killer wished to steal must be the key to everything else. As we don't know what it is, it is very difficult to determine the motive."

"I think the opposite is true," Bella helpfully responded. "I think the fact that he left behind Lady Sheridan's jewellery collection shows that he didn't really know what he wanted. He'd hoped to find one incredible item but didn't have the knowledge to steal the ring that Lord Sheridan mentioned. He must have become overwhelmed and not known what to take."

I didn't have the energy to talk anymore, so I let them take the reins.

"I'm sorry, Lady Bella, but I remain unconvinced." The inspector is nothing if not polite. "There would be no point in killing two people if he didn't have a very clear objective in mind."

"What a terrible hobby we picked for ourselves, Bella," I leaned forward to tell her. "Why couldn't we have taken up tennis rather than a largely unpaid job which exposes us to the very worst of humanity and generally leaves us frustrated for days at a time?"

"Don't be like that, Marius. I know you love the challenge of it all."

"There are perfectly good challenges on page two of the *Daily News*. I could answer a riddle or solve a crossword if I was so inclined." I admit that I sounded glum.

"Then solve this puzzle. It's more of a conundrum, in fact." Lovebrook paused for effect. We both paid him our full attention. "Why would the killer go to all the trouble of incriminating Dennis Apps and then kill again to undo that work? Especially if he didn't end up taking anything. It's pure madness."

I expected Bella to answer and, when she didn't, I thought more carefully about what the inspector had asked. Slowly, as my brain worked its way through the labyrinthine trail of evidence which we'd tried and largely failed to follow, something dawned on me.

"My goodness, Valentine. You've done it!"

"I have?"

"Most spectacularly. You've got to the heart of the matter in one question." I was up on my feet and already dashing away through the garden. "Hurry up, you two, I'll explain everything on the way."

"Where are you going, Marius?" Bella demanded, with a bewildered expression that suggested she didn't expect me to provide a satisfactory answer.

"To tell Lord Sheridan who killed his wife."

THIRTY-THREE

We raced up the bank to cut across the highest lawn before taking the grand stone staircase that led to the top terrace in front of the house. On hearing the evidence, Lovebrook broke off to do what was required of him, and Bella and I continued on to the library. I felt a touch nervous heading there. I know we'd already been to see Lord Sheridan once, but we'd heard so much about his sanctuary in the house that it had come to resemble a fortress, and I doubted we would ever step inside again.

"Come," he called when we knocked, and we entered the room to find him sitting in his chair, gazing off into the distance over the woods of his estate. It took him a few moments, but he eventually turned around to see us. "Ah, Lady Bella, Mr Quin. I'm glad you're still here."

His sentiment was concise and businesslike, but the emotion running through the man was impossible to overlook. It appeared that someone had siphoned off all the energy and resilience that I'd noticed in him the day before. It was not that the murder of his maid had left him unaffected, but the death of his wife had drained him dry.

"We have something important to tell you, Lord Sheridan," Bella began as he pointed us to the chairs in front of the desk, just as he had on our first visit. "We believe we know what led to the terrible circumstances in which we find ourselves."

We took our places as he'd silently instructed. I could have taken charge of the conversation, but Bella had filled in just as many gaps that week as I had, and I felt she deserved to start the sad, inevitable process.

"Are you saying that you know who killed my wife?" His voice was hoarse, his cheeks gaunter than they had previously been, and his always-pale hair had turned a shade closer to transparent.

"We believe so, yes." Bella paused to give him the time he needed to comprehend this simple, terrible fact. "It hasn't been easy, mainly because the killer has gone out of her way to hide the truth."

He pulled back from the desk in one brusque movement. "'Her'? Are you saying that my wife was murdered by another woman?"

I imagined the list of possible suspects forming in his head.

"That's right." Bella kept her voice steady. She didn't want to upset the man any more than he already was. "I know this will be difficult for you to hear, but we feel we must tell you what really happened. Inspector Lovebrook has gone to arrest the woman we believe to be responsible."

She glanced at me in the chair next to hers as though to encourage me to continue.

"It's not easy for us to tell you," I said, to avoid an awkward pause. "It's a strange case, and we wanted to explain the situation as soon as we could."

I don't believe that Lord Sheridan had the strength to form an audible response then, but he nodded to show his appreciation.

Bella started talking again, like a gramophone that had been wound up and was ready to play. "Of all the crimes we've investigated, this may be the most beguiling." We have probably said this about all our cases at one time or another, but I couldn't disagree with her. "From the very beginning, we have found ourselves exploring dark alleys that led nowhere. Even as we gained an understanding of what had happened, we constantly grappled with the knowledge that nothing was quite as it seemed."

Lord Sheridan cleared his throat, smoothed down his black tie but said not a word, so Bella got to the facts of the case. "When we arrived here, our focus was on what had been taken and whether Dennis Apps really was to blame for the crime, regardless of the presence of the weapon with his fingerprints on it in the room where Penny was found. We soon realised that someone could have arranged the scene to make him look guilty. In fact, we found certain factors which suggested that was the case. First of all, it would have been a great risk for one of the gardeners to come into the house. His presence here, had it been observed, would have immediately told whoever saw him that he was up to no good.

"Furthermore, Dennis and his colleagues would have been less likely to know what was happening – and who was where in the house – than almost anyone else. It would be far easier for a footman or maid to have carried out the burglary. But then the question would have remained, why commit the crime when there were so many people here? Assuming that Penny's killer was a resident or guest, why not wait until later at night to snatch whatever it was that the killer wanted?"

Lord Sheridan sighed and finally found the spirit to reply. "I have asked myself the same thing often since it happened and even more so today. I understand why someone would steal from another person to improve his lot in life, but why kill? Why did two people have to die?"

He wasn't the first to ask this, and he wouldn't be the last.

"That was a question we couldn't easily answer." I believe that there was a hint of a tremor in Bella's voice. The case had affected us both in unusual ways. It was only a few months ago that her close family friend had been murdered, but she'd somehow shown more resilience back then than today. I had to question whether the feelings she'd pushed down as far as she could were finally coming to the surface.

All the same, she composed herself and continued with the

explanation. "It was only in the last hour that we confirmed two important points. First, we became quite confident that Dennis Apps had nothing to do with the killings. In itself, this wasn't enough to point us in the direction of the actual culprit, but it helped us to concentrate on several relevant details. Most importantly, we knew that the events of Friday night had been staged to cast blame on Dennis. We couldn't say at first whether the killer's ultimate objective was to steal something or there was an entirely different motive which we'd failed to divine, but we knew the seemingly haphazard nature of that night was a sham."

"Presumably my wife's murder played some part in your understanding." We'd heard from the beginning that Lord Sheridan was a smart man, and in his quiet, serious way he'd proved it. "Dennis couldn't be the killer if he was up in Scotland at the time."

It must have occurred to Bella that there were certain things we'd discovered that morning which had not yet been relayed to our host. "That's right. In fact, he was on the train on his way back here at the time that Imelda was killed. We discovered when he arrived that it was Penny herself who had handed him a note on Friday night telling him to leave the grounds and get on a train at King's Cross. It was written in your name, Lord Sheridan, and the killer gave it to Penny to pass on to your gardener. Can you confirm that you weren't the person who wrote it?"

One eyebrow moved higher on the baron's forehead. "No, of course I didn't."

"Very good." Bella smiled a little as though happy to be making progress. "The writing was in a childish hand, and the envelope even contained a five-pound note for the expenses he would accrue. Every move that Dennis made until the police located him in a hotel near Edinburgh Station was directed by the killer."

"It made us question what else had been staged," I felt I had to add.

Bella picked up this point and expanded it. "Your staff and family took consolation from the idea that the maid you all loved was simply in the wrong place at the wrong time, but it was no accident. While it didn't really matter who ended up in Lady Sheridan's boudoir, someone had to die. It was what the killer had always intended to happen."

We heard a noise out in the hall then, and Bella paused to see whether we would be interrupted. From the slow, steady sound of footsteps, I could only conclude that it was Ponsonby. Much as in our investigation, he came close then left without having any noticeable impact.

"One crime led to another." Her tone had become more resolute. I don't know whether she'd gained confidence or the rhythm of her story had loosened her tongue, but she no longer held back her emotion. "Just when we accepted that Dennis was to blame, and everyone here at Cherkley Court started to relax, your wife was murdered. It was a shock to all of us, and I can't begin to comprehend what you and your son have experienced today, but I'm certain that the two crimes were planned together. This was not a burglary gone awry which led to a hasty second attempt. Lady Sheridan's murderer knew exactly what she was doing from the beginning."

I don't know whether Bella intended to reveal the killer's name just then, but she was interrupted by the sound of footsteps, which were followed by three slow knocks. The door opened and there was Detective Inspector Lovebrook pushing my handcuffed ex-girlfriend into the room.

THIRTY-FOUR

"You? Why would...?" Sheridan said, looming over his desk in dismay when he saw the Spaniard. "I knew you couldn't be trusted. I should have dismissed you when I had the chance."

With Constable Watson at his side, Lovebrook held Nerea by the chains between her wrists. She was surely only making the situation worse by struggling like that, but she wasn't the kind of person to do what was in her best interests.

"You're lying," she shouted at the inspector, before a string of Spanish swear words and some particularly graphic phrases involving milk, goats and dead people spewed from her lips. "Marius, you know me. You must believe I wouldn't do this."

I rose to look her in the eyes before responding. "Yes, my dear Nerea. I do know you. I know exactly what you're like, even if you've spent the last couple of days doing your very best to help me forget it, but I should have trusted my instincts when I first saw you outside my house."

The scream that tore out of her seemed to ring around the glass lampshade that hung from the ceiling. Lord Sheridan lacked the strength or composure to remain on his feet and dropped back down into his chair.

"You have deprived a young boy of his mother." His words

were only just audible, but they must have reached Nerea, as she immediately stopped fighting and stared in horror.

"No, this is wrong. This is all wrong. It shouldn't be like this."

"Then you shouldn't have chosen to kill someone." I was surprised to hear Bella say this. She looked at the culprit with such fire that I thought Nerea might melt where she stood.

I knew that the time had come. It was a tragic tale, and I would have much preferred to let Bella or Lovebrook tell it, but Lord Sheridan deserved to hear what had happened, so I began the final part of the story.

"Your language mistress befriended a nice, innocent, hard-working man in order to push the blame onto him. I should have known from the very beginning that she would never choose good character or steadfastness over more material concerns. We learnt that she began to show an interest in Dennis Apps a month ago, which shows just how long this plan was in the making."

As the prisoner had now settled somewhat, Lovebrook brought her to stand by the desk, and I sat back in my seat.

"With Dennis won over, she was well placed to obtain a blunt object with his fingerprints on that could be used as a weapon. I've described much of what else went on prior to the fatal attack on Penny, but not what happened in the early hours of this morning. I'm sorry to go into detail, and I hope your son never has to hear this, Lord Sheridan, but I believe you should."

This was too much for Nerea. She turned towards the book-shelf behind her to hide her face. From the way her shoulders convulsed, I could see that she was crying. It just so happened that the painting of Lady Sheridan's father was hanging above her. He looked down disapprovingly as though he knew just what she'd done.

"Nerea waited until everyone was asleep, then knocked on your bedroom door to persuade Lady Sheridan to accompany her downstairs. It didn't have to be last night. Had your wife stayed up talking to a friend, it could have waited until any moment when you weren't at home to get in the way, but as fortune would have it,

Imelda was alone. I'm sure Nerea told her some tragic story about why she needed to talk to her. We only knew your wife for a short time, but the staff here were clearly fond of her. It seems likely that she would have listened to the concerns of a distressed employee, and I believe she followed Nerea downstairs to the tropical house of her own accord."

My voice had become breathy and uncharacteristically harsh. I paused for a moment to calm myself. "I don't know exactly how it happened, but I assume that Nerea went ahead to hide somewhere so that she could garrotte Imelda from behind with a length of wire. It wasn't so very different from the first killing, in fact, and it led to the same result: an innocent woman dead. These despicable murders were separated by a fraction more than two days."

She'd had time to think by now, and Nerea turned back to me with tears in her gorgeous brown eyes. At one point in my life, I could have lost myself in them for hours and not felt as if I were wasting a single moment, but I could barely stand to look at her now.

"I asked you to come here," she said by way of a defence. "Why would I have gone out of my way to bring two detectives to the scene of a crime, especially if I was planning another murder?"

I imagine she thought she'd caught me out with this question, but it did not preclude her guilt. "You wanted to make it look as though you were only concerned with proving the innocence of the man you claimed to love. In reality, Inspector Lovebrook had already asked Lord Sheridan whether we could assist in his investigation. Your sentimental performance was just that: a show you put on for us. You didn't need our help, just like you didn't truly love Dennis Apps. You're an excellent actress, Nerea, and I'm certain that, while it might have interfered with your initial plans, you were only too happy to have us here as an audience."

She wouldn't give up so easily. "Then tell me how I could have killed Penny when I was with my cousin in Guildford at the time she died?"

I scratched my head a little exaggeratedly, but then I've never claimed to be much of an actor myself. "What a good point you make. You evidently had help."

Young Constable Watson, who had been standing beside the door this whole time, glanced at it briefly, and I wondered whether he knew what would happen next.

Nerea's mouth had fallen open just a crack, but she had nothing more to say for herself, so I kept going.

"There were two things that stood out to me as I walked here a short time ago. The first was the point that Nerea just made. Why would a killer invite any more surveillance of her actions than necessary? Well, I've already explained that mystery, though the ramifications of this proved to be important in another way."

"Speak plainly, Marius," Bella reminded me, and I must admit that I had slipped into the voice of the ever-enigmatic Inspector Rupert L'Estrange, who leads the investigations in all three of my published books.

"A second point, which we should have noticed far earlier, was that Thomas Smith – or Thomas-Richard Harrison as you know him, my lord – spent a great deal of time on Friday planning out the game your wife and her guests played."

I waited to see whether anyone would comprehend the relevance of this, and it was our host who finally showed that he hadn't. "Surely the fact that he was here under a false name is more significant than his efforts to entertain his friends."

"That would be the obvious conclusion but, in this case, we discovered his true identity so easily that he couldn't have relied on it to provide any protection over the course of a murder investigation. The police were bound to uncover it eventually." My chair squeaked as I moved. It was a little off-putting. "What I found interesting was that he had been able to hide the clues for the game in so many places without the participants knowing. There was one all the way down in the woods. Several were scattered about the gardens, and there was even one here in this library."

Nerea's head had dropped at some point, her shoulders were hunched and she knew that there was no way back for her or her accomplice. Even after all that she had done, I found it dispiriting to see her in such a pitiful state. Love never dies completely and, as much as I'd come to regret the time I'd spent with her, brief happy memories peppered my thoughts.

"It's significant because Thomas was quite confident that his friends didn't know what he had planned or when he would do it. But to get into this library, which you keep locked when you're not here, my lord, he would have had to tell you what he was doing."

Lord Sheridan looked confused about why this would be relevant, but he responded all the same. "That's right. He knocked on the door in the afternoon. He asked me whether I wished to participate in the game he was planning. I laughed and politely told him that I would be busy with my work that evening. By way of a consolation, he asked whether he could leave a clue in here for Imelda to find, and I allowed him to do just that."

"Precisely," I said, getting to my feet again and signalling to the young constable. "Watson, the door, please."

He looked a bit nervous but did as instructed. Approaching it cautiously, he pulled the door open to show the empty hallway.

"There's no one there," Bella muttered as I turned back to Lord Sheridan.

"What a shock." I counted to three, and I'm sure it wasn't just my own heartbeat I could hear pounding. "It seems that no one else is coming because the other killer is sitting behind that desk."

THIRTY-FIVE

"You're talking gibberish," Sheridan tried, before addressing the inspector in the hope that his appeals might hold more sway with him. "The man's lost his mind. Why did you ever think that involving a novelist in all this was a good idea? They're professional fantasists." To his credit, he did sound suitably distressed, but then that didn't require any acting; he was surely terrified. "Did you not think it was enough of an ordeal for me to tell my son that his mother is dead? Is that why you've set this reprobate on me?"

"Would that be the wife you conspired to murder? Yes, I can imagine how difficult it was for you to explain that she'd been killed." Lovebrook knew all of this in advance but still sounded horrified by the contemptible man's actions.

I thought it best that I finish the account. "Of course, you couldn't kill her yourself. That would have been too obvious. You needed an alibi and therefore you needed an accomplice." I'd probably become a mite too arrogant by now, but if there's one type of person to whom it is acceptable to feel superior, it's a murderer. "My former love, Nerea, has always had grand ambitions. You killed Penny to provide her with an alibi so that she could get rid of your wife when you were in the city. I wonder whether you told your co-conspirator that you loved her. I wonder whether you actually believed it."

It came as no surprise that the insanely rich, disproportionately powerful man before me wouldn't lie down and accept defeat. His ire was up. "Prove it. Prove any of this and I will hold out my wrists for the shackles." He paused, and when I didn't immediately list all he wanted to know, he laughed at me. "You see, you can't do it. You really are a fantasist."

"The evidence, Marius," Bella or perhaps Lovebrook but most likely both of them prompted me.

"Oh, very well. From the beginning, I found it hard to accept that Nerea Barriuso –who left me for a rich fellow with the personality of an earthworm, simply because he could take her to nicer restaurants than I ever could – would settle down for a cosy, humble life with a gardener. I tried my very best to believe that she had changed, but deep down I was never convinced. Don't misunderstand me; she played her part to perfection, but then she only knew to visit us in the first place because you told her we were coming."

He had no answer to this, but I could see from a slight flicker in his pale eyes – and a pulsing of one vein in the side of his neck – that he appreciated the significance of what I'd just said.

"Nerea begged us to investigate after you told her that Lovebrook wanted us to come here. You could have said no to the inspector, but that would have looked suspicious, and you couldn't risk any attention being directed your way. It was fine when Penny was the only victim. Although you were alone at the time of her murder, you had absolutely no motive for killing your maid, but there must be a million ways in which you would gain from Imelda's death."

Lovebrook was watching the man's reactions with a stern, calculating expression which showed just how capable an officer he is – a fact he often hides behind his easy demeanour. I knew that, even though Sheridan huffed and complained and would not confess to anything that I was saying, Lovebrook could see through his pretence and would arrest him when the time came.

I selected the next piece of evidence to put to the culprit. "On Friday night, you saw Penny through the window here and called for her to take the message to Dennis in the annexe, no doubt with instructions not to say anything else. It didn't have to be her. You could have called a servant from elsewhere in the house, but she happened to be passing, and so her fate was sealed. She was to report back to you when it was done, and then you asked her to meet you upstairs on some flimsy errand."

My anger peaked, and I felt true hatred towards this man for his cruelty and cowardice. "I don't need to tell you what happened next. If you have any kind of conscience, it will stay with you for the rest of your life. You took the box to implicate Dennis in the first instance, and for Nerea to place it in another suspect's quarters this morning when the gardener could no longer be your scapegoat. You made a mistake when choosing Louise's room, though."

I was on less firm ground at this point, as I couldn't say for certain what he knew about his wife's affair, but that didn't change the basic facts. "I bet you hated Imelda for bringing those people here. It wasn't just that she was in love with one of them; they weren't your sort at all. I saw it when Thomas spoke out of turn at lunch yesterday. I saw how his talk of keeping the little people in their place vexed you like itching powder."

I extended my hands to gesture to the luxury in which he lived. "Despite all of this, you came from humble beginnings. We learnt how you went to work for an earl whose daughter took a shine to you. Without Imelda, you'd never have been able to build up the empire you created. So tell me: how much of the money you made did your wife and father-in-law retain?"

I looked up at the painting of the Earl of Clonmel, who continued to peer down gloomily at us from his spot among the bookshelves. "I bet it's galled you your whole life that the wealth you've accumulated is yours in name only. Imelda told us that she inherited her father's wealth when he died. Am I right in thinking that, had you divorced your wife, you would have kept little more than you had back then?" He didn't have to tell us. The police would soon search the library and find the relevant document. "The only way for you to lose the woman who had betrayed you but keep your fortune was to make it look as though you were twenty miles from here with plenty of witnesses to attest to your presence when she died."

Bella had been quietly seething throughout my speech. I'd told her the main details before we'd entered, of course, but some of Sheridan's motivations were still unfurling in my brain as I spoke. A similar explanation occurred to her at this moment.

"You tried to hide your connection to Nerea by pretending to dismiss her from your service so publicly. If we hadn't come to her defence, I'm sure that you'd have found another reason to reinstate her."

I had something to add. "I saw how much you enjoyed exercising the power you had over her. It wasn't just megalomaniacal; it was lustful. I should have known then that there was something between you."

Nerea's long brown hair, which had been hidden away so primly in a ponytail for most of our time there, had fallen down in front of her face. She jerked her cuffed hands away from the inspector, and I believe she must have recognised what I'd described. Whatever she had hoped to achieve by aligning with the murderous baron, she must have been aware that he was the one in control. To call her a victim in any of this would be going too far, but I truly believe that their plan was hatched by Lord Sheridan.

As she sobbed, her accomplice did his best to appear resilient. "This evidence isn't even circumstantial. You have no way of proving that I was the one who attacked Penny Baker." He sat straight-backed, with his fists resting on the desk before him, but nothing he'd said would aid his cause.

"I'll accept that to an extent," I told him, sounding every bit as confident as he wasn't. "However, as Louise was with your wife at the time, and the staff all have alibis, that only leaves Quentin and Thomas, neither of whom would appear to gain from the outcome of your various crimes."

"That's not enough!" He really bellowed these words, but they would have no impact. The room was too well upholstered for them to bounce back to us. They were absorbed by the thick carpet and countless books that lined the walls. "You have no way of proving to a jury that I was the one in the room when Penny's skull was shattered."

"I wouldn't say that. For one thing, I already showed that Nerea came to us on your recommendation. But even more importantly, if my old friend wishes to avoid hanging alongside you, she'll tell us exactly what you did to convince her to kill. Did you promise to take her as your wife? Once the dust had settled and you'd got away with murder, did you plan to install her as the mistress of Cherkley Court?"

She finally looked up at me and, despite everything, a faint trace of relief could be seen on her features.

"At the very least, I believe she pushed you to spare Dennis Apps. He may have taken the blame initially, but the pair of you did nothing to incriminate him after your wife was killed. I can only think she'd grown fond of the pleasant young man over the month she'd been pretending to be besotted with him. I'm sure it was a nice change from having to put up with you."

"You're a swine, Quin. A stuck-up little know-nothing." His features seemed to group together in the centre of his face then. His eyes became pinpricks, and we got to see the ugly creature that lived within that outwardly respectable gentleman. That was when I knew he'd given up the pretence of innocence.

"I told her it was a mistake." Even his voice had changed. He sounded crueller and rougher. It was his death gurgle, months in advance of his trial and final punishment. "I said that we should direct the police's attention to Dennis and Louise both, but that fool wouldn't have it. She knew how Imelda had made use of me for so long. She said she felt my pain, but she wouldn't let me do things my way."

Nerea looked like a witch as she tipped her head back and laughed with manic glee. "I may come out of this better than I'd hoped." Her eyes were fixed as she looked across the room at him. "Even if I'm locked up for the rest of my life, I'll spend every minute thinking how lucky I am never to see you again."

Clearly whatever had passed for love between them was now extinguished like a campfire in a rainstorm.

"Just arrest me and put me out of my misery." Sheridan rose imperially from his desk, but he couldn't resist one last look at the painting that had haunted him for decades. "I made that mouldy old family richer than they'd been throughout centuries of sponging upon the peasants who farmed their land, and what did they give me in return?"

"A perfectly comfortable existence that the vast majority of people would envy?" I hazarded a guess, but I don't think it was what he wanted to hear.

"Nothing! Even in the last weeks of his life, my father in-law, the kind and benevolent earl you see on the wall over there, talked as though it was his genius in employing me that led to the family's change in fortune. Everything you see here belonged to him until he died and generously left it to Imelda – making sure in his will that I would receive nothing. He gave me a salary, but the assets of the company remained in her name. I have stashed away every-thing I could for years, and it is a mere fraction of the wealth I created for them. I was trapped in a marriage with a woman who had more interest in running around with children than obeying her husband."

His finger trembled as he pointed in my direction. "So don't talk about suffering or right and wrong, because I did what I did to escape from the cage that those heartless individuals had forged for me."

I waited a few moments to see whether he would say anything

more. "Right. Have you finished? Wonderful. You can arrest him now, Inspector. I think we've all heard enough. Besides, I haven't eaten anything since breakfast and I'm becoming rather peckish."

THIRTY-SIX

We weren't afforded a grand lunch in the dining room that afternoon. We had sandwiches in the kitchen with the staff, and they may have been the tastiest things I ate all weekend. The atmosphere there wasn't exactly a happy one, but Penny's colleagues were relieved that her killers had been brought to justice, and everyone who passed our table offered their thanks.

Obviously, there was some shock that their employer had turned out to be the killer, and I'm sure some of them feared for what would happen to their jobs now that he was gone, but the general feeling was that justice had been served.

"I never trusted that Spanish woman," the plump, cheery cook said, and just as I was thinking that such criticism was based on her nationality rather than any personal failings, she listed the reasons why. "From the day she got here, she talked down to us like she were the lady of the house. Just think how it would've been if she'd got away with murder and been the one to order us about in place of her ladyship! It i'n't worth considering."

The scullery maids agreed with her, but then talk turned to other matters. That's how long it took them to forget Nerea Barriuso.

It was interesting to hear their thoughts on the case, and I should probably have spent more time down there before, listening to the rumours and gossip at the heart of the house. When the subject of their fallen mistress arose, the odd criticism was uttered for the way Imelda had raised her son but, on the whole, it was clear she would be missed. Inevitably, though, much of the discussion centred on Penny Baker. She was just as loved as everyone had said, and her death seemed even crueller than Lady Sheridan's.

When Dennis came in for his lunch, there were cheers and applause, which made the reserved gardener blush. He shook hands with the men, received a few kisses on the cheeks from the ladies and, once the noise had died down, he came to speak to us.

"I must thank you again," he told us, his cap clutched tightly in both hands. "I don't like to think what would have happened if you and the inspector hadn't taken up my cause."

"You're very welcome, Dennis," I told him sincerely. He reminded me of several of the men with whom I'd served in the war. Under different circumstances, I could have imagined us getting on rather well. "I'm just sorry that Nerea used you as she did."

He grinned at this and looked a little mischievous. "I'm not. It's not every day a beautiful young lady takes an interest in me. It only lasted a month, and she turned out to be more rotten than a maggot's dinner, but I certainly enjoyed m'self while it lasted."

He let out a thundering laugh at this point. The cook tutted and shook her head, whereas her young assistants looked at him as though he were the most handsome man on earth. Somehow, I didn't think he'd have too much trouble finding a replacement for his now-shackled former sweetheart.

"I'm glad to hear it," Bella said with a cheeky smile of her own.

Dan and Derek, or Bill and Bobby, or whatever his colleagues' names were, had just arrived for their lunch, so he put his hat back on to tip it to us and hurried off to receive their congratulations.

It was odd to see the Duke of Hurtwood's daughter eating her ham sandwiches in that unglamorous setting, but we enjoyed our meal, and once we'd explained all we knew for a second time to

Lovebrook, it was time to go. Well, there was one more thing I felt I had to do. It probably shouldn't have fallen to me, but just as we were preparing to leave, I noticed Lionel through the grand salon. He was sitting alone on the back step of the house, so I decided to talk to him.

"We got off on the wrong foot, you and I," I said as I reached him. "I'm truly sorry for that."

He looked up at me and shrugged. "It wouldn't be the first time. I have a habit of annoying people."

"Has someone explained what happened?" I thought I should confirm before I said anything more.

He picked up a tiny stone from the step beside him and threw it into the garden so that it bounced down onto the first lawn. "My father is a killer, and my mother is dead." He said this quite stoically, but then a sigh came out of him that I wasn't expecting. "The thing that makes me saddest is that I didn't care for either of them too much, but I loved Nere. I foolishly thought she liked me too."

I allowed a few seconds to pass before sitting down on the step to reassure him. "I'm sure that she did. You know she was my friend too once, and I still remember how wonderful it felt when we first met. But I wouldn't worry about her. She and your father did some terrible things, and now it's your job to build a life that's better than theirs."

With his eyes pointed at the scrabbly ground in front of us, he sniffed. "I'll do my best, but perhaps I'm a bad person too. My governess always complains that I waste her time and don't concentrate on my work. Mother was normally too busy to notice what I was doing, and Father often told me that he had no interest in me. So perhaps I'll turn out to be just like him."

"No, Lionel," I said more forcefully. "You can't think that way. We spend our childhoods being told how naughty we are, but when we grow up everyone expects us to be model human beings. The truth is that we're all born good, I promise you that. It's up to each of us to make sure that we continue on the right path."

I realised that I sounded like any one of the adults who had spent so long telling him what to do, and so I changed the tune I was singing. "You know, I was only eight years older than you when my father disappeared. He walked out of our house one morning to go to work, and I haven't seen him since. The pain of losing him has never healed, and I wish every day that I could see him again. He wasn't perfect, though time may have smoothed the edges of his occasionally prickly personality, but that doesn't take anything away from how much I miss him."

I waited to see how he would respond. When he said nothing, I took a deep breath and tried to explain myself better. "What I'm trying to say is that, whoever your parents were and however they treated you, you're allowed to feel whatever it is you are feeling. If you miss them, that's to be expected. And if you hate your father, that's perfectly understandable too."

The boy looked away for a moment, and when he finally mustered a response, he turned back to me with such a serious expression that I realised I'd misjudged him. "The truth is... I don't think I'm going to miss either of them. I'll probably be sent to live with my father's sister, or she'll come here perhaps. I've always loved my auntie Sally more than my parents. When we're together, she wants to talk to me and play games. They only wanted to see me if there was a party and they needed to pretend we were a happy family."

It was at this moment that I noticed Bella lingering in the room behind us, but I didn't turn to see her.

"Well, Lionel, I hope that you'll be happy, whatever happens. I'll leave my telephone number with Ponsonby, and you can call me if you have any trouble. I'm not as rich or powerful as your parents were, but I normally find a way to solve problems."

He fell terribly quiet then. I don't just mean that he offered no reply; something about the way he was sitting became more self-contained. He seemed to make himself smaller, as though he had no wish to be noticed.

"Thank you, Marius," he finally said, and I realised that Nerea must have told him who I was. "That's very kind of you, and I'm sorry if I was obnoxious earlier. I never mean to annoy people, but sometimes my silly mouth says the wrong thing."

"Then, if you don't mind my offering one more piece of advice..." I waited for the nod that I was fairly certain would come back to me. "If you wish to have an easy life, you'll learn to keep some things to yourself. It took me long enough, believe me, but I generally find that making rude comments in your head is the best way to go about it. That way you can say all the snide things you like, and no one gets hurt."

He needed a moment to consider his answer. By the time it arrived, I was up on my feet.

"I'll try that and see what happens." He had to squint as he looked up at me. The previously grey sky above us had turned so bright that it felt as if the spring had finally arrived. "Perhaps I'll call to tell you how it goes."

I smiled down at him. "Good lad. You do that."

I didn't know whether to ruffle his hair or give him a pat on the back, so I nodded and moved to leave.

"That was very kind of you, Marius," Bella said as I looked for a pen to do as I'd promised. "Genuinely, that was very kind indeed."

"Well, we were lucky, weren't we, Bella?" I didn't leave her a moment to ask why. "We were brought up by people who loved us and showed that to be the case every day. It's a gift that many children don't receive. For Lionel, at least, I hope that will change."

She didn't praise me again or confirm her agreement. She looked at the little boy in the bright doorway who must have felt as though a tornado were blowing through his head.

On our way out, we saw Louise, Quentin and Thomas lingering at the top of the stairs. Louise was undoubtedly still heartbroken, but she was young and would find someone more suitable for her than a married baroness who took to people the way children enjoy a new toy. Quentin stood stone-faced, perhaps considering his thwarted ambitions, and Thomas just looked grateful that he hadn't ended up in a police cell. It was hard to know which of us would learn the most from this strange encounter. I truly hoped it wouldn't be me.

"Another case closed, Inspector," I called to Lovebrook as we walked out of the house to Bella's car.

He was busy talking to the footmen but came to speak to us a few moments later.

"All thanks to you," he claimed, and I disagreed.

"We all played our parts. If you two weren't around to tell me off when I'm obnoxious and calm me down when I get overexcited, I'm sure I'd brood like a spoilt little boy and get nothing done."

"I was talking to Lady Bella," he quipped, which earned him a kiss on both cheeks from the lady in question.

"Do get in touch if you have any more adventures for us, Valentine. Marius spends far too much time alone. He needs to get out of the house more."

I knew she was going to elbow me in the ribs before long, so I thought I might at least take the time to insult her first. "Whereas Bella spends far too much time worrying about me. At least when we're investigating crimes, she can poke her nose into other people's business instead of mine."

As expected, Bella elbowed me in the ribs. And it was just then that a large, freshly washed basset hound came waddling out of the house, barking as if to suggest that we'd forgotten he was there – which, admittedly, we had.

We got into Bella's car and Lovebrook, Constable Watson, not to mention Ponsonby and the similarly named footmen, waved us off before we mounted the hill to cross the estate. We went first to our village to say goodbye to our families and pack a bag or two, and then Bella drove us back to London.

We didn't say a great deal in the car, but we didn't have to. There was a feeling of peace between us that I imagine occurs quite frequently with old married couples. Not the couples who wed for money or convenience, like the Sheridans, but the people who are still in love after twenty, thirty or even eighty years. They say that familiarity breeds contempt, but in my experience, *they* are wrong about a lot of things.

"Will you stay in London for long?" I asked Bella, as the Sunbeam pulled into St James's Square.

"I haven't decided yet," she said a little mysteriously, and her words stayed with me as we came to a stop in front of my house.

For a moment, I didn't know what to say. I felt that there was something we needed to discuss, but I couldn't decide how to begin.

"I think..." I muttered just as she said, "Don't you agree..."

"Please, after you," I told her, and suddenly the peace I described had evaporated.

"I was just going to say..." she began before a long pause cut through her sentence. "I was just going to say that I enjoy investigating murders with you, Marius." She immediately saw how terrible this sounded and corrected herself. "Not that I want people to be killed or anything like that. I just mean..."

"I know what you mean, Bella," I said in the hope I could make the atmosphere in the car a little less painful to bear.

"No, let me finish what I wanted to say." She flicked her fingers then, as though she had touched something hot. "If it weren't for these cases over the last year, I don't know what I'd have become. They've helped me in more ways than you know. And... And that's all I really have to say."

The car came to a stop, she smiled a terribly polite and terribly false smile, and I did not know how to respond. My very clean dog was asleep on the back seat and moaned to break the silence.

"I feel just the same," I told her, and then, as she apparently had nothing more to say, I climbed outside and opened the door to let Percy out. He was either too tired or too stubborn to wake up, so I had to carry him to my house, which made unlocking the door a real ordeal. I put him on the floor and finally managed it, just as Bella called out to me.

"I'm sorry, Marius." She was already running towards me. Her manner was different again. I felt that she had lost some of her usual polish and self-control. "There's something else. You see... I wasn't telling the truth last night. I was unkind to you, and I shouldn't have been. I assumed that you were unfair to Nerea because you couldn't see past the life you had shared together. I should have been more generous, and I'm sorry."

She was standing under my front porch, just a foot or two away from me, and I could tell that there was something more. "Is that really all you wanted to say?"

This was terribly boring for Percy, who had woken up but still wore a dazed expression. He lumbered into the house to look for somewhere warm to sleep, and I tried again. "It's been clear for some time that we haven't been honest with one another, but perhaps it's time that we were."

I could hear the air go rushing into her mouth as she inhaled. "I don't know, Marius. I really don't." She looked away, but only for a moment and, when her eyes landed on mine, a surge of energy shot through me. "I think so much about the past, so I know how diffi-cult it must have been for you to see Nerea again." Every sentence was followed by a cautious pause. "I think about how all I wanted to do as a child was to be a grown-up, and now that I am one, all I want is to go back."

"But we can go back, Bella," I insisted in the voice I'd heard a few times that weekend which surely wasn't my own. It was too forthright. It belonged to a person who lived without fear and took what he wanted. "We don't have to live our lives in the fog of nostalgia when everything we've ever wanted is still here."

Her eyes looked so sad then that I was worried I'd made a terrible mistake. "Do you really believe that, Marius? Do you really think that—"

She couldn't finish that sentence because I leaned forward and kissed her. I did what I'd been wanting to do for the last fifteen months since she found me on a cold pavement in Bloomsbury and made me believe there was any sense in living again. I kissed her, and I knew that this was what I should have been doing every day since the war had ended. I kissed her, and I felt so alive and so free that my body turned weightless, and I had to open my eyes for a moment to make sure that I hadn't risen off the floor.

I kissed her, and she brought her fist crashing down on my shoulder. "We can't, Marius. I'm sorry, but—" She interrupted herself this time. She put her silk-soft lips on mine, and it was even better than the first time. I've never had any desire to try opium or cocaine, but I know that no drug could compare with how I felt at that moment.

Just as I was about to take to the air and fly about the rooftops of London, she pulled away again. She looked at me, and the intense sorrow that she'd carried with her for so long had returned.

"I can't, Marius. I'm sorry, but I can't let this happen."

The very thing I'd been dreading had come to pass.

She was already leaving. She backed away at first, but once she'd stepped down from the porch, she ran towards her car. I wanted to tell her that she was wrong and that the two of being us together was the only thing that made sense. I wanted— No, I needed to tell her that I loved her in every imaginable way, but I was frozen where I stood. My tongue wouldn't do as it was told. My jaw clamped shut, and I couldn't make a sound.

And so I just watched as the woman I've loved since I knew what that word meant got into her car. Her beautiful green eyes were full of tears as she drove away from me, but I did nothing. I stood there with my heart breaking, thinking, *That's your life in a nutshell, Marius Quin. Now wave goodbye to happiness.*

THIRTY-SEVEN

I remained standing in that exact same spot even after Bella had disappeared around the corner and out onto Pall Mall. Perhaps some part of me thought that, if I just wished hard enough, her sweet little camel-brown car would drive straight back to me. I imagined her stopping in front of the house and running out to me. I could practically feel her lips on mine, and I knew that, this time, I would never let her go. I would ask her to marry me there and then and not let her out of my sight until our dying day.

But she never came back. I stared into space until I realised how cold it was and had to pull my officer's coat tightly around me. I would probably have continued staring for a while longer – or perhaps until the winter returned and I froze to death – when the door behind me blew open in the wind.

I didn't have the courage to go inside. The world wasn't the same as it had been minutes earlier, and the thought of returning to normal life was unbearable, so I pulled the door closed and I walked. I didn't know where I was going at first, but I knew that was what I needed to do. I would walk across the city to absolutely nowhere. There was surely a place for hopeless cases like me – some earthbound purgatory where the broken-hearted can live out their days in bland indifference. If it existed, I was determined to find it.

I walked from the far-too-luxurious neighbourhood of St James's – which I should have accepted long ago was no place for a man like me. I cut between the royal parks to end up in the even more luxurious environs of Buckingham Palace. I longed for the grit and grime for which London had been famous for centuries, but even Victoria Station looked too grand as I continued my journey south-west. I crossed the Chelsea Suspension Bridge with a vast clear space to the east, which had once been covered by a piecemeal selection of wharves, sheds and coal yards, but would now be occupied by London's most technologically advanced power station that they had just started to build.

It was almost as if the city were fighting back – as if London had cleaned up its act just to spite me. I thought that the sight of its less salubrious side would suit the feeling of desolation that coloured my every thought, but it was only when I got south of the river that I saw anything approaching the grey and barren cityscape I craved.

I walked, and I kept walking, and I doubted for some time that I would ever stop. I thought of my Bella, knowing that she was, at that very moment, in floods of tears for what I'd done to her. I thought of all that she had gone through after her fiancé was murdered, and I knew how selfish I had been to disturb her mourning.

I wasn't the hero of the story. I was a vulture, waiting until she was weak enough before swooping down to claim my prey.

I walked because I didn't know what else to do. I walked, and I really wished that I had gone east through London, as the area I'd chosen was far too leafy and pleasant to do any real brooding. I avoided Battersea Park and left the main roads to follow the railway tracks. The sidings were just about dirty and litter-strewn enough to suit my purposes, and the sound of the wheezing, puffing trains as they rolled past me was the perfect accompaniment. I was struggling, just like them. Struggling to build up a head of steam or the confidence to speak to my beloved Bella ever again.

I walked for so long that I left the tracks behind without even noticing that I'd done so. The unmistakable smell of yeast and beer told me that I was near the brewery in Wandsworth, but even that distinctive aroma was mixed with the acrid scent of the nearby gasworks as the wind rushed about me. When I'd been walking for the best part of two hours, and I'd found the stench and grunge of industry that I so desperately required, I had to stop to wonder what good it had done me.

I was about to turn for home or simply sit down on the pavement where I was, when a smart black car came to a stop in front of a dirty old building that had once been an abattoir or a factory of some sort. It had a shabby façade that made it look as if someone had tried to hide it in plain sight by painting the sandstone bricks a shade of grey. It was because of that expensive vehicle – a sparkling new Wolseley 16-35, if I wasn't mistaken – that I even noticed it, but as soon as I did, I found myself pulled towards the grim spot.

I'd only taken a few steps when a chauffeur in his neat blue livery stepped out to open the back doors. A few moments later, a short man with a bony face and pockmarked skin emerged from the building. I was close enough to see his shifting gaze, and I felt quite certain that he was looking around to ensure no one was watching him.

I knew this because I recognised him as a killer. I'd never seen him in full daylight before, but Lucien Pike was the man who had murdered Bella's fiancé the previous summer. He'd nearly trapped me in a criminal plot, too, and he definitely knew more about my father's disappearance than anyone else.

Some stupid part of my brain, which I'm proud to say I usually ignore, suggested I should shout to him. I could have issued a nice British, *You there!* Or, *What's your game?* But I'm happy to say I ignored that instinct and crept along the road, hugging the red-brick wall so as not to stand out. Lucien Pike turned his back to me, and so I moved a little faster as he and the driver guarded the right-hand passenger door of the Wolseley.

I came to a crossroads, and two more men rushed out of the old building. The first was a slight, rather bent figure. He was perhaps sixty years old, with a long, straggly beard and a similarly unkempt overcoat. Striding close behind him was his polar opposite. The second man was a giant. His thick arms stretched the sleeves in which they were encased, and he marched the skinny individual ahead of him with such speed and determination that their short journey to the car was over before it began.

As soon as I saw them climb inside, I ran. My body worked without my brain getting involved. I ran because I had no other choice – because my instincts had fired and this was my chance. I heard the engine of the funereal car roar into life, and I tried to accelerate, but I had no higher gear. I was only yards away when the tyres spun on the dusty road, and I shouted out to them.

"Stop!" was just about short enough for me to muster, and as I said it, the man who'd been bundled into the car turned to bang on the rear window. He saw me chasing after the vehicle, and his fists pounded with all the strength he possessed.

"No," I wailed, out of frustration rather than any hope he would hear.

It was no good. The car darted off down the street, and my father stared back at me through the window with a look of pure misery on his emaciated face.

ABOUT THIS BOOK

Cherkley Court is the name of a real house in Surrey, the English county where I'm from. It is now a very expensive hotel where I've eaten lunch a few times (in the cheapest of their many restaurants). On our last visit, I went to ask whether I could use an image of the house on the cover but sadly I haven't heard back from my subsequent enquiries. The hotel is called Beaverbrook, and I highly recommend it if you happen to have a ton of money – or can slum it like me in their still very nice pizza restaurant!

What particularly drew me to the hotel was its history. It is now surrounded by a golf course and caters for the richest of travellers, but there was a time when it... well, it belonged to one of the richest of men. Max Aitken, now better known as Lord Beaverbrook, was a Canadian who came from a fairly poor family but worked his way up to be one of the most influential men in Britain. By the age of thirteen he'd started his first newspaper (at school, naturally enough) and was already doing a number of odd jobs to make money. He never completed a university degree, and he wasn't born with extensive connections, but he would become a millionaire by thirty – at a time when such people were extremely rare. He became the head of an important stock brokerage firm and made his fortune buying and selling businesses. He soon started more newspapers, which is the industry he is still associated with, but he also started engineering and electricity companies in his home country.

In 1910, aged thirty-one, having pretty much dominated the business world in Canada by controlling much of the cement and steel industries, he figured he'd leave his mark on the Old World too and moved to Britain. It was here that his political influence was particularly felt. As well as making friends with prime ministers and famous names of the day, he would become a politician himself – serving in the cabinet during both World Wars – and he continued his interest in the newspaper business by gaining control of the *Daily Express*. Known as a formidable press baron, Aitken employed very modern techniques to present the First World War to the general public, including sending photographers and even cameramen to document the fighting. His approach to the news made the *Express* an important and popular paper through much of the century. He used it to promote his own interests and could make his friends and break his enemies with a front-page headline or a cutting leader. During the Second World War, Churchill made Aitken the Minister of Aircraft Production, and he ran a successful campaign to get ordinary people to donate pans and scrap metal to aid the war effort, which made him an even more significant person in the eyes of the public.

He was good friends with people like Winston Churchill, Harold Macmillan, Rudyard Kipling and H.G. Wells, all of whom he entertained at Cherkley Court, which he bought the year he arrived in Britain. The house had originally been designed as the retirement home of a man named Abraham Dixon from Birmingham, who had made his fortune in the wool trade and by exporting metal goods. Lord Beaverbrook came across the estate by chance one day when he was motoring about with Kipling and bought it immediately for the bargain price of £30,000 (or the equivalent of £3m today). He spent another £10k doing the place up and even installed a swimming pool and the first home cinema in the UK, where you can still watch films if you stay at the hotel. During Lord Beaverbrook's tenure, the house was used for grand parties and important political events. In 1931, Britain's first coalition government was formed in the library there, and the house hosted famous names like Ian Fleming, Charlie Chaplin, Elizabeth Taylor, Somerset Maugham and the artist Jean Cocteau, all of whose visits are marked in the hotel today.

Marius has already described the house for you, but it really is an interesting property for its different architectural influences. Originally built in a French château style, it also has Tuscan columns, mansard roofs and an unusual layout. But it's the grounds of Cherkley Court that are particularly impressive. The house was built on a hill overlooking a wide, wooded vista, which was embellished with Italianate gardens, an arboretum with several record-breaking (for Britain at least) trees, a grotto, terraced lawns and a large pond. The greenhouse and tropical house that are so important in this book were destroyed in a fire in 1942 – whereas the house itself was nearly destroyed by a rocket two years later as the Germans tried to kill Aitken and other members of the British government. I read about how vast and impressive the glasshouses were, so I went looking for more information and found something really interesting.

I managed to locate an online scan of the April edition of the magazine *Country Life* from 1900. It has a long feature on Cherkley, then still owned by Abraham Dixon (more on him in the next chapter), including plenty of photos of the grounds and green-houses. Together, the two adjoining glass buildings occupied an acre of land. They were incredibly elaborate constructions, with "the Victoria regia house", or tropical house, shaped somewhat like a cathedral with a high, sloping roof. Each of the glasshouses had a large pond and they were lit by electric lights with globe-shaped shades in different colours that hung from the high ceiling. The larger of the ponds had Victoria regia lily pads – the world's second largest, which originated in the Amazon basin. When I discovered that they could support the weight of a human being, I could hardly resist murdering a character and placing her body there now, could I?

Because of the way I research as I write and fit pieces of history and fiction together, funny coincidences often dictate the flow of the narrative. This was certainly the case with the opening of this book as I first picked a grand theatre from a list. It turned out to be five minutes' walk from Marius's house and then, when I checked in the newspaper to see what was playing in the Theatre Royal Haymarket in March 1929, it turned out that there was a mystery on. Even better, *The Fourth Wall* was written by A.A. Milne, the author of *Winnie-the-Pooh* and also one of my favourite books, *The Red House Mystery*. That book, which is Milne's only mystery novel, has an introduction in which he goes into his love of the form and his concept of the key ingredients that make a great whodunnit. Despite whatever Raymond Chandler may have said to the contrary, it's a very enjoyable read.

The play itself was filmed the year after this book was set. As an early sound film, 1930s *Birds of Prey* is a bit clunky by modern standards, but it is still a fun watch, and I greatly enjoyed being able to experience the story that my characters (or at least Bella) had watched at the theatre. One of the best things about it is that the actor C. Aubrey Smith, who plays the victim, would make the most perfect Lord Edgington should anyone wish to adapt my other series for the screen (and have a time machine, as Smith died in 1948). He was also a high-level cricketer, once captaining England to a win against South Africa, and he even set up the Hollywood Cricket Club, playing alongside actors like David Niven, Laurence Olivier and Boris Karloff. His career as an actor lasted fifty-four years, and he appeared in at least two classic mysteries in Hitchcock's *Rebecca* and the first film adaptation of Agatha Christie's *And Then There Were None* from 1945.

As for the theatre where the opening scene of this book takes place, the Haymarket Theatre (sometimes known as the Theatre Royal or a combination of the two) was built in 1720 then rebuilt where it now stands a century later. It was the third theatre to receive permission from King Charles II to perform serious drama, after such frivolity had been banned under the pious and puritanical interregnum of Oliver Cromwell. The restoration monarch was a great supporter of the theatre (and its players, wink wink) and his presence at the Haymarket one night drew such a crowd that twenty people were killed in the crush (and, according to reports, countless people were bruised) trying to catch a glimpse of him.

It fared better in the following century when redesigned by John Nash, who is best known for being the architect behind the Brighton Royal Pavilion, Marble Arch and Buckingham Palace. Although the interior has been altered many times over the centuries, Nash's building is largely unchanged. In 1881, the novelist Henry James described the most recent refurbishment by saying that it had "transformed the Haymarket into the perfection of a place of entertainment." In the twentieth century, Queen Elizabeth would go incognito to matinees with her children there. Rather than sitting in the royal box, she would enter through a side door and sit in the stalls. It is still an incredibly luxurious and impressive theatre, and one of London's most beautiful.

An important turning point in this book comes after Marius sleeps on the case. I've probably mentioned this before, but this is a reference to my favourite ever Marius twist which came to me in my sleep. There is a certain play on words in the first book in this series which had quite improbably formed in my head when I woke up in the middle of the night. I was so pleased with this subconscious-to-conscious revelation that I decided my detective could benefit from such good fortune.

Before I move on to the even more loosely connected points in the next chapter, I must mention the delightful Nerea. Seeing as we knew that Marius had lived in France after the war, I'd originally intended to make his ex-girlfriend French, but Chrissy is busy falling in love with a French girl in the Lord Edgington books, and I didn't want my readers to think that I was obsessed with French women (even if I am married to one), so I named the guest star of this book after a good friend of mine from my home in Spain. I should mention that the real Nerea Barriuso is a lovely person. She was one of my adult students when I was teaching, and we're still friends a decade or more later. She and her partner Ana even went to live with my mum in London for a month and became part of the family.

I suppose that having so many much-loved gay friends in my everyday life was one of the reasons I wanted to at least hint at a lesbian romance in this book. By sheer chance, half of my friendship group is made up of gay people. Like Bella, I grew up with two unofficial aunties who lived together but never revealed that they were a couple until I was an adult. I think it's terribly sad that my aunties Sheila and Usha felt they had to keep their love a secret, even though they have now been together for over fifty years. For anyone who dismisses such a plot in a 1920s mystery novel as overly modern or *woke*, there are plenty of allusions to gay characters in Golden Age detective fiction. There are a lot of not so subtle references in Agatha Christie's books to characters and scenarios which, even at the time, would have been understood as *unconventional*, and other authors like Dorothy L. Sayers and Josephine Tey are more explicit (within the realm of what was permitted by censors and societal norms of the day).

The week I write this has been marked by my brother Daniel's death after a long fight with cancer. He was supported throughout by his boyfriend, Darek, who also talked him through his final breaths as several of their best friends stood at the end of his bed to offer support. Unfortunately, I didn't get to Britain in time to say goodbye, but all the people who called to see Daniel over his last few days have told me just what love and dedication Darek showed to my brother, and I am so thankful for his presence in our lives.

Beyond any doubt, this has been the hardest week I can remember. I've cried more than I have in the rest of my life combined. The only thing that has helped distract me from the pain of losing a brother – whom I idolised as a child, argued with endlessly as a teenager and came to love as my best friend as an adult – was writing (and playing with my kids). Amelie and Osian have just gone to bed, so I have no other option than to get on with the next chapter.

RESEARCH

I'm always amazed at the interesting things I discover when checking facts, reading up on history or just falling down an online rabbit hole while researching my books. Please don't expect much of a through-line in what follows, but I hope you enjoy this little treasury of knowledge nonetheless.

Let's start with those massive lily pads. Even though Victoria regia (or Victoria amazonica) may only be the second largest in the world, the record for weight held by a single pad is 226kg (that's 498lb). The leaves can grow up to three metres in diameter, and the stalk that supports them grows to the riverbed some seven or eight metres down – which is just a little longer than the green anacondas you might find swimming amongst them. What I found particularly interesting was that they inspired something of a craze in Victorian Britain. After the plant was discovered by European botanists in 1801, wealthy gardening enthusiasts began a competition to see who could first grow a flowering plant, with the Dukes of Devonshire and Northumberland tying for first place – well, the men they paid to do it for them tied for first place, at least. They recreated the tropical conditions of the lilies using gas boilers, and one of the first flowers to bloom was presented to Queen Victoria before the species was named in her honour. The cell-like underside of the gigantic lily pads are said to have been the inspiration for one of those gardeners, a man named Joseph Paxton, when he designed the Crystal Palace for the Great Exhibition of 1851. He is also famous for cultivating the ever-important Cavendish banana, the descendants of which make up about half of all bananas now eaten.

Sticking with sweet treats, I had to look up the history of British confectionery and was pleased to find that a company I remember well from my own childhood – I was something of a sugar addict – formed way back in 1848. Barratt & Co. was the largest sweet manufacturer in the world by 1906, though it was started by one man with a sugar boiler who delivered his produce across England by horse and cart from Hoxton in East London. By the end of the twentieth century, the family business employed two thousand people, and their factories occupied five acres of land. The company was well known for their stickjaw toffees, and in the 1920s, it started producing black jacks, fruit salads and sherbet fountains, which are all still available today. One of the oddest products they ever made was Tichborne rock, which was a stick of rock with the image of the Tichborne Claimant inside.

Oh, fine. I suppose I should explain who the Tichborne Claimant was. The case had a major influence on mysteries and fiction of all kinds, with authors as diverse as Agatha Christie, Josephine Tey, Anthony Trollope, Jorge Luis Borges and Zadie Smith all writing versions of the case. It started with a shipwreck in 1854 in which the heir to the Tichborne baronetcy was said to have drowned. His mother refused to believe her son Roger was dead, and she offered a reward and focused her search on Australia, where it was rumoured that survivors of the wreck might have ended up. After her husband died and the title passed to her younger son, who would soon die too, a man known as Tom Castro contacted the family claiming to be the long-lost heir. His mother was desperate to believe that Roger was alive and accepted Castro as her son, even though he was far heavier than the missing man, did not speak French and couldn't remember much about his family or home. Other relatives were less accepting and, after a spot of investigating, discovered that Castro had been born in Britain and his real name was Arthur Orton.

Orton won influential backers, and the case became an obsession of the day, with newspapers making the most of the mystery and two clear camps of believers and cynics emerging. It was often depicted as a fight between the stuffy upper class and a humble but plucky challenger. Orton tried to prove his claim in court, but after a year-long trial, his inability to speak French – as the real Roger had been born in Paris and even spoke English with a strong accent – would prove his undoing. Things were to get worse for him, as he was then prosecuted for perjury and sentenced to fourteen years' hard labour. For a while, though, he'd lived in the lap of luxury. With his supposed mother paying for his life in London, he was a regular guest at high-society events, where his presence was guaranteed to spark interest. There was even a souvenir industry that grew up around him with photos and caricatures in high demand and even, as I may have already mentioned, Tichborne Claimant sweets.

Such cases of false representation are common throughout history. There's the supposed Russian princess Anastasia, though two other people also claimed to be her sisters. A few centuries earlier, three different men claimed to be the youngest son of Ivan the Terrible, and one of them even served as Tsar of Russia for almost a year before he was overthrown. A famous case, which also inspired countless books and films, is the story of Martin Guerre from seventeenth-century France. This was quite a similar incident to the Tichborne Claimant, although the motivation of the imposter was harder to understand. It started when a French peasant was suspected of theft and ran away, abandoning his wife and child. Eight years later, a man with some knowledge of the missing husband took his place in the household and even fathered children with Guerre's wife, who believed the imposter was her husband. Some members of the family eventually became suspicious, and the imposter was identified as Arnaud du Tilh. Tilh was put on trial, found guilty and sentenced to death.

However, in a twist worthy of (and later used by) Hollywood, he appealed against his sentence and was found innocent – leading his supposed wife and uncle to be arrested in his place. At their trial, though, a one-legged man appeared and proved that he was the real Martin Guerre and Arnaud du Tilh was the fake. The imposter was sentenced to death, at which point he confessed to his crime and explained that he had been mistaken for the real person by two friends of Guerre and so he picked their brains about the missing man's life and then took his place in his home.

We like to think that people in the past were more gullible, and such things could never happen today, but there was an even more incredible case from 1997, when a Frenchman appeared claiming to be Nicholas Barclay, a missing boy from Texas. He was flown to the States by authorities and succeeded in convincing Nicholas's family that he was their son, even though his eyes were a different colour, he spoke with a French accent, and, in truth, he was seven years older than Nicholas. He lived with them for five months before someone noticed that his ears were different from Nicholas's and his true identity was uncovered. It turned out that he was Frédéric Bourdin, a twenty-three-year-old criminal who is said to have impersonated five hundred people. He was sentenced to six years for fraud but after his release, he went on to impersonate at least three more missing teenagers. He claims that the reason he kept doing this was to make up for the love he never received from his real family. Which is kind of sad – and really weird.

From missing schoolboys to a famous one who has made an appearance in my books before. Billy Bunter gets a mention in this book and one of the early Lord Edgingtons, but I can't imagine he's as well known abroad or, indeed, in the present in general. Bunter is a character who first appeared in stories in the boy's weekly magazine *The Magnet* in 1908. He was created by the writer Charles Hamilton who is credited as being the most prolific writer in history. I'm not doing too badly, as I've written about three million words in six years, but Hamilton managed 100 million over the course of a sixty-six-year career. Though he mainly wrote serial stories for magazines, that's the equivalent of 1,200 novels. I'm up to 37 novels, and even if I continue at my current rate for another sixty years, I won't get close!

He is best remembered today for his Greyfriars boarding school stories and, in particular, for Billy Bunter, who is something of an antihero. Bunter is mendacious, greedy, selfish and deluded, but very funny with it. His primary motivation appears to be eating, and he's not against helping himself to the other boys' food, but he is blissfully unaware of his own failings. My father loved the Greyfriars stories, and they were still being written when he was a boy. They are very much of their time, but I read a couple of them before writing my own boarding school book, and they are still very entertaining.

From schoolboys to school shoes. I knew the name Mary Janes for the type of shoes worn by little girls in America in the middle of the twentieth century but didn't know what they were called in the UK. It seems they were best known as bar shoes and were originally worn by men and women. What I found interesting about all this was that the name Mary Jane came from fiction. I'm surprised how often I find that the origin of phrases is from books or films. One good example is the Trilby hat, which comes from the stage adaptation of George du Maurier's novel *Trilby* (which also gave us the word Svengali). Mary Janes, meanwhile, originated in the American comic strip *Buster Brown*, created by Richard F. Outcault. Outcault was a successful marketer and sold the rights to use his characters to two hundred different companies at the 1904 World's Fair. Something else I like about him is that he helped me to learn the name of something I often do.

Tuckerization is the process of using real people's names as characters in stories. Outcault did this even before the term had been coined, as Mary Jane was the name of his daughter in real life. The word comes from a science fiction author called Wilson

Tucker, who often used his friends' names in his stories. I imagine that most authors have done so at some point or another, but H.P. Lovecraft, Kingsley Amis and Evelyn Waugh are known to have done it. Coincidentally, Evelyn Waugh also used the appearance and personality of the actor C. Aubrey Smith (mentioned above) for his character Sir Ambrose Abercrombie, an elderly British actor in Hollywood, in his 1948 novel *The Loved One*, which I remember enjoying. Oddly, the book about the funeral and film industry in LA inspired a 1965 episode of the classic British science fiction series *Dr Who*.

As you've probably noticed, I employ tuckerization all over the place. In addition to my friends – Nerea being one example but also Christopher from the Lord Edgington books and even Delilah his dog – I've used all my cousins' names, plenty of readers' (both those of competition winners and others whose names stood out to me) and I also have a penchant for hiding rock star names in among the cast list. Off the top of my head, I've had characters named after members of the bands Blur, Television, My Bloody Valentine, the Stranglers, Sleeping States and probably a bunch more I've forgotten. And why do I do this? I hear you ask. Well, I write a lot of books, and it's sometimes not easy to come up with names I haven't used before, so I have to get inspiration where I can find it.

Inspiration also comes from such places as the deceased former owner of the house where I set this book. Abraham Dixon was born in 1820 to a family of wool merchants, but he made his money in metal goods in Birmingham. He moved to Surrey and built Cherkley Court because of his poor health. He said that one day in the country air adds ten years to your life – though I don't believe this claim stands up to scientific testing. With his fortune made, he retired to his luxurious home and set about having a positive impact on the local community. He and his wife Margaret established the Leatherhead Institute to provide education to the people of the nearest town, and the building remains a registered charity to this day. The trustees recently paid to refurbish the Dixons' grave in the town, and it's nice to see on their website that the contribution he made is still recognised. I'm amazed how often the historical figures I read about have a link to mystery fiction, and the Dixons are no different as Abraham's brother, George, was a politician who did a lot to promote education in the late nineteenth century. There is still a school that bears his name in the area, and that school gave its name to the long-running BBC police series *Dixon of Dock Green*.

Another interesting connection to Cherkley Court comes in the form of Lord Beaverbrook's third wife Marcia Anastasia Christoforides. Thirty-one years his junior, she was the widow of his good friend who had left her a large fortune, which Beaverbrook helped her to distribute to charitable causes. Beaverbrook had remained single for thirty-six years since the death of his first wife, but the two became close and married a year before his death in 1964. The first thing that caught my attention about Lady Beaverbrook, as she became, was that, despite bearing a Greek name, she was born in Sutton – the very same place as the person writing this sentence. The second was the fact that she became good friends with the Spanish surrealist Salvador Dalí and was even painted by him on multiple occasions.

She was apparently quite the eccentric in her own right and, shortly before her second husband's death, she organised his eighty-fifth birthday party at the Dorchester hotel for six hundred and fifty guests. Then, a short time before it was due to take place, and perhaps wisely considering her husband's history of womanising, she uninvited all the female guests. She was also nearly killed in an assassination attempt by a terrorist group with the rather funny name, the Angry Brigade. Because of her prominent position in society as a philanthropist, they attached a bomb to her Rolls Royce, but it was detected before anyone was hurt. I wonder if the bomb was detected by sniffer dogs. Speaking of which...

I had to look up the history of police dogs, and I was surprised to discover that they were still not common in the 1920s. The first canine police programme was in Belgium in the 1890s, and they even gave some thought to breeding the right kind of dog for the job. There had already been one case in Britain of dogs being used for law enforcement, but it was not particularly successful. In 1889, the commissioner of the Metropolitan Police was criticised for his failure to apprehend Jack the Ripper, and the public thought he should at least have used bloodhounds to follow the killer's scent. He obtained two dogs for this purpose, but one of them bit him and they both tried to run away. It wasn't until the 1930s that police dogs became more common in the UK, where there are now 2,500 active doggy officers.

The word sleuth for a detective comes from sleuth hound, which is another name for a bloodhound, and I had to look them up, too. Percy is a basset hound so he should be perfectly capable of following a scent, but he's rather a temperamental creature, and I decided not to rely on him in this investigation. I just watched a recent Oscar-winning film that was hugely enjoyable, but its central mystery was undone by the fact that the police in the story could have found the missing children who are actually in the town the whole time if they'd simply used scent dogs. Bloodhounds can be traced back to a specific monastery in Belgium a thousand years ago, where the ancestors of many different modern breeds were kept. They have been used for following human scents – at which they excel – right back to the fourteenth century, when Scottish heroes Robert the Bruce and William Wallace were probably pursued by them. In the seventeenth century, Robert Boyle, often considered the first chemist, proved just how effective bloodhounds are by having a dog follow a man's scent for seven miles along a path which a lot of different people had used. The dog even took its handler all the way to the upstairs room where the target was hiding. There's a good boy!

Sticking with innovations in crime fighting, I know I've looked at fingerprints before in one of these chapters, but I learnt a little bit more this time about the difference between latent and patent prints. From what I understand, there are three categories of fingerprints left on surfaces. There are those which impact the surface itself, leaving a 3D impression behind on, for example, a bar of soap or a mound of clay. Then there are patent prints where a substance such as ink or soot is transferred to another surface, leaving a print, and the last kind are latent prints where they are largely invisible but can be highlighted with fingerprint dusting powder, iron filings or, back in the day, lampblack. The reality of fingerprints is that they are not always clear enough to identify a culprit, and the kind of surface on which they are found makes a big difference.

I was interested when reading newspaper articles about finger-printing in the 1920s to discover the opinions that people already had towards them. One article from Washington DC, but reprinted in the *Belfast Telegraph* in 1924, discusses the possibility that the technique would eventually become standard and lead to the police solving mysteries at record speed. Meanwhile, *Woman's Dreadnought* magazine in September 1922 was already cautioning its readers over the limitations of the technology and the room for nefarious individuals to "frame up" innocent suspects. The article claims that, through a clean process of transference, it is easier to plant fingerprints than it is to fake a signature. The expert the magazine consulted claimed "...as evidence in court, fingerprints are utterly worthless". I think that's going a bit far, but there are limitations to them, and anyway, in a whodunnit it would be pretty boring if the answer came from simply finding a fingerprint.

One interesting prediction that the first article made was that, before long (they imagined two years would be enough), police would have access to the fingerprints of every criminal in the land and crime solving would happen in seconds. The current FBI fingerprint database, which is the biggest in the world, has over a hundred million people's records, so they weren't far off.

I knew that forensic crime-solving techniques were coming into their own in the twenties, but one article from August 1927 in the *Saturday Record* showed me that they really were put to good use. I reproduce the opening here for your reading pleasure...

TEST TUBE SLEUTHS BEAT BURGLAR

The newest kind of sleuth is the French "laboratory detective", who solves mysterious crimes by using test tubes, ultra-violet rays, micro-photography, electro-chemical baths, and a host of other new scientific processes. "The criminal always leaves behind him his signature." This is the watchword of the modern Sherlock Holmes. "It may be only a microbe, a wisp of hair, a powder stain, a bit of mud, a scrap of burned paper, a tooth mark, a foot track, or fragment of fingerprint, but the signature is there for the man who has learned to read it."

It gives examples of two cases that were solved using these techniques, including a murdered bank collector whose body was found in a sack with a handkerchief in his mouth. Because of some irregular stitching on the hanky, the detective identified the sewing machine and tied the crime to the two killers. The second was the burglary of an office in which red hairs were found on the keys of a typewriter, and the genius Frenchman realised they came from the cat of the suspects. Why they decided to bring their mog with them on the job, I cannot say. In any case, good kitty!

Despite the fact I've written, at least tangentially, about them many times, I was surprised to discover that coroners didn't actually have to know much about science or medicine to fulfil their duties. The role dates back to the time of Richard the Lionheart, and it's interesting that it hasn't changed a great deal since it was introduced. To this day, coroners are legal rather than medical examiners. It is their job to determine who a dead person is, along with where, how and when the person died. If the deceased has seen a doctor in the two weeks prior to death, and there are no suspicious circumstances, the coroner is unlikely to be called at all, and the doctor will issue the death certificate. In other cases, it is the coroner's job to determine whether a post-mortem is necessary.

Despite my previous assumption that a coroner would require medical training, they are more accurately described (in the UK at least) as a type of judge who will have studied law and must have worked as a barrister or solicitor for at least five years. I was interested to discover that the term *hue and cry*, which can mean *to raise an alarm* or *a general clamour*, comes from the requirement for the public to take action, *or raise the hue-and-cry*, when a body was discovered. It was later the name given to the weekly newspaper which, between 1772 and 2017, was used by the police to report serious crimes.

One famous coroner in the neck of the woods in which this book is set, was Athelstan Braxton Hicks. His name was already famous, as it was his father, an obstetrician, who identified Braxton Hicks contractions in pregnant women. The son, however, studied law and became known as "the children's coroner" for his work in London and Surrey investigating infanticides and particularly addressing the unfathomably evil issue of baby farming and the killing of children to claim on life insurance policies. When he started his career, the problem was shocking. In 1870, 276 murdered babies were found in London, most of whom would never find justice. Athelstan worked hard to end these nefarious practices and made a lasting impact on British law and society. Another significant statistic which shows the terrible conditions in which children were raised is that, in the span of a mere ten months in 1895, five hundred died from suffocation due to overcrowded beds. Shockingly, on the morning I wrote this, I read in the newspaper that, due to the ever-widening poverty gap in the UK, bed poverty is a problem once more and, in 2023, 226,000 children in Britain were required to share a bed because of a lack of resources. That's in the country with the sixth-biggest economy on earth. Come on, Britain! Pull yourself together.

Going back to Braxton Hicks Jr., in 1901, thirty years into his career, of the 201 inquests he held, forty-two related to the deaths of infants under one year of age. Three of these were found to be murders, and three more were down to "want of attention" at birth. This is still a terrible statistic, but it suggests that things were beginning to turn for the better. His work helped improve conditions for children, but he also tackled quack doctors, the original Hooligans (a Lambeth street gang who threatened his life when he pursued charges against them) and several famous cases including the Pimlico Poisoner, Adelaide Blanche Bartlett.

Right, I only have one last gory topic to discuss – I promise. Let's move on to the nice, light matter of rigor mortis! This must be one of the areas I have checked most often in my books, and in this one I needed to see what state the second victim would be in after a night in the conservatory. There's a very helpful graphic on Wikipedia showing the various stages of deterioration which can be used to determine the time of death. Along with body temperature, these include corneal clouding – a haziness to the eyes which can appear almost immediately – pallor mortis, or pale skin, livor mortis, as the blood settles in the lower part of the body, putrefaction, decomposition, skeletonisation and even fossilisation. I won't go into the ways in which empty pupae can be helpful to scientists, but these elements combined offer a timeline to coroners and forensic examiners. As he is a mystery novelist like me, Marius knows this stuff. As he is far more morbid than I am, and he can't consult the internet on a whim, he knows it off by heart.

Enough more or less sequential topics! Let's switch to bullet points...

- A crown in Britain never had a value marked upon the coin, but it was worth five shillings from 1544 to 1965. And I was surprised to learn that crown coins issued since 1818 can still be spent with the value of twenty-five pence – so long as the total payment is not more than £10. This was particularly noteworthy as the previous iteration of the recently redesigned pound coin can no longer be spent. However, the Royal Mint's website explains that any British coin, even if it is no longer in circulation, remains legal tender to pay debts in court, though not for everyday transactions. So hold on to your ha'penny bits, ladies and gentlemen! You never know when you may have a speeding fine.

- Rin Tin Tin was a famous German Shepherd who was discovered near a bombed-out town by an American soldier in 1918. Saving a whole litter of puppies and their mother, the soldier, Lee Duncan, kept two for himself and smuggled them home with him the following year. He trained the male dog and found him work in silent movies, with Rin Tin Tin becoming a major star for Warner Bros and (possibly) saving them from bankruptcy. The star dog continued in the business until he died nine years later, after which time his son took up his mantle. I remember reading somewhere that one of Rin Tin Tin's films was a favourite of both Adolf Hitler and Anne Frank, but I can't find anything to back up this hazy memory. Another apocryphal tale states that the Academy wanted to give the dog the best actor Oscar at their first award ceremony, but this myth has since been dispelled. Duncan went on to train many dogs and even helped prepare 5,000 of them for use during the Second World War.

- One of the main websites I use for information on old British theatres is arthurlloyd.co.uk. I've spoken before about this wonderful site which is full of amazing images and fascinating facts. It is run by the great-grandson of nineteenth-century music hall act Arthur Lloyd, and I was happy to come across Lloyd in another context. It turns out that the word toff, meaning a rich person, was popularised by the singer/comedian. It comes from the expression *toffee nosed*, but Lloyd's song "The Shoreditch Toff" brought the shortened form to the public at large.

- Bella makes a passing reference to seedy seaside postcards and, while the heyday of the cheeky postcard was a bit later, they definitely existed in the twenties. Even in Edwardian times, you can find examples complete with humorous captions, bright, caricatured images and a saucy undertone. The master of the form was Donald McGill who, between 1905 and his death in 1962, designed around 12,000 postcards, of which two hundred million were sold. One example in particular, with an innuendo-filled joke about Rudyard Kipling, holds the Guinness World Record, having sold six million copies. He made no money from the rights to the images, but he was famous enough to attract the attention of George Orwell, who wrote an essay on "The Art of Donald McGill", and the Kipling joke travelled so far that it was repeated in *The Beverly Hillbillies*, *The Muppet Show* and the spoof whodunnit film, *Clue*.

- Pansies don't grow naturally in March in England, but I removed a reference to them being grown in the greenhouse as it got a bit wordy (and I've seen plenty there in gardens at that time of year). The name pansy comes from the French word *pensée*, meaning thought. It was chosen as a name for a type of viola as they were associated with remembering the dead. Other interesting things I discovered about them include the fact that Scarlett O'Hara in *Gone with the Wind* was originally called Pansy O'Hara. The love potion in Shakespeare's *A Midsummer Night's Dream* was made from the juice of heartsease, the pansy's progenitor. However, until the nineteenth century, when two British aristocrats busied themselves developing crossbreeds and popularising the pansy, the plant was treated as a weed.

- In the late eighteenth and early nineteenth century there was a popular spectator sport known as pedestrianism. It first developed as races between footmen, who could walk no faster than the carriages they accompanied. I suppose it's not so dissimilar to

Olympic race walking today, but it sounds as though it was popular at all levels of society, as races began to be held in fairs and then long-distance walking races became popular. Its popularity was buoyed by people's ability to bet on the outcome, and the sport spread to the New World in the nineteenth century. By 1878, Baron Astley had established the "Long Distance Championship of the World" which took place over six days.

- I was unsure whether someone like Lord Sheridan would actually have been a millionaire in the late 1920s. Luckily enough, the British Inland Revenue carried out a study the very year that this book is set and they determined that there were just under five hundred millionaires in Britain at the time. Most of them were businessmen rather than landed gentry, and Britain's richest man was the shipping magnate Sir John Ellerman. His annual income was a whopping £1,553,000 – or about £84 million today – whereas his father had left him just £600, which already wasn't bad for an immigrant corn broker who died in the 1870s.
- The hotel in Edinburgh which is mentioned in my book was known at the time as the North British Station Hotel but is now called the Balmoral Hotel. The interesting coincidence I discovered, though, was that the site had previously held a shop which sold James Young Simpson, the controversial figure I have mentioned in several of these chapters before, the chloroform he used on himself and his friends to test the substance before his experiments with it as an anaesthetic. His unconventional methods led to widespread use of the substance in childbirth before people came to their senses and saw how dangerous it was. Chloroform was also the chemical that the

Pimlico Poisoner, mentioned above, used to kill her husband (allegedly, at least).

- Battersea Bridge, which Marius crosses at the end of this book, was the last-standing wooden bridge to cross the Thames until it was rebuilt in 1887. It was never much loved by Londoners, not least because, located as it is on the bend of the river, it was prone to vessels smashing into it. Even since its redesign, there have continued to be disasters, with the last major one occurring in 2005. Despite that, it has featured often in paintings, most notably *Nocturne in Black and Gold – The Falling Rocket* by James McNeill Whistler, which is an abstract and murky depiction of fireworks descending over the once-spectacular Cremorne pleasure gardens near Chelsea. The painting achieved notoriety when art critic John Ruskin accused the artist of "flinging a pot of paint in the public's face". Whistler was so incensed, and financially disadvantaged by the remark, that he took Ruskin to court for libel and attempted to prove the artistic merit of his interpretative work. Things started badly when the painting was placed upside down in the court. He won the case, but his victory would prove Pyrrhic, as he was only awarded a symbolic sum. His legal costs were great, and his reputation was in tatters, so poor Whistler was soon declared bankrupt.

- When Marius visited in 1929, he could see the work just beginning on Battersea Power Station on the south bank of the river. The immense project was started that year but would not be completed until 1955. It still stands today and has had an oversized impact on London. It was always the first major landmark we would spot on the train into the city from my home town of Wallington, though to many people it will be most recognisable for appearing on the cover of Pink

Floyd's 1977 album *Animals*. It was designed in part by Sir Giles Gilbert Scott, who was already famous for the ubiquitous red K2 telephone box. The building was actually made up of two identical stations which worked in unison, with the first being completed in 1935 and the second coming online twenty years later. After it was decommissioned in 1983, the future of the site was up in the air for decades, but it was finally sold in 2012 and rebuilt with offices, housing for fifteen hundred people, a shopping centre, theatre, cinema and various other swanky facilities which opened in 2021.

- There were also two new railway stations opened to serve the new development, the mention of which brings us on to the topic of... trains! The *Flying Scotsman* was named because it went really fast and travelled to Scotland. In fact, the service still exists, though the 1924 locomotive with the same name is no longer used, and the modern electric equivalent can do the journey in half the time it managed back then. Four hours and eight minutes! That sort of speed would blow Marius's little mind. It goes non-stop between London and Edinburgh, and the first such service was run in 1928. Covering 392 miles, it broke the record for the longest regular train journey at the time. I was pleased to discover that there was a film named after the famous train which was released right back in 1929. It was memorable for having a mixture of spoken dialogue, intertitles and synchronised sound effects. The thriller really was filmed aboard the train and featured then-groundbreaking stunt work.

- As for the 1924 train I mentioned, *Flying Scotsman* holds a number of records, including being the first train to reach the speed of 100 miles an hour, way back in 1928. Decades later, it also set a new record for the longest steam-train journey when it was taken to Australia and managed 422 miles without stopping. It remained in service for thirty-nine years and covered over two million miles in that time. It has since been restored and now runs occasional services for special occasions or luxurious tourist routes.

Right. I think you've heard enough from me. I was going to tell you about the roaring twenties in Spain, but I'll finish with a song and then say ta-ra for now. This book is, admittedly, fairly light on musical numbers, but then my audiobook narrator is currently appearing in a musical, so I thought I'd give his voice a rest. I couldn't do without entirely though, so two of the young artists got to sing a verse of "And Her Mother Came Too." Written by Welsh 1920s pin-up (not to mention, singer, composer and actor) Ivor Novello and the Australian actor and composer Dion Titheradge, it featured in the 1921 West End revue *A to Z* where it was sung by the actor Jack Buchanan – who would later make a name for himself in Hollywood. It tells the tale of a young man courting his sweetheart but continuously finding her mother on her, and sometimes his, arm. It features one of the best puns I've come across in a song, as the sense of her mother coming too (accompanying them) and coming to (regaining consciousness) comes into play by the end. I chose the verses included in this book for their mention of the Paris restaurant Maxim's where I recently dined and which will feature in my next Lord Edgington book, *The Paris Library Murders*.

So now you know. I'm off to help plan a funeral. I hope you have something jollier to occupy your time. Ta-ra for now.

<h1 style="text-align:center">WORDS</h1>

Nutria – a type of fur taken from coypus. They were introduced to Europe through the fur trade in the 1930s and are now quite common in the wild, as so many breeding programmes were abandoned. I saw them for the first time near my wife's house in France, not far from where I wrote this book. The ones we saw were quite tame and came up to us in search of food. However, they are an invasive species and, in some areas including Louisiana swampland, they pose a risk to ecosystems and other species.

Check-taker – an old-fashioned expression for the person who takes the tickets in the theatre.

Fantods – a word I like which means to give someone the willies/apprehension.

High cockalorum – an important (or self-important) person.

Brained – I was surprised to find out that this verb (meaning to bash someone about the head) dates way back to 1382.

Hopped the twig / absquatulated – different ways of saying that someone ran away.

Box the compass – reverse your opinion on something.

Pandora's box – in the ancient Greek myth, the box was more likely some kind of jar, but there was no time to slip this titbit into the text.

Dressing down – there are a few different possibilities for the origin of this phrase. One is that dress simply means to punish someone, and another is that it comes from sailing, in which sails would be taken down to recoat with oil and wax before rehanging. Figuratively, therefore, a sailor who was "dressed down" would have his own behaviour or performance corrected by his superiors.

Custard / shrimp-hearted – both mean cowardly. Custard retains this meaning in the expression *cowardly custard.*

Toledan – from Toledo. There was a great European renaissance of silver making, and one of the epicentres was in this city, near Madrid in Spain. It retains a lot of its medieval architecture and is a nice place to visit if you're passing through.

Harangue – a tirade or angry speech.

Hunter watch – a pocket watch with a spring-mounted cover that could be operated with one hand. For this reason, it was popular with hunters on horseback as they could hold on to the reins and check the time.

Rooms of one's own – I'd intended this as a reference to Virginia Woolf's essay on the process of writing, which was published the same year this book is set, but the expression dates back to at least 1869.

Bacchic – referring to Bacchus, the Greek god of wine, fertility, festivity and madness, who loved a good party. As a child, I was in a play of Euripides' *The Bacchae* playing, if I remember correctly, the all-important "Second Messenger" in an amateur dramatic competition. Possibly the strangest man I've ever met, who had latched onto my family during a previous production, came a long way to watch the play and tell me in front of my friends that I wasn't very good. He really was a nasty man, and I don't think I took it to heart.

Take her in a lie – in the twenties, this expression would have been used, as *catch someone in a lie* had not caught on.

Scot-free – according to the online version of the OED this term is an evolution of the phrase *shot free,* which meant to get away with something and not have to pay *shot*, an old-fashioned word meaning a payment, debt or tab. However, one of my most important beta readers who is a Doctor of History debated the origin of the term and says the online version is plain wrong. I trust her judgement.

Hell's delight – pandemonium.

No te preocupes – Spanish, meaning "don't worry".

Rin Tin Tin – a canine movie star from the twenties onwards. See the research chapter for more information.

Banquette – the French word for a bench. I took a gamble and looked it up in the OED and, sure enough, it exists in English too. It means an upholstered bench, which is exactly what I wanted it to mean.

Racket sports – I wanted to check whether the common spelling was with ck or cqu. The former is definitely the most common in English, as it was in the twenties, though the French-derived variant also appears.

Party hound – an old-fashioned expression for a party animal.

Chronograph / crown – the word stopwatch seems to have caught on later – though it did already exist. And as for crown, it took me ages to find what the small wheel/knob on the top was called, but that's it!

Proximately – not a typo. A colloquial version of approximately.

The butler could have done – the butler being the killer wasn't yet a cliché in murder mysteries, but there are plenty of articles in the papers detailing crimes that real butlers perpetrated.

Royal Academy – Royal Academy of Arts: an important institution founded in 1768 which is unique as it is run by artists and continues to have a significant impact on the art scene in the UK.

Peter Paul Rubens – seventeenth-century Flemish artist. I have no idea why I picked him.

Chenille – a yarn so named because its furriness resembles the hairs on a caterpillar (which is what *chenille* means in French).

The fish stinks first at the head – there are two things worth noting here. First, the expression *the fish rots from the head down* formed later. And second, this is true metaphorically but not literally. In fact, dead animals' organs start to rot and smell before their exteriors. Oh, and third, this metaphor dates back to at least thirteenth-century Turkey, when the poet Rumi mentioned it in his writing.

Looking daggers – another phrase that has developed over time. Shooting daggers is now more common.

Tom, Dick and Harry – I did worry towards the end of this book that this phrase might have originated far later, but I was okay. It dates back to 1730. Meaning, any random fellow; other common names are sometimes used, like *Bill, Bob and Jim.*

Imbroglio / Sang-froidical – The former means *a state of great confusion* or difficulty. The latter comes from the French for *cold blood* and, in English, the noun sang-froid means cool indifference. I must admit that I made up the adjective to suit my needs.

Settee – this is one of the words which Nancy Mitford drew attention to for being Non-U (i.e. not upper class) in her jokey but snobbish article, "The English Aristocracy" in the 1950s. Other words included *mirror* (filthy commoners) vs *looking glass* (the refined higher echelons of society) and *serviette* (Non-U) vs *napkin* (U).

A mare's nest – a common enough expression in 1920s fiction, it means a terrible mess. It originally meant an incredible discovery which turned out not to be true – presumably with the idea that one might think they've found a nest that a horse made, but no.

Con artist – dating from 1878, this was originally an American expression but would have been known in the UK.

Corpse Reviver Number Ones – a cocktail with a storied history. Its sequel appeared in the last Lord Edgington, and I go into the story of it there.

Graphic phrases involving milk, goats and dead people – as much as I love the Spanish language, I'm really not a fan of the expressions they use as swear words. I won't go into them here, but there is a lot of talk of spoilt milk. I don't use much bad language personally, but I'm not actually that bothered by swearing in English because we're not nearly so graphic!

CHARACTER LIST

Old Favourites

Marius Quin – he's there on the cover! You must know him by now!

Lady Bella Montague – Marius's former girlfriend, sleuthing partner and close friend.

Inspector Valentine Lovebrook – a normally happy-go-lucky officer who befriended Marius & Co. in the first book of the series.

Marius's mum – Marius's mum, Mary.

New Favourites

Nerea Barriuso – Marius's former love from his days living in Paris. She is the language mistress at Cherkley Court.

Penny Baker – the maid who is attacked in Lady Sheridan's boudoir.

Dennis Apps – the missing gardener.

Virgil Dixon – Lord Sheridan – a wealthy industrialist and master of the grand estate.

Imelda Dixon – Lady Sheridan – his youthful and lively wife.

Thomas-Richard Harrison – one of the young artists Lady Sheridan patronises. He is exceedingly posh.

Quentin Urquhart – another of the artists and the brother of an old friend of Bella's.

Louise Thorneycroft – the third of the trio, she is more reticent than the other two.

Ponsonby – the estate's elderly butler.

Lionel Dixon – the ten-year-old heir to Cherkley Court.

Gareth and Gavin – two other gardeners

Francis and Frederick – two footmen.

Hilary – the nursemaid.